TRUST AND TRICKERY

- HIVITES -

LIGHT OF NATIONS
BOOK THREE

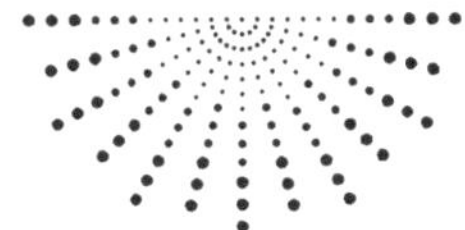

CHRISTINE DILLON

LINKS IN THE CHAIN PRESS

www.storytellerchristine.com

Trust and Trickery - Hivites (Light of Nations #3)

Scripture taken from the HOLY BIBLE, NEW INTERNATIONAL VERSION®. NIV®. Copyright © 1973, 1978, 1984 by International Bible Society. Used by permission of Zondervan. All rights reserved worldwide.

Epigraph scripture quotation is from The ESV® Bible (The Holy Bible, English Standard Version®), copyright © 2001 by Crossway, a publishing ministry of Good News Publishers. Used by permission. All rights reserved.

Cover Design: Lankshear Design

ISBN: 9781923012035

With grateful thanks to my team especially Joy Lankshear (cover designer), and my editors, Laura Tharion and Iola Goulton.

Thank you also to the proofreading team and early readers. Not all of you can work on every book but you are still much appreciated. Lizzie, Kate, Stephanie, Suzanne, Elizabeth (making sure our US formatting, spelling, and word usage is correct), Roe, Anne, Kim, Erin, and Linda ... Each of you have different specialties and I've come to rely on you all.

I am greatly blessed. I could not do this without the team.

I will make you as a light for the nations,
that my salvation may reach to the ends of the earth.

Isaiah 49:6b (ESV)

Your servants were clearly told how the Lord your God had
commanded his servant Moses to give you the whole land and
to wipe out all its inhabitants from before you. So we feared
for our lives because of you—

Joshua 9:24 (NIV)

LIST OF CHARACTER AND PLACE NAMES

Fictional Characters

Danel - baker, and citizen of the Hivite town of Gibeon.

Donatiya- Danel's younger sister, assistant in the bakery.

Keret - Danel and Donatiya's grandfather.

Uncle Hammurapi - brother-in-law to Keret.

Yassib - Danel's best friend. One of the chief of Gibeon's many sons.

Rivkah - Israelite, grand-daughter of an Egyptian who left Egypt after the ten plagues.

Zeb - Rivkah's brother.

Biblical Characters (found in Joshua 2-10)

I have chosen to use more Hebraic-anglicised versions of the familiar names. This helps us approach the story with different eyes and hopefully makes the biblical parts, feel less familiar.

Yehoshua - new leader of the Israelites after the recent death of **Mosheh** (Moses) - legendary leader of the Israelites. He dies at the start of this story and is replaced by Yehoshua.

Rahab - rescued from Jericho.

Sihon and Og - Amorite kings, east of the Jordan River. The reports of the battles are found in Numbers 21 and Deuteronomy 2.

Place Names:

Gibeon - 5 miles (9 kilometres) north-west of Jerusalem. It was later part of the territory of Benjamin (Joshua 18:25) and became a Levitical city (Joshua 21:17). Joshua 10:2 says it was an important city, larger than Ai, and its men were good fighters.

Kephirah, Beeroth, Kiriath Jearim - sister cities of Gibeon and also part of the treaty agreement.

Jericho - the first city on the western side of the Jordan River that the Israelites conquered.

Ai - near Bethel and the city that the Israelites attacked after Jericho. Joshua 7-8 give the account.

PROLOGUE

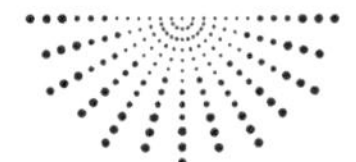

Gibeon, Ancient Canaan

"Take that!" Danel swiped his best friend, Yassib, with his makeshift sword, a small branch he'd selected that morning.

Yassib blocked Danel's swing with his own stick. Danel's stick splintered, and he growled in frustration. If only they could use real swords. Yassib had asked his father, but he had only laughed.

"Swords are for real men, not boys," he'd said.

It was so frustrating to be a child. Growing up took too long. Danel and Yassib often watched the older boys training in sword and pike fighting. When Yassib had asked his father how long until he and Danel could join the training, his father had clapped his son on the shoulder.

"You're just like I was when I was your age. Eager to be a hero." He gestured at those in training. "When you are strong enough to wield a sword, you can join in."

Yassib had puffed out his chest. "I can do it now."

"Me too," Danel had said, not wanting to be left out.

Yassib's father had grinned and whistled. When one of his men came over, Yassib's father took the man's sword and held it out to Danel. Danel's eyes widened, and he grinned as he went to lift the weapon from Yassib's father, only to stagger backwards and drop the sword. He'd had to jump out of the way to avoid it hitting his toes.

"It's heavier than it looks, isn't it?" Yassib's father had said.

Danel had nodded, red faced. After that, he and Yassib had practiced with sticks. They'd started with mere twigs and slowly progressed to longer and heavier versions. In the bakery, Danel's father always said skill came with much practice, and Danel intended to apply the principle to sword fighting. His father might only be a baker, but Danel had no intention of kneading dough for the rest of his life. Danel was going to be a hero and flatten the armies of their enemies, and the first step to being a hero was being able to use weapons—swords and pikes and bows and arrows.

He and Yassib practiced every afternoon they could, down by the stream. They parried back and forth, training their hands and arms and feet and even their eyes. If Danel didn't pay attention, Yassib would break through Danel's defenses and give him a bruise to remember. In the early days, Danel had received lots of bruises. Now they were more evenly matched.

Yassib's branch thwacked Danel's arm, drawing him back to the present. They continued parrying back and forth until exhausted, then plunged into one of the deeper pools in the stream to cool off.

"When will we be big enough to fight with real swords?" Danel asked.

"Look." Yassib flexed his elbow. "My muscles are growing."

Danel hadn't the heart to tell Yassib that his bulky muscles were only in his imagination. Yet Danel trusted that one day their puny arms would show off toned muscles and their sticks would be replaced with swords.

Maybe by the time he and Yassib had grown, there would be a task worthy of them. Something to ensure they'd be remembered forever, like the mighty men of Gibeon's past.

CHAPTER ONE

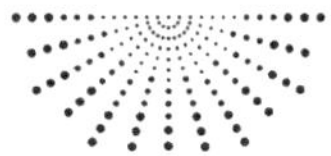

Ten barley harvests later

"*H*elp, Danel! Help me," his sister screamed.

Danel whirled around. Donatiya was struggling to free herself from two battle-scarred men. Anger surged until it nearly choked him. He wasn't going to lose any more family members. He had been careless. Of all people, he should have known it was no longer safe to go outside the city walls without his hunting bow, given he'd lost his father the same way. As his father lay bleeding in Danel's arms, his final words had been an entreaty for Danel to look after his sister. Danel had vowed to do so and it was a vow he was determined to keep.

"Yassib!" Danel yelled. His best friend had disappeared behind the nearest tree to relieve himself.

One of the men slapped Donatiya, leaving a red mark across her face. She twisted away from her captors and bit him as hard as she could. The man took a hurried step back, wringing his hand. "None of that," he growled.

Good one, Donatiya. Bite him again. Danel desperately searched for a weapon. Anything would do. A stout branch lay under the closest tree, but could he make it there and back before Donatiya was taken?

Danel sprinted to the tree and stooped for the branch. Something hit him on the side of the head with a stinging blow, and everything went black.

He blinked as he regained consciousness, squinting into the searing sunlight, head pounding. Where was he? Danel struggled to get up, but his limbs were tied. *No! Donatiya. Was he too late?* Pushing against the pain, Danel forced his eyes open.

Two men stood over him, ready to knock him out again if necessary. Next to him, Yassib, hands also tied, was being dragged into the open by a third pair of men, who were keeping well away from Yassib's lashing feet. Another man followed, carrying Yassib's dagger.

"Kick us again, boy, and I'll find a use for your knife," he said.

The two men threw Yassib aside like a sack of grain but remained close enough to prevent him being of any help to Danel.

Danel's heart sank. Now they were weaponless. Or were they? *Think, Danel, think.*

Donatiya stood beside a lone large man, untied, but cowed by his sheer size. Her face was pale, and her hands trembled. She knew what was coming if they couldn't save her. Girls had been disappearing for years, never to be seen again. *Think.*

Yassib made no sound, but Danel could tell he was burning with anger at being caught unprepared and tied so easily. When Yassib was angry, the scar on his forehead glowed red.

Think.

What had Yassib once quoted at him? Something about a warrior had many weapons besides bows, swords, and pikes. Danel hadn't understood at the time.

"Witch." Danel's voice came out in a croak. He took a deep

breath. "Witch," he repeated. "My sister is a witch. Leave us or she'll curse you."

The largest kidnapper snorted, clearly unconvinced.

Using his chin, Danel pointed toward Yassib. "See that scar. He teased my sister once too often. She made his dagger rise in the air and slash him."

Donatiya's eyes widened. *Come on, little sister. Play along.*

Her eyes rolled back in her head, and she mumbled in the childhood language she'd made up to annoy Danel.

"I never dared again." Yassib somehow managed to look as though the memory terrified him. "No one around here dares."

The man behind Yassib shuffled his feet. With a quick glance to ensure the large man beside Donatiya wasn't watching, he tossed Yassib's dagger into the bushes as though it had burned him.

So at least one of the kidnappers was spooked. Good, but they needed something more. They'd been warned not to risk this walk, but they were tired of being enclosed within Gibeon's high stone walls. If only they'd listened to the warnings.

Donatiya kept mumbling. Hopefully some of her mumblings included prayers. Danel's prayers were never answered, but maybe hers would be. The gods were fickle in both their cruelty and kindness.

A raven swooped and landed on a tall rock nearby, fixing its eyes on the group. The man to Danel's left gave a superstitious shiver. Ravens were regarded as harbingers of evil. Danel felt a flicker of hope—the city ravens were a tight-knit flock, defensive if provoked.

"Ravens obey my sister's commands," Danel called. *Keep acting, little sister. Keep acting.* He tried to make his voice tremble with the fear of what might happen. "Please, I beg you, get away before she calls up more ravens."

Donatiya straightened her spine and stared at the raven with narrowed eyes, as if she was communicating with the bird, controlling it. She'd always loved pretending. If Danel hadn't known she was acting, her look would have convinced him.

With a howl, the dagger thrower turned and ran.

The leader of the group snarled, picked up a stone, and threw it at the bird. It spread its wings, gave an angry squawk, and flew straight toward its tormenter, forcing the man to stagger sideways. Another raven landed on the rock. It gave an indignant hop sideways as two more landed.

"Gah!" the leader shouted, raising his arms to scare the birds. They lifted off the rock but landed again, unperturbed. Now there were twice as many ravens, with more descending from the skies as if the whole flock had been summoned for battle. If only the city gods were as dependable as the city ravens.

Two more captors took off running back to wherever they'd come from, leaving only one man with Danel. Danel could smell the man's sweat.

"Birds, come!" Donatiya yelled. "Peck out the eyes of these evildoers."

Danel's remaining guard howled and took off, forearm held up to protect his eyes. Yassib's guard followed suit.

The leader cursed and ran after them. "You cowards!"

"Quick, Donatiya," Danel said. "Find that dagger and cut the ropes."

Yassib scrambled to his feet and rushed toward the bushes, parting the branches so Donatiya could find the dagger. Danel's heart pounded. They weren't safe yet. They needed to reach the city wall before the leader rallied his men.

Donatiya peered under several bushes and finally gasped. "Found it."

Yassib held up his hands and stretched the bindings to make it easier to cut. Donatiya's hand shook as she sawed through the ropes. She nicked him once, but Yassib didn't flinch. Then Yassib took back his dagger and easily cut through Danel's bindings.

"Come on." Yassib helped Danel to his feet.

Danel felt as if the weight of the sky had lifted from his chest. "Donatiya, run in front," he said, and she took off like a young deer. Danel caught Yassib's eye as they ran behind her, sharing a glimmer of fear at all that might have been.

CHAPTER TWO

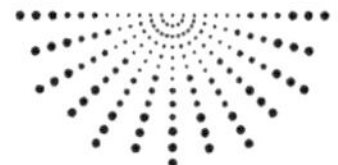

"Our doom is coming. We will all be wiped out!" the familiar voice boomed.

Grandfather.

Danel's cheeks burned. He'd only let the old man out of his sight for a moment while he haggled for some olive oil.

Danel looked from side to side. There. His grandfather had found a large rock and was perched precariously on top of it, ready to repeat his pronouncement. He must be stopped.

Danel muttered an apology to the seller and dashed toward the rock. Grandfather took a deep breath.

"Be careful up there," Danel yelled.

His grandfather looked at him, confusion clouding his eyes. He shook his head as though to clear it and Danel reached the bottom of the rock.

"Come down, Grandfather." Danel extended his hand.

His grandfather took the offered hand, and Danel helped him safely down. If he was lucky, Grandfather would have forgotten why he'd climbed the rock.

"You need to keep a closer eye on the old man," a nearby pome-granate seller said.

"I try," Danel said.

"Well, it's not good enough." The seller scowled. "Your grandfa-ther is always disturbing the peace."

Danel flushed. This was the third time in as many weeks that Grandfather had shouted his predictions of doom. What had set him off today?

He took Grandfather by his elbow. "Please stay close to me. I need to buy oil and arrange for its delivery."

Danel had never expected to be in sole charge of the bakery at nineteen summers old, but his father's murder by bandits almost twelve moons ago had changed his plans. Now Danel ran the bakery, their livelihood. Danel's life was dictated by the rhythms of bread making. Mixing the dough in the afternoons and letting it rise in the warmth near the ovens overnight. Well before the sun rose, he'd set the fires beneath the clay ovens, slapping the uncooked dough on the inner surfaces of the oven, and making a fire under the flat stone on which they cooked flatbreads. He'd turn into a flatbread soon, as the pace never let up. He baked every day until he could almost bake bread in his sleep.

Danel would never have been able to manage if Grandfather didn't do the kneading. It was one task the old man could still manage. Donatiya was a quick learner who loved to flip flatbreads, adding poppy seeds, herbs, or sesame.

Danel turned to his grandfather. "Please don't move from this spot. I need to concentrate."

His grandfather lowered his eyes, looking like a sheepish little boy.

Danel turned to the oil seller. "Sorry about that."

The oil seller passed Danel the first jar of oil, sensing a sale. Danel sniffed it, poured a thin stream into a dish for the purpose, then placed one drop on his finger and rubbed the oil between his finger and thumb.

The oil passed all the tests. Danel was looking for a new supplier after his previous supplier had thought he could fool someone less experienced by substituting oil of lesser quality.

"If I need five of those jars each moon for the next three moons, can you supply and deliver them?"

"It would be my pleasure." The man squared his shoulders.

Danel wasn't going to enter into any agreements without a trial first. That had been the first major mistake he'd made as a baker, simply continuing with the suppliers who had dealt with his father. The grain merchant had proved reliable, but some of the others had not.

Behind Danel, he heard a big intake of breath. He spun around.

"Our doom is come. We will all be wiped out," Grandfather shouted.

Not again!

"Grandfather, stop." Danel took three rapid strides and grabbed his grandfather's arm.

Grandfather wrenched his arm out of Danel's grasp and stumbled backwards into a basket of fruit. It tipped over with a crash, and fruit poured out in a golden cascade across the ground.

"Keep that crazy man under control," the fruit seller yelled.

What more could Danel do?

The fruit seller rose to his feet and pointed at the fruit. "You'll have to pay for it. Every last piece."

No doubt at an inflated price.

As anger swirled around them, Grandfather wrapped his arms around his body and whimpered.

Oh, Papa, why did you leave us?

With his face burning, Danel collected the fruit and paid the seller, who agreed with reluctance to deliver it to their home.

Danel took his grandfather's hand. "Come on, Grandfather. Time to go home."

Grandfather, his head down, shuffled beside Danel as they headed home. This would have to be their last visit to the market together. Somehow Danel had to find someone to keep an eye on the old man. It was that or close the bakery and give up.

CHAPTER THREE

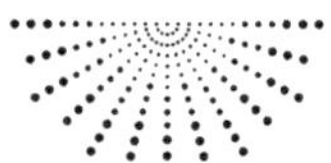

he cock crowed, as reliable as the sunrise. Danel turned over and pushed himself into a kneeling position before rolling up his sleeping mat. Their family always slept on the flat roof during the warmer seasons.

Grandfather gave a snort but soon settled back to snoring. The longer he slept, the better. A sleeping man required no looking after, couldn't knock things over, and didn't make embarrassing pronouncements.

In the bakery below, the dough would be waiting. Another day, like another rock in the sack that seemed to hang around Danel's neck ever since his father's death. He sighed and headed down the outside stairs to the courtyard below. At the bottom of the stairs, he took the tiny oil lamp he'd prepared the night before, stooped to the still-warm coals in the outside fire, lit a twig, and held its flame to the wick in the oil. A crescent moon gave a little light outside, but inside would be dark.

Danel entered the cool darkness of the central building. Using the oil lamp, he lit some incense and bowed as he offered it to the wooden carvings of Baal and Astarte, god and goddess of fertility. If drought or fire or flood struck, there would be no barley or wheat and with no grain, there'd be no bread. Without bread to sell, Danel's family and their neighbors would starve. It was as simple as that, so Danel never missed making his daily obeisance and muttering a prayer for protection from all such disasters.

Danel crossed the courtyard to the clay ovens and fanned the still-warm coals into life before adding new kindling and wood. Yassib usually scoffed at this having to wake so early every morning, saying Danel should have chosen a profession where he didn't have to get up before the sun. Yassib couldn't conceive of there being no choice of profession but Danel quite liked the hour of quiet in the morning, an hour before the burdens of the day dragged him down.

Outside, the scuff of a footstep made him jump.

"I woke early." Donatiya poked her head through the doorway. "I'll wash my face and come and help."

"There's no need to rush," Danel said. Donatiya had had such a short season to be a child. None of her friends were working as hard as she was at a mere eleven harvests old but Donatiya had been cursed to lose both parents so young.

Danel carried a flaming twig across to light the fires under the giant stone slab where Donatiya would flip the flatbreads. He didn't want her to have to lean into the clay ovens and slap the bread on the inner surface, as one of the neighbor's children had fallen into an oven and been so badly burned that she'd died.

Donatiya came toward him, face still damp. "Grandfather is still asleep."

"Good," Danel said shortly. Grandfather had kneaded extra dough last night and maybe more exercise would help him sleep longer. It was hard to know how much Grandfather understood, but if dough was placed in front of him, he kneaded it and kneaded it well.

Danel moved the bowl of dough toward his sister. She took the first portion, rolled it flat, then brushed it with oil. Once she'd rolled six portions, she flicked a little water on the flat surface. It sizzled and she laid all six circles of dough on the stone's surface, then started rolling the next batch.

"Did Mama use to do this?" she asked.

Donatiya was always wanting to know about their mother. Danel had only been eight when their mother died. He'd seen his mother's joy at finally being with child again, but he'd been too young to know childbirth could be dangerous. He knew now. When his sister was learning to walk, Papa had told him that Mama had lost many babies, which was why she had been so both terrified and excited to be carrying his sister.

"She learned to make bread from her parents when she was even younger than you are now," Danel said.

The business had belonged to his maternal grandparents. Papa had often reminisced about how busy the bakery had been when all four of them were working together.

Donatiya used a round piece of wood to roll more dough into flat circles. "I like working here. It makes Mama more real, because I'm sitting where she sat and doing what she did."

Danel wished he had more memories himself because Donatiya always wanted more. He remembered his mother kneading and rolling and cooking the breads. He remembered going with her to market or to collect water. And he remembered her laughter and her love of flowers. If he'd paid more attention, he might remember more. Mama was simply there until she wasn't. He remembered being resentful helping her with chores, longing to escape with Yassib to go fishing, swimming, tree climbing, or stick fighting.

How was Danel to know he'd regret not memorizing every line of his mother's face? Now he struggled to even picture what she looked like.

* * *

*D*anel grinned as Yassib sat down on one of the benches lining three sides of the courtyard, shaded by the canopy of a fig tree. Many customers gathered out here to escape the heat, chatting to friends and neighbors.

"I heard your grandfather caused a ruckus at the market yesterday," Yassib said.

Danel grimaced. "He's been much worse lately. Sometimes his cries wake us up during the night."

"Any idea why he's doing it?" Yassib asked.

Danel sank down on a convenient stump. "Ever since the barley harvest he's been muttering that it's the fortieth year."

Yassib raised an eyebrow. "Fortieth year of what?"

"Your guess is as good as mine. This town is much older than forty years and there's nothing in the local area that's linked to forty years, but when I ask him, he gets confused."

"Is he the reason why you never come fishing anymore?" Yassib asked.

Yassib and Danel had first met on the banks of the river, and they'd spent many afternoons fishing since.

"That and trying to run the bakery. We lost a lot of customers after Papa died."

Papa's body had barely been cold before a competing baker had been suggesting that Danel was too young to run a bakery. Danel had been striving to prove them wrong ever since. Slowly, as he provided a steady supply of good quality bread, some of Papa's former customers were returning.

"If I catch any fish, would you like some?" Yassib asked. "I've just been throwing them back."

"Please." Danel tried to keep his eagerness out of his voice. The family had always eaten Danel's catch, and they missed fish now he didn't have time to accompany Yassib. Yassib might be a younger son, but his father was chief of Gibeon. His family did not need the fish.

It was hard not to envy Yassib. He had the perfect life. He was not an oldest son, bound by expectations, nor the youngest, and thus totally ignored. His father ensured he had the same education as his older brothers in archery, reading the stars, sword fighting, and business, but he didn't have to work around his home as there were plenty of slaves. Yassib had time to fish and ride and hunt, and he took full advantage of his freedoms. If Yassib was lucky, he might even get freedom in the matter of his marriage. Danel would be lucky to get married at all. His grandfather wasn't in a fit state to arrange a marriage, and Danel never had a spare moment to look at a girl, let alone talk to one.

The only way Danel was likely to get married was if he did something so spectacular that parents would compete to gain him for their daughters. But Danel was a baker. He looked down at his calloused baker-burned hands and chuckled grimly to himself. When the town gathered for Yassib's father to tell them stories of their great ancestors, they were not stories of winning wars by kneading bread.

CHAPTER FOUR

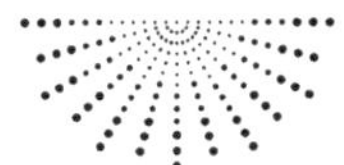

"Danel, have you heard?" Yassib dropped onto the bench in the bakery.

"Heard what?" Danel wiped the sweat off his forehead. "I haven't sat down all day, but it's been the best sales day since my father left us." The warmth of the accomplishment settled in his belly, and he allowed himself to take a swig of water as he flopped down near Yassib. He deserved a bit of a rest. Maybe Yassib would help him prepare tomorrow's dough. Sometimes it amused Yassib to help.

"There's been trouble. Out on the road toward Mount Hor."

In Edom? Considering Danel had never traveled beyond the next town, Edom seemed a long way from Gibeon. Of what relevance was news from such a place?

Yassib rubbed his eyebrow. "My father is worried."

Danel offered Yassib a drink which he refused.

Danel took another swig himself. "What's worrying him?"

"I don't know, but he tensed up when the messenger arrived on horseback. He's been in huddles with the council ever since." Yassib shook his head. "Father even snapped at my mother, and he never does that."

Yassib's father had wisely allied himself through strategic marriages with many of the surrounding towns and peoples, and Yassib's mother was a favorite among the six wives still living.

Danel stretched out his legs and prepared for a longer break. "Do you have any hint about why your father is worried?"

"Only that it concerns Edom and something about Israelites."

"Israelites?" Danel had never heard of them.

Inside the house behind them, there was an unearthly moan. "Our doom is upon us," Grandfather said. "No one listens to me. Fools!"

"Your grandfather seems to know who they are," Yassib muttered.

Maybe, but would Grandfather be willing—or able—to tell them anything? Danel got to his feet and went through to peer into the entrance to the main part of the house. "Grandfather, come and sit with us for a while."

His grandfather's few remaining teeth gleamed in the gloom as he shuffled toward the doorway. Danel took his hand, led him into the bakery, and handed him a cup of water.

"What do you know about Israelites?" Danel asked.

"Israelites?" The old man frowned and there was a long silence.

They waited but it was as though shutters had been locked in Grandfather's mind. Eventually, Grandfather staggered to his feet and wandered back toward the main house. "Donatiya, bring me my meal."

"Sorry," Danel said. "I don't think we'll get a sensible answer from him."

Yassib frowned. "Maybe not, but your grandfather knows something."

"Yes, but his reaction might have been a coincidence."

Yassib stood. "I will see what I can find out. Tomorrow, I'll bring you some fish."

"We'd appreciate that. Fish is tender enough for Grandfather to eat."

* * *

It was the middle of the next afternoon when Danel heard Yassib's whistle. Danel wiped his hands on the cloth tied around his waist, sneezing as a cloud of flour hit his nose, and hurried out to the courtyard.

Yassib had brought them four good-sized fish, enough for two days. Danel called Donatiya, who came and took the fish.

"I'm nearly finished mixing the last batch of dough," Danel said to Yassib. "Come and tell me what you've discovered."

Yassib followed Danel into the room, squatted on his haunches, and watched as Danel combined the ingredients. "I've found out a little. Enough to help us find out more. The Israelites are the descendants of a wanderer called Avraham. Apparently he lived around Kiriath Arba many generations ago."

Kiriath Arba was an Amorite area. Maybe Avraham was related to the people of the area. "I've never heard of them."

"That's because they've been slaves in Egypt for generations."

The dough was almost mixed. "They don't sound like much of a threat."

"I'm not sure about that." Yassib cleared his throat. "I've been listening to every conversation I can and heard a lot more than I want to know about the women in various council members' lives."

Danel laughed and continued mixing the dough to the right consistency. Once it was done, he covered it with a heavy cloth to keep the dough warm and to keep any creatures out of it. "Did you find out anything more?"

"Whoever they are, there's a lot of them. More than in Gibeon and Edom. More than the eye can see. They're led by an old man called Mosheh."

The numbers explained why Yassib's father was nervous. It wasn't as if there were large areas of vacant land around Canaan for these people to settle in and call home. Settlers would put pressure on pastures and water sources. Gibeon had two large pools of water and would be the kind of place that would attract attention but they should be able for repel any attack for they were surrounded by a thick wall and the Hivites were good fighters.

"Father has called in the great Talliya to read the bull entrails."

Danel shivered. It was said that the diviner's curses could make flocks infertile or fill a person's bowels with fire. The chief must be worried. Talliya was the only diviner in the surrounding towns capable of interpreting bull entrails and Talliya's fee would probably be a bull's weight in silver.

* * *

*D*anel had taken part of the afternoon off to watch the divination. It seemed as if many others had done the same, for there was a big crowd outside the city gates, all looking toward a small hill.

A bull bellowed and the crowd craned their necks, looking for Talliya. She didn't disappoint, for she came from behind, standing in a chariot that allowed her to be seen by one and all. Her dress was scarlet, and her arms loaded with gold bangles. Walking behind her chariot was a young man, torso bare and gleaming with oil, and carrying a polished knife on a black cushion.

The bull was led forward by some of the chief's men, protesting the whole way as if the beast knew what was to happen. In front of the procession, the crowd parted to let them through and then pressed in again once the chariot and knife-bearer had passed.

"Impressive, isn't she?" Yassib said with awe in his voice.

"If you're going to call yourself 'The Great' you'd better look the part," Danel said.

Talliya had obviously told the men what to do prior to the ceremony, for they had efficiently bound the bull in a standing position so it couldn't move and obscure the reading. A large tray was placed on the ground under the bull's belly.

The crowd fell silent as the youth carrying the knife knelt and presented the cushion to Talliya. She took the knife off the cushion and raised it above her head on open palms. The sun flashed off the gold bracelets.

"Great Baal and Astarte, rulers of all in these lands and provider of all good things, you know a new people approach the borders of our lands. We ask for your reassurance that we have nothing to fear. That victory, if we need to fight, will be ours."

Fight? Excitement churned in Danel's belly. Maybe this was the opportunity he'd been waiting for his entire life.

Talliya ended her prayer with words spoken in another language. A language Danel had never heard and which sounded mysterious and powerful. She ended with an ear-splitting scream, lowered the knife, and handed it back to the youth. The sun gleamed on his oiled body. Moving swiftly, as though in a dance, he stepped in, drew back the bull's head, and cut its throat. The blood poured on the ground, and the men struggled to hold the bull still.

The youth had obviously been helping Talliya for a while, for at precisely the right moment, he opened the bull's belly and the entrails fell onto the tray. The dying bull was pushed onto its side, out of the way. Once it was dead, Talliya stepped toward the slimy mass of entrails.

She did not turn her back to the crowd but allowed them to see her every move. She peered, and murmured, and moved her arms as she performed her incantations. At last, she raised her head and gave a triumphant smile in the direction of the chief. He clambered up the hill, bowed before her and listened as she spoke quietly. Then he turned to the crowd.

"The gods have smiled on us," the chief said, projecting his voice so all could hear. "These Israelites will not prevail. We have nothing to fear."

Danel let out his breath with a whoosh. His family was safe.

But the ongoing movement near the bull drew Danel's gaze and he saw Talliya's face as she turned back toward the crowd. For the briefest of moments he saw the pale haggardness of her expression before her mouth twisted back into a victory smile.

Danel's gut twisted. Something wasn't right. As Talliya passed him, Danel looked past the smile into her eyes. They were hard and lifeless.

His throat tightened. What had she seen that she had not revealed?

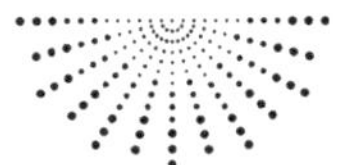

*D*anel woke in the darkness for the second time that night, his panting breath loud in his ears and his body slick with sweat. Sitting up, he bent up his knees and grasped them, relieved to feel his bones and flesh, to know he was alive.

He took a deep breath, willing the fear that gripped him to loosen its hold.

Breathe. In, out. In, out.

Every time he breathed in, the dream pushed in too. The rats, the birds pecking at him, the utter devastation.

Just a nightmare, nothing unusual but he failed to convince himself. The dream hadn't felt like any ordinary nightmare, and he feared it. He feared it predicted yet another disaster for his family. A disaster that would leave Grandfather and Donatiya alone.

He would not sleep again. He didn't dare.

Danel got up. He'd go and pray for peace from the gods, for only gods could grant peace to troubled minds.

anel barely acknowledged Yassib as he pushed through the gate and crossed the courtyard two days later.

Yassib raised an eyebrow. "Girlfriend trouble?"

Danel snorted. "You know there's no spare moments in my life for girls."

"Well, what then?"

"Let me put this sack down before I drop it on my toe."

Danel carried the full sack of flour toward the bakery, put it in a heavy box, and covered it with a lid so nothing could get into it. Coming in here also allowed him a moment to think. What should he tell Yassib? Would Yassib laugh at the fear that had gripped Danel since the previous night?

Yassib was a friend—Danel's best friend—but what did their friendship consist of? A few childhood games, fishing, and horsing around. Danel knew nothing of Yassib's feelings or fears. Was theirs a friendship that could share deeper things?

Danel turned back toward the courtyard and took a deep breath before he stepped from the cool darkness back into the blazing sunlight. A cicada thrummed its song from the fig tree. Danel used a ladle to scoop up some water from the barrel and carried it to Yassib.

Yassib slurped a mouthful. "Sit and tell me what's bothering you."

Danel looked at the ground and felt again the terrible fear from the night before. Fear with talons to rip at his heart.

"Two nights ago, I had a dream," he said.

"Obviously a bad one if it's still bothering you."

Danel nodded.

"Then you're in luck. Talliya's divining tent is set up," Yassib said.

"I'm not sure," Danel said, stomach churning. After his glimpse of Talliyah's face at the entrails reading, he wasn't sure she could be trusted.

"Not sure she can help you? Lots of the diviners are frauds, but she predicted Father would become chief even though he wasn't the oldest son."

Predicted? Or had the prediction encouraged Yassib's father to take matters into his own hands?

"Don't look so skeptical. You know she predicted the famine, which meant we had plenty of time to prepare. It's not just one or two lucky guesses. People swear by the accuracy of her palm readings, and—"Yassib's voice grew animated, "—she specializes in dream interpretation."

And Danel had a dream that he was convinced held meaning. He just wasn't sure he wanted to know what it meant. If a dream had a good outcome, everyone would love the resulting happy anticipation. But what if the meaning of a dream was bad? Who'd want to live with the burden of dread?

"I came to ask you to go with me and find you actually need a dream interpreted. It's obviously meant to be," Yassib said with enthusiasm.

Danel looked at Yassib. "What do you need to consult her about?"

Yassib shrugged. "Nothing really, but she is old and doesn't move far from Kiriath Jearim. I was curious, that's all. It would be something to tell my children one day, that I met the great Talliya."

The woman or her parents didn't suffer from lack of modesty. She'd been named after the goddess of the dew, one of the daughters of Baal. Had that been her name from birth, or had she taken it on as her power and fame grew?

Should Danel go? Talliya might be the answer to his prayers for peace. Papa had told Danel not to waste his money on diviners, but that was because people had pushed Papa to go to a diviner when Danel's mother was sick. Papa had spent money he could ill afford to lose, and it had made no difference. Mama had still died. Afterwards, Papa had refused to go to the temple or participate in festivals. He said he wouldn't worship any gods who didn't answer prayer or demanded the blood of children.

"You go if you want to," Danel said. "I'm not sure it's a good idea."

"I'm not going without you." Yassib stood.

And he wouldn't. Yassib's absolute confidence that Danel would follow made it extremely difficult for Danel not to do so.

Tension knotted in Danel's stomach. What excuse could he give? "She'll cost more money than I want to spend." He knew the moment he spoke that his excuse wouldn't work.

"Don't worry about that," Yassib said. "I'll pay."

"No. If I go, I'll pay for myself," Danel said.

"Whatever you like, but we need to leave now. There'll be a crowd waiting."

Other people believed in the woman. Why was Danel so loath to go? He groaned as the dream flooded back into his mind again. This might be his only chance. Even if she only told him what she knew he wanted to hear, maybe it would be enough. Anything to be able to sleep again.

Danel fetched his silver and followed Yassib toward the hillock where the diviner had set up her tent.

* * *

There was indeed a long line of people waiting to consult Talliya. Danel sighed. He strove to look relaxed and happy. He didn't want others to know about the fear that kept coiling in his stomach when he least expected it.

He and Yassib inched forward. The closer they came to the tent, the more Danel's feet dragged. The fear he'd felt last night once again sunk its talons into him again, and his stomach churned.

The line contained equal numbers of men and women. Most were silent, minding their own business, but their faces reflected different emotions. Some were bright with curiosity and hope, others beset with worry or fear. Could the people waiting see Danel's fear?

The line continued to move forward. Danel couldn't help noticing that people looked different when they emerged from the tent. Some looked more fearful, some more anxious, some more somber. All looked—he searched for the word—all looked somehow more drained, more lifeless, as though something was missing. Dread coursed through him. He still wanted to run, but running would never give him peace.

"You first," Yassib said as they reached the front of the line, as though he knew of Danel's reluctance and didn't trust him not to dash away at the first opportunity.

Taking a deep breath, Danel pushed up the flap of the tent. He waited for his eyes to adjust to the gloom. There was a spark from a tiny oil lamp. Danel couldn't help drawing in a sharp breath.

"And why do you want my help?" a woman's voice asked.

Danel blinked. Talliya's voice was honeyed, seductive. It somehow suggested she knew him and had his best interests at heart.

Again he wanted to run, but Yassib would never let him forget it if he did. Instead, he stammered, "I had a dream."

"Well, honey, dreams are my-y specialty," Talliyah's voice purred.

His face warmed.

"It might not be important," he said, squirming,

"Let me be the judge of that." There was something mesmerizing about her voice, and suddenly it felt the most natural thing in the world to pour out his fear.

"I dreamed." He licked his lips. "I dreamed I went into my bakery and it was empty. No bread, no flour in the bins. The rats had devoured everything. There was no oil in the jars, for they had been smashed and the oil had seeped into the earth floor."

The despair and fear he'd felt during the dream swept through him again. "I looked and knew it was all gone and I didn't have the strength to do any more. I fell to the ground in a faint or death, I know not which. The birds of the air poured in through the doorway and descended, pecking, pecking, pecking. I woke in the dark, shaking."

There was a long silence. "I can see why you were concerned."

The last thing Danel wanted was for her to agree with him. "But that is not all, for I fell asleep again and dreamed the same thing."

"Let me ponder your dream's meaning." The woman began to hum. The humming continued for a long moment.

Then a voice spoke. "Disaster. Disaster and death are coming. And loss. Total loss."

The hair on Danel's neck stood on end for the voice was not the smooth purr of a woman's voice, but the deep, guttural tones of a man. A voice that made his mouth dry and his palms sweat.

"Death," the deep voice said again. "Death."

Danel started to shake. This was what he'd feared. This was why he hadn't wanted to come. He'd feared the dream predicted nothing good. It was worse, much worse, to have his fear confirmed.

Danel lurched to his feet, slammed the payment on the table, and dashed toward the exit from the tent.

"Death," the voice intoned again from the darkness behind him. "Death and destruction."

Danel stopped in the entrance of the tent, temporarily dazzled by the sunlight outside. The first thing he saw was Yassib, mouth open and eyes wide.

"Come on," Danel said. "We're going."

"What happened in there?" Yassib asked.

"This is not the place to talk about it," Danel said, heading away from the tent.

Behind them there was an indignant shout. "What do you mean you're closed?"

Danel turned. A man, bare arms folded, barred the way into the tent. "Talliya is unwell. She cannot see anyone else today."

Unwell? Danel would not have said she was unwell. Terrified at what she'd seen, perhaps, but not unwell. Did Talliya often react to dreams in this way?

Without looking any further, Danel turned and headed for the stream outside the town. If Yassib insisted on hearing what had occurred in the tent, then Danel wanted to be in the bright sunshine. They were not words that should be uttered in his home.

CHAPTER SIX

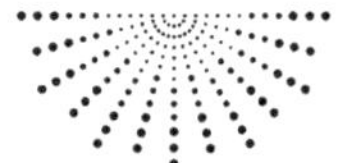

"Grandfather!"

Danel had been running late all day after yet another night of poor sleep. Out in the back garden, collecting more wood for the fires, he heard Donatiya cry out.

"Don't take him." Donatiya cried again.

Take him? Danel dropped his armful of wood and dashed toward the courtyard. It was filled with soldiers clad in the distinctive tunics of those who served Yassib's father.

Danel strode forward. "What has my grandfather done wrong?" He couldn't think of a single reason for Grandfather to be taken by the soldiers.

"He hasn't done anything wrong," one of the soldiers said. "The chief just wants to speak to him."

Why? Grandfather was a baker, not a soldier, not someone qualified to advise the town leaders. Danel turned. Grandfather had his arms clasped and his head lowered as if he was trying to make himself small enough not to be noticed. "Grandfather, shall I come with you?"

Grandfather nodded and uncurled himself to walk toward Danel.

"Donatiya, just sell the remaining bread and tell any other customers I'll bake more this afternoon."

Donatiya nodded as Danel took his grandfather's arm and followed the soldiers.

* * *

The chief's hall was on a small hill in the center of the town, surrounded by large trees. The group climbed the broad stairs. A pair of soldiers peeled off to each side to line the stairs while the commander pushed open the huge doors at the top and they entered the coolness of the large hall.

Once Danel's eyes had adjusted to the dimness inside, he took a keen look around. A series of pillars allowed the span of the roof to be wider than any he'd ever seen, with narrow windows running down the length of the building leading to a dais where Yassib's father sat.

This was where the serious business of the town was conducted, where important guests were welcomed. The family would live behind this public edifice.

Yassib had never invited Danel home, and Danel had never expected an invitation. Yassib had always come to Danel's home, or they had met at the stream, or beside one of the pools.

Danel's neck and shoulders were tight with a mixture of excitement and apprehension as he and his grandfather were led forward.

Yassib's father fixed his gaze on Danel's grandfather. "I am told you can tell me about the Israelites."

Danel blinked.

"The Israelites are coming." His grandfather threw back his shoulders as though he was speaking to a room full of people instead of just a few. "Our doom is here."

The chief turned to the soldier. "Is this what this man has been saying in the market, stirring up the people?"

"Yes, but no one believes him."

Danel's face warmed.

"The time has come," his grandfather burst out. "Their god has told them to destroy all within Canaan."

"All?" the chief said, leaning forward. "We are strong. We are not so easy to defeat."

"All are doomed," his grandfather repeated.

"Tell us more," the chief said, with skepticism in his voice.

But Grandfather's now-familiar shuttered look was back. No matter how many questions the chief asked, Grandfather said nothing.

Danel hung his head. If the soldiers had told him what they wanted with Grandfather, he could have told them this would be the result. What had been an occasional incoherency after Mama died had only worsened with the years. Since Danel's father had been murdered, Grandfather had seldom said much beyond these repeated predictions of doom.

There was the sound of hoofbeats outside, then voices. The soldier who'd brought them slipped out and came back almost immediately. "One of the messengers is back."

"Bring him in," the chief commanded.

Danel moved himself and Grandfather over into the shadows.

The messenger entered, covered with dust. He bowed his head to the chief.

"Well? What message do you bring?"

"The king of Edom has refused the Israelites permission to cross his land."

The chief raised an eyebrow. "Aren't the two peoples related in some way?"

"Yes, my lord. Mosheh claimed kinship by saying, 'This is what your brother Israel says: You know the hardships we've endured.

Our ancestors went down into Egypt, and we lived there many years. The Egyptians mistreated us and our ancestors, but when we cried out to the Lord, he heard our cry and sent an angel and brought us out of Egypt.'"

Danel didn't doubt the accuracy of the words, for messengers were trained to memorize the words they heard.

"Now we are at Kadesh, on the edge of your territory," the messenger continued. "Please let us pass through your country. We will not go through any field or vineyard, or drink water from any well. Any water our livestock drinks we will pay for. We will travel along the King's Highway and not turn to the right or to the left until we have passed through your territory."

The chief leaned forward. "But Edom refused?"

The messenger nodded. "They threatened to march out and attack the Israelites if they entered Edom's territory."

"And then?" the chief asked.

"The Israelites turned back toward Mount Hor, and they seemed to have stopped there. Several men went up the mountain. The elderly one stayed up on the mountain, and did not return with the others."

"Does that mean the old man is dead?" The chief stroked his beard. "That might work in our favor for if Mosheh is dead then we might have more time."

Time for what?

"They will come. They will destroy us." Grandfather's voice rang into the quietness, urgent and disturbing.

"Grandfather!" Danel tugged at his arm, anxious to get away before they were thrown out. Anxious not to be humiliated in front of the soldiers he'd admired since childhood. Anxious not to irritate Yassib's father, the chief who had made Gibeon great with his wise decisions and alliances.

"So you think the Israelites will come another way?" The chief's eyes were alert and piercing.

Danel looked up. Was the chief more worried than he appeared?

"Forty years are complete." Grandfather seemed clear for a moment, but even as Danel looked, his eyes clouded with confusion again.

"Take your grandfather home," the chief said. "Whatever this man once knew about the Israelites is now hidden. We will have to find out more another way."

CHAPTER SEVEN

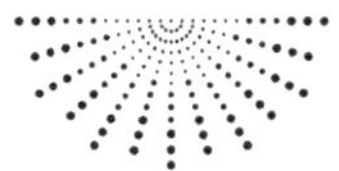

"*D*anel, I didn't expect to see you here." Yassib was fishing under their favorite tree. "I thought you couldn't get away from the bakery."

Danel sighed loudly. "I had to get away from things for a while." He was tired of dealing with all his responsibilities, and now there was the threat of the Israelites hovering in the air. He'd like to think the threat was far away, but the chief was obviously concerned.

Two evenings previously Donatiya had grumbled that Danel wasn't fun anymore, that he didn't spend time with her. Danel had brushed off her complaint but found it difficult to sleep that night. She was right. He behaved like an old man instead of a young one.

Yassib handed him a hook and line, and Danel searched around for a pole. It didn't matter whether he caught something or not, he just needed to be out of the bakery.

The sun danced on the water, and Danel felt some of the tension easing as he baited his home-carved hook, dropped it into the water with a plop, and settled himself on the riverbank.

"The fish aren't biting." Yassib gestured at the sky. "It's too bright."

"It is a little early for you to be fishing."

Yassib grunted. "Things are a bit tense at home."

Maybe Yassib wasn't carefree after all. Danel kept quiet. Yassib would speak when he was ready.

"Father is keeping a close eye on the Israelites. He's pretending to be relaxed and confident, but a chief remains chief by being alert to all possible threats."

"And your father thinks the Israelites are a threat?"

"It seems so. I've been talking to some of the older folk. Apparently, the Israelites were on the borders of our land some forty years ago."

Forty. Danel bit his lip. Was the number a coincidence? "Where have they been the past forty years?"

Yassib cleared his throat. "Wandering around the desert. No one seems to know why."

Danel frowned. "Why would they wander in the desert rather than settle?"

Yassib blew out a big breath. "That's part of what Father hoped your grandfather would tell us."

Danel drew in his line and tweaked the bait before throwing it out again. "I don't understand how Grandfather could help. He's no soldier."

As far as he knew, Grandfather had worked in the bakery from his youth. Danel had never delved any deeper. Never seen a reason to. He couldn't imagine Grandfather's scrawny body ever being of use to a fighting force.

"Father hasn't said anything in my hearing about why he thought your grandfather could help."

And even if Danel's grandfather could have helped in the past, he was no longer able to communicate. They'd probably never know, but the mystery gnawed at Danel.

"Father is receiving messengers from all over. He is checking if the old man who went up the mountain and didn't return was the Israelite's leader, Mosheh."

Even Danel could see that if such a leader died, the Israelites would be in unsettled for a while, with less time to be aggressive toward others. Yassib's father had been chief for all Danel's lifetime but Papa had said the years before had seen a rapid changeover of leaders and much instability. If the gods smiled on Canaan, the Israelites would wander elsewhere and leave them alone.

A breeze rippled the surface of the water, and there was a pull on Danel's line and almost simultaneously on Yassib's.

They busied themselves hauling in their fish and did not talk again about people who were far away and so different from themselves.

* * *

"What are you doing, Grandfather?" Danel asked.

Grandfather was trying to push a large pottery urn aside.

"Got to see," grandfather muttered.

"Got to see what?' Danel asked.

His grandfather didn't answer but kept trying to move the urn, the muscles in his neck sticking out like cords.

"Let me help you then," Danel said, a tinge of frustration in his voice. He didn't want Grandfather to overstrain himself.

Together they tipped the urn over and rolled it on its edge to a new position. Grandfather squatted with some difficulty and ran his finger along something scratched into the wall. Danel squatted next to him. There was a long line of marks, with every fifth mark taller than the others.

"Forty, aren't there?" his grandfather said. "Forty?"

Danel counted, then counted again. "Yes, there are forty."

"Then I'm right."

"Grandfather, what are you right about?"

"It's been forty years."

Danel took a deep breath to control his frustration. "Forty years since what?"

Grandfather tried to rise, teetered, and almost fell. Danel helped Grandfather stand, steadied him, then followed as he set off for the outside benches. He liked to sit and warm his bones in the sun.

"Who made the marks?" Danel asked once they were seated.

His grandfather thumped his own chest.

"You did? Why?" Danel could have kicked himself. Asking why was too complicated. Asking why usually resulted in a blank look.

His grandfather didn't seem to notice Danel's question but kept right on speaking. "Forty marks, forty barley harvests."

Forty obviously had significance, but what? What had forty years to do with anything?

"Our doom is come."

Grandfather was back to the same theme he'd been going on since the barley harvest. The urn. They'd moved the urn during the barley harvest because it had been in the way. Thinking back, Grandfather had been agitated ever since they'd performed the ritual offerings at the start of the harvest. Offerings to ensure good weather and protection of the grain. Danel recalled Grandfather leaning down toward the spot just before they'd pushed the urn into its new position. Had Grandfather made the fortieth mark on that day? If each mark was a year, had the harvest offerings been the signal to make the mark?

Grandfather jiggled his leg, something he often did. He had indeed been far more agitated since the last barley harvest, and his public proclamations had started at that point. If only they had the key to unlock what was hidden in Grandfather's mind. For it was increasingly obvious Grandfather knew something about the Israelites and something about the significance of forty years.

But how could a man's mind be opened?

CHAPTER EIGHT

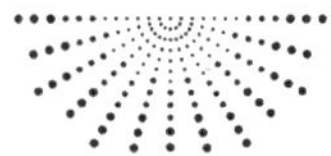

The market was always full of gossip, but today there were little groups of people everywhere and the hum of conversation was tense and urgent rather than the usual relaxed chatter.

Danel ignored the gossip and headed toward the corner where the sesame seed sellers sold their produce. Donatiya's sesame breads were in high demand, and it was time to settle on a supplier. The market was the easiest place to see all the sellers together and play them off against one another.

The sun was high overhead, so Danel had expected the market to be almost finished for the day. The news, whatever it was, had kept people here longer than usual.

"Danel, good to see you," called the first sesame seller.

Danel nodded to him. He already knew the man's prices and the quality of his product, so he proceeded to visit five other sellers. He let the sesame run through his fingers, checking whether it was clean without added stones or chaff. He squeezed individual seeds and tasted a few. Then he asked questions about the prices and whether it could be delivered to the bakery. After much deliberation, he made his decision and negotiated the deal with the seller.

"Shocking, isn't it?" someone said from behind him. "King Sihon is defeated and Heshbon is occupied by the Israelites."

A shiver of fear ran down Danel's spine. Sihon wasn't a mere tribal chieftain. He was a king and a warrior. Under his leadership, the Moabites had been driven out of Heshbon and the surrounding area. Danel and Yassib had reenacted the battle in one of their pretend games of war, chanting the words of an old poem. "Fire went out from Heshbon, a blaze from the city of Sihon. It consumed Moab. Woe to you, Moab! You are destroyed, people of Chemosh!"

Danel turned to the speaker. "Why did the Israelites attack Sihon?"

"They didn't. They asked permission to travel through Sihon's land and promised they would stick to the King's Highway and not turn aside into any field or vineyard, or drink water from any well."

Similar to the promise the Israelites had offered Edom.

"But Sihon answered by mustering his full army and marching out into the wilderness. He attacked the Israelites at Jahaz."

"Surely these Israelites couldn't be more powerful than Sihon?" Danel said, wanting skepticism to color his voice, but hearing fear instead.

"They must be," the man said. "They defeated Sihon, and now Sihon's capital, Heshbon, and his other cities belong to the Israelites."

Danel's shoulders relaxed a little. Heshbon was a long way away, and the Jordan River ran wide and swift between there and here, a longstanding natural protection for all peoples and cities to its west. Sihon might have been powerful once, but perhaps his power had waned or he had become overconfident. It happened to the best of kings.

There were other kings, more powerful than Sihon in the area, kings like Og of Bashan who ruled sixty cities. Cities with high stone walls and secure gates. Og himself was rumored to be a giant, with a bed made of iron, nine cubits long and four cubits wide. Danel and Yassib had once paced out the size of the bed and tried to imagine what it would be like to be that big.

The conversation moved away, and Danel turned to his chosen merchant and agreed to a trial period. Some would have called him overly cautious, but the responsibility to care for his sister and grandfather was always heavy on him. His sister might still be young, but she would be betrothed in a few years, and Danel would need to come up with a dowry. The bigger the dowry he could provide, the better chance she'd have of marrying into a good family and being cared for.

The sun scorched the top of Danel's head. Once his business was concluded, he headed home. Home, where Donatiya would give him a cool drink of goat's milk, and where he could sit under the fig tree for a while before starting the preparation for tomorrow's bread. The day-to-day work had been so constant that he had little time for other work, but soon he had to replace some of the mud bricks in the corner where water had leaked during recent heavy rains. This year's figs were now ripening well and soon there would be the picking and drying to do.

One day, if the bakery was successful, Danel would like to buy land and grow their own barley, wheat, and sesame, and hire people to help him. Danel sighed as he came to the gate into the courtyard. If he had to be a baker, he intended to do well. A wave of fear rolled over him. Try as he might, it was impossible to forget the diviner's words. He stroked the amulet hidden around his waist, one of several amulets he'd bought after his encounter with Talliya ... just in case. What if after all his striving, he died? He swallowed and squared his shoulders. No matter what, he would keep working as hard as he could. The gods could be arbitrary, granting one person's desires and crushing another. He was unimportant. Maybe they would forget him.

Passing through the gate, Danel bowed and offered incense at the new shrine he'd placed under the fig tree. "Great Baal and Astarte, grant a good fig harvest and may our goats have twins and triplets. Give me wisdom on where to use my efforts."

Backing away from the shrine, he discovered Donatiya had already placed a cup of goat's milk and some of the last of the dried figs ready for him. She stood nearby, clutching a cloth bag with an expectant look on her face. He'd hoped to have time to relax but she obviously had a question to ask. He gestured for her to sit next to him.

She sat down on the edge of the bench, "Can I show you something?"

He nodded and she drew some bread out of the bag.

"I tried something new."

He looked at the loaf, if that was what it could be called. She had made an intricate plaiting of the strands of dough and formed a circlet with it. Then she'd brushed the top with olive oil to make it shine, and sprinkled sesame across it.

She was an artist, this little sister of his. He'd have been content to keep making bread as his parents and grandparents had been making for generations, but Donatiya was always trying new things.

Most households still made their own flatbread. It was the fancier breads that they bought. As the city grew, more people were willing to buy bread rather than make their own.

"Do you like it?" Donatiya gnawed her lip.

"It's amazing."

Her face glowed. "I keep trying to improve it."

He indicated the loaf. "What do you do with bread that isn't as pretty as this?"

"I give it to beggars." Her voice shook as though she'd done something wrong.

"You're a kind girl," he said. He had wondered why there'd been more beggars around lately.

She grimaced. "I didn't think they would all start coming."

"We'll think of something. We can't feed all the beggars in Gibeon, but maybe we can choose a few to help and tell the others we can't do more."

His father used to say their mother was the same. Always feeling sorry for this beggar or that one. He could not scold his sister for being like their mother, but they couldn't afford to support too many. If King Sihon truly had been defeated, they could expect more beggars to make their way west, away from the Israelites.

Did the Israelites plan to live in the lands and cities that had belonged to Sihon, or were they looking beyond the land they'd already conquered? And if the Israelites wanted more land for their people, would they cross the Jordan River?

Danel's heart pounded in his chest. He'd always wanted to be a soldier and fight for his people, but what if Talliya meant he'd die achieving that dream? He'd promised his father he'd look after Donatiya, but that would be impossible if he was dead. The way things were currently in Canaan his death might mean hers too for without him she had no protector.

Danel rubbed the smooth stone of the amulet. *Keep me safe.*

CHAPTER NINE

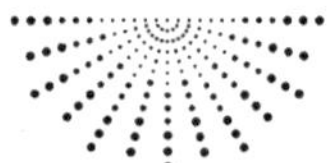

A horse thundered past their gate while the night was still dark, well before the cock would crow to signal the beginning of the new day. Danel sat up, heart pounding. Another messenger? No one traveled at night unless it was absolutely necessary. Grandfather said his own grandfather had talked of days when night travel had been safe, but nowadays there were too many bandits. As their family knew all too well, bandits were not content to merely steal. Too often, they murdered their victims. Danel shuddered, seeing again his father bleeding from his stab wounds.

Up here on the roof, a cool breeze blew. The rough rasp of Grandfather's breathing was loud in the darkness. Danel drew his cloak more tightly around him as though to block out the images in his mind. He put his hand under his mat and touched another amulet resting beneath. *Keep me safe.*

What news could possibly require someone to travel at such a pace during the darkness, as though the demons of hell pursued him?

The cock finally crowed and Danel got up, shivering in the predawn air. He shook out his cloak and felt the dampness of dew on the cloth. There would be a storm later in the day.

He said his prayers and made his offerings, then set to work. He smiled to himself as he remembered the beautiful bread his sister had surprised him with the day before. He'd suggested she only make the fancy breads for special occasions and feast days. That way, they could make her breads more desirable and charge higher prices.

Danel might still daydream about being a warrior but he didn't fool himself that it was likely. It was better to resign himself to being the best baker he could.

Danel was leaning into the fiery blast of air from the mouth of the clay oven when Yassib hollered from the courtyard. Danel pulled out the last of the bread and dropped it into a basket to carry through to where they sold it. He took a long swig of water and then poured the rest over his head. He was hot enough that it should have turned to steam.

Yassib was standing under the fig tree. He didn't wait for Danel to walk across to him but came quickly toward Danel. "Have you heard?"

"I haven't had time to talk to any of the neighbors this morning." Danel wiped the sweat from his still overheated skin. Yassib didn't seem to understand how much time and effort it took to run a bakery.

"There's been another battle." Yassib dropped onto the nearest rock. "King Og attacked the Israelites, just as Sihon did."

"Og must have been confident he'd win," Danel said.

"Any king that rules that large a territory and is as tall as the giants of old is confident." Yassib shook his head. "It was no use. The Israelites obliterated them. Killed everyone."

Danel touched the amulet at his waist. "Surely not everyone?" Sometimes Yassib exaggerated.

"Every man, woman, and child. Then they carried off all the livestock and plunder."

Danel shuddered. He and Yassib had played at war often as children. Now he was older, he didn't want war to come to Gibeon itself. It was one thing to want to fight, but he'd always imagined fighting on a plain or in the hills, not right here in Gibeon. Would the Israelites be content with two kingdoms?

"The messenger witnessed the battle from afar," Yassib said. "He walked through some of the empty cities. Said it was eerie to see the gates sagging open and not to hear anything inside except scavenging animals. He swam the river at its safest point and came to warn us."

Danel gnawed his lip. "What do the Israelites intend to do next?"

Yassib shrugged. "No idea. They'll have to make sure of their victory first. They can't leave the towns empty, or others will move in."

And occupation took time. The Israelites would have to repair walls and gates and distribute houses. Maybe they'd all be lucky and the Israelites would settle over the Jordan River, well away from Gibeon and the other Hivites.

Danel turned to Yassib. "What does your father intend to do?"

"Keep a good watch and push forward with repairing the town walls and older gates."

The tension in Danel's jaw relaxed.

"Today, some will start work ensuring there is enough water within the town walls and enough food stored," Yassib continued.

Many a strong town had been starved out in the past. *May the gods have mercy on us all and keep these people far away from us.*

Danel's insides knotted at the thought of what might happen to grandfather and Donatiya should things go wrong.

"I wondered whether you would like me to teach you what I have learned about fighting." Yassib looked at the ground, then met Danel's eyes.

Danel cracked a half smile, "Just like the old days."

Yassib smiled grimly. "Except we won't be fighting with sticks, and it won't be play."

Danel's mouth went dry.

Yassib stood up. "Meet you at the fishing spot when the shadows are longer than the trees." He slapped Danel on the back. "I'll bring the weapons." Yassib chuckled. "We'll see if you can finally beat me."

Danel doubted it. Yassib had been training with his father's men since they'd ceased their childish games.

* * *

"We'll start with short pikes," Yassib said. "I can't give you one of these to keep, but you should be able to find your own."

Danel's stifled his disappointment. He'd known he couldn't hope for a sword, but old dreams died hard. He'd never even held a real sword apart from the one failed attempt as a child. People like himself were allowed a small bow for hunting. He'd mastered that with years of practice but he'd need a bigger one if it came to war. That would only be possible if the chief was willing to trust more men, or if he needed every man to fight.

Yassib had chosen a flat piece of ground among some trees, out of sight of the women coming to fetch water.

"You always were skilled with the longer sticks, so you should find the short pike easy. Make sure your feet are the same width apart as your shoulders. Then you can step forward or back like this."

Yassib demonstrated a few times and had Danel mimic him. As Yassib demonstrated how to block and attack with various thrusts, Danel watched carefully. It didn't look difficult, but he'd thought the same about making bread. The practice of any skill was much harder than talking about it.

Yassib had Danel try the moves separately, giving them their appropriate names. Soon Danel could do each move without hesitation.

"Now I'll call out the moves in different orders." Yassib said. "Try and do them as smoothly and quickly as possible."

The short pikes would be used to parry sword thrusts or stun enemy soldiers so they could be finished off with a sword. Longer pikes with pointed ends were only used against horses, and horses were rare.

"Now you're ready to fight me," Yassib said.

Danel didn't feel at all ready, but he wasn't going to say so. Yassib's pike whizzed through the air while Danel's moves were more clumsy. Soon sweat was prickling along Danel's hairline, and he would have two bruises where he'd been too slow. Yassib was a hard taskmaster and the sun was nearly set before Yassib said, "That's enough for today. Can you come tomorrow?"

"I'll get up a little earlier and try to work a little faster," Danel said. "It was good to train with you."

"You have natural ability, and all that kneading of dough has toughened you."

Toughened him maybe, but nothing beat the long, constant practice with actual weapons. Weapons that, despite this training, Danel still might never touch.

CHAPTER TEN

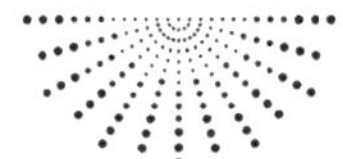

One moon later, a messenger from the chief's hall arrived at Danel's gate. "The chief wants to talk to you and your grandfather."

Danel glanced nervously at the messenger. Had the chief heard about his and Yassib's weapon practices? Maybe he was angry that his son was spending time with a baker and passing on the secrets of weaponry.

Danel dusted his hands on the cloth around his waist. He could not appear in front of the chief covered in flour.

"My grandfather is inside. Please seat yourself and have a drink while I fetch him. I must warn you, he is old and does not move quickly."

"There's a donkey outside," the man said.

The matter must be urgent then.

Danel hurried inside, helped his grandfather clean his hands and face and took the chance to do the same.

"Grandfather, let me get your second tunic." Grandfather often spilled food down the front of his clothes.

Getting his grandfather onto the donkey was an awkward task

involving a stool and the messenger's help. Danel walked alongside, holding the bridle in case Grandfather needed to hold on to his shoulder. Grandfather seemed calm, but Danel felt sick as he considered all the reasons why they might have been summoned. Grandfather had not yelled in the market again, because Danel hadn't taken him anywhere near it. If Danel was in trouble over the weapons training, there was no reason for his grandfather to come. An old man, whose mind was gone, could not be held responsible for Danel's misdemeanors.

"Do you know why the chief wants to see us?" Danel asked the messenger.

The messenger looked straight ahead. "The chief will tell you when you arrive."

Anxiety surged in Danel's belly as they reached the bottom of the hill. Danel helped his grandfather off the donkey. The messenger handed the donkey's bridle to another man and escorted them up the stairs. Once the guards allowed them through the entrance, the messenger left them.

Danel squinted across the dark expanse of the room, trying to gain a hint of why they were there.

"Brother, it is good to see you," a voice called out from the far end of the room.

Grandfather gripped Danel's hand as he turned his head to look for the man whose voice he seemed to recognize.

"Brother, here I am." A man strode toward them. He gripped Grandfather by the shoulders, looked long into his face, then enveloped him in a hug.

Grandfather choked and Danel heard a sniffle. Did his grandfather know this man? There were so many he no longer recognized.

"Brother, I am sorry the gods have chosen to afflict you." The man ended the hug. He turned to Danel, kissed him on each cheek, then held him at arm's length. "You have your mother's eyes."

Who was this man?

Behind them, the chief cleared his throat.

"Come, brother." The man led Grandfather forward. "Your chief wants to hear your story."

Grandfather's story? Could this relative, a man Danel could not recall ever meeting, know something about Grandfather's earlier life? Could this man explain the marks on their wall at home and Grandfather's ravings?

The man led them forward, indicating they should sit on stools below the dais. What could Grandfather's story have to do with the chief?

The chief clapped his hands, and several servants scurried in to lay a cloth and offer a selection of dried fruits and nuts and watered wine. This unknown visitor must have some status. Certainly, his clothes were of finer quality than the simple tunics Danel and Grandfather wore.

The servant poured each of them some wine then withdrew. In the shadows, there were guards but they were far enough away that they'd hear little. Not that it mattered—like the messenger who had brought them, the guards were chosen for their ability to keep their mouths shut.

"Now we have waited long enough. Tell us what we need to know," the chief said.

It was interesting that the chief had not demanded the man's news first, but instead had waited for Danel and Grandfather's arrival.

"I am Hammurapi from Kiriath Jearim. I was married to Keret's sister."

The chief tapped his finger on his knee.

"Forty years ago, I was a young man who didn't want to settle down in my father's bakery."

Not wanting to settle down to baking seemed to be a family trait.

"My father sent me to Gibeon to learn more of our trade. Here I met my now-brother and eventually his sister. Like most people, we had little interest in matters outside our own lives and families and paid no attention to happenings in far off places."

Uncle Hammurapi took a sip of wine.

"But then momentous news reached us."

Danel scratched an itch on his nose. What news would be considered so momentous?

"We did not know much of Egypt, but we did know it was a powerful country ruled by great pharaohs, rich beyond our wildest imaginings. It was a place of dreams and legends. All of a sudden, news from Egypt flooded over our land."

"I remember hearing about this." The chief leaned forward. "Plagues and disasters raining down on the Egyptians."

"Yes, that is what I speak of. By the time the news reached us in Canaan, three disasters had already struck Egypt. First, the mighty river Nile had been turned to blood."

Even Danel had heard of the Nile River, which was so much bigger and longer than the Jordan.

"Frogs had invaded people's homes, and then people had been bitten by swarms of gnats."

"Wasn't this man, Mosheh, the cause of all their problems?" the chief asked.

"I would not call Mosheh the cause of the plagues," Uncle Hammurapi said carefully.

"If not Mosheh, then who?" the chief asked with a frown.

"Mosheh claimed to be the mouthpiece of a hitherto unknown god. He claimed this god created the heavens and the earth and commissioned him to speak to Pharaoh and demand that Pharaoh let the Israelite slaves go free."

The chief snorted. "What king would let his slave force go?"

It did indeed sound crazy.

"Every time Mosheh made his demand, Pharaoh refused it, so

the Israelites' god sent plagues to force Pharaoh to change his mind."

Danel wished he could ask questions, but he had no right to speak unless the chief invited him to participate. He was only here to accompany his grandfather, although he still did not know what all this had to do with Grandfather.

"How many plagues did this god send?" the chief asked.

Danel leaned forward. This was one of his many questions.

"Ten in total," Hammurapi said. "Our leaders had messengers waiting in the south, waiting to carry the news from merchants of what was happening in Egypt."

Uncle took another sip of wine. "After the third plague, Pharaoh's magicians admitted they were powerless, that they were already defeated, but the plagues kept coming. Each time a plague hit Egypt, Pharaoh would tell Mosheh the Israelites could leave, but once the plague departed, he would change his mind."

Uncle Hammurapi paused and ticked off his fingers. "Flies were next, then boils, then a plague that killed the livestock." He clicked his tongue. "I am not sure I have the order right but you get the idea. There was a plague of hail that killed all living things left outside in the fields, including many of the Egyptians, and a plague of locusts that destroyed everything the hail had not destroyed." He closed his eyes and then murmured. "And darkness was the second last."

"The Egyptians worship the sun god, do they not?" the chief asked. "Why could Ra not deal with this unknown god of the Israelites?"

"An excellent question," Uncle Hammurapi said. "Each plague was like a series of battles against the gods of Egypt but the Israelites' god saved the worst for last."

"Hmm," the chief murmured. "My father talked about these plagues. I thought he was drunk, but he said something about the death of all the sons."

"Just the oldest sons," Uncle Hammurapi said.

Danel gulped. He was an oldest son, as was his father, and grandfather.

"Did no one escape?" the chief asked. "I seem to remember there was a way to avoid death."

"You have a good memory," Hammurapi said. "It was a strange rescue plan. Each household was instructed to choose a lamb without defect, kill it, and use its blood to paint the lintels of their door. If this god saw they'd painted the blood, he would pass over the door, and the sons were safe."

Danel blinked. Blood sacrifice and substitution he understood, but painting blood over a doorway? Was it a visible sign of submission to the rescue plan or a sign of allegiance or something else?

"Did Pharaoh's son die?" the chief asked.

His uncle nodded. "That night, Pharaoh was finally brought to his knees. He expelled the Israelites from Egypt and they headed this way."

"Why toward Canaan?" The chief rubbed his eyebrow. "And why have they taken so long to get here?"

"It's a long story but I'll try to be as brief as I can." Uncle Hammurapi took another sip of wine. "Why here? Because four hundred years ago, their god promised their ancestor, Avraham, that one day all this land would be his."

"But this land is ours," the chief growled.

Uncle nodded. "And that causes a problem, for in order for them to move in, we will have to be pushed out."

Danel swallowed.

"And if we don't want to be pushed out?" the chief asked.

"Sihon and Og didn't want to be pushed out either," Hammurapi said quietly.

There was another long silence.

If Yassib hadn't spoken to the messenger who had seen the desolation of Og's cities with his own eyes, Danel would have thought Hammurapi's tales exaggerated by time and distance. But there was Sihon as well, abandoned by their gods and mown down by the Israelite hordes. Had Sihon and Og wronged their gods, or was the Israelite god just too strong? If this new god had promised the Israelites all of Canaan, presumably they would soon try to cross the Jordan River.

But what did all this have to do with Grandfather?

CHAPTER ELEVEN

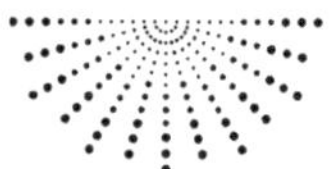

Serious conversation ceased while the servants brought in more refreshments.

"You have given us good background to these people, but this is not all you know," the chief said once the servants withdrew.

Hammurapi shook his head. "I was a young man when the multitudes of Israel arrived on our southern borders."

The chief stroked his beard. "I was just a carefree boy, but my father spoke of it."

"Mosheh sent twelve spies into Canaan. They traveled north and south and east and west for forty days." Uncle inclined his head toward the chief. "Your father was a wise man. He cautioned everyone to be alert for these spies. Keret and I were young and looking for adventure and spy-hunting sounded much more exciting than baking bread."

Danel looked across at his grandfather. It was strange to think that he and Grandfather might once have had a lot in common. Had Grandfather also had the desire to do something worth remembering? Maybe those shaky hands and weak knees once bent, and leaped, and wielded a weapon.

"We talked among ourselves and took to scouring around the town and out into the surrounding areas. Looking, looking, looking for anyone who was foreign and didn't belong."

"And did you find anyone?" the chief asked.

Uncle nodded. "We saw two men. Two men who looked remarkably like us, but their eyes were the eyes of those who have wandered far and seen much. They were alert and watchful, strangers to the rhythms of our town."

Like most Canaanites, Hivites seldom traveled out of the safety of their local area. Danel had never been more than a quarter of a day's journey from the sheltering walls of this town.

"The men we saw did not have anything to sell and they were noting things like the width of our walls and the strength of our gates."

"And trembled in fear I hope," the chief said with a wry smile.

"I don't know about trembling, but once we identified the men, we weren't going to let them out of our sight. I sent Keret to gather our cloaks, waterskins, staves, and a few provisions. Nothing was planned." Uncle Hammurapi chuckled. "Perhaps I was trying to impress my future wife by doing something adventurous."

The chief burped. "And you followed them?"

"We did. For days and days." Hammurapi turned to Grandfather. "Brother, do you remember? Sleeping under the stars and trying not to be seen."

Grandfather nodded. "Wolves."

"That's right. We wanted to head home whenever we heard them, but once the sun was up, we changed our minds."

So there was still some understanding trapped behind Grandfather's often expressionless face.

"Eventually the spies turned back toward their camp. The closer we went, the more we were afraid, for soaring into the air above the camp was something like a column of cloud."

The chief raised an eyebrow.

"It was not anything natural. We began to fear that the tales about Egypt had been nothing less than the truth."

The chief selected a dried fig. "What happened next?"

"The twelve spies returned to Mosheh, laden down with produce, and gave their report."

"Which presumably you couldn't hear?"

Hammurapi chuckled. "We spent an entire night getting into position so we had the best chance to hear. We crawled into a dry riverbed, covered ourselves with leaves, and waited, hoping we were in the right place." Uncle shook his head. "It was hot and we were bitten by ants. In the end, all our work was wasted because Mosheh called a huge assembly and we were too far away."

Danel's shoulders slumped. He'd been so sure Uncle Hammurapi and Grandfather would have succeeded in their mission.

"Keret was always a clearer thinker than me," Uncle said. "He said, 'The spies don't look any different than us, do they? Why don't we just mingle with the crowd? If we remain silent, they won't hear that our accents are different.' So we brushed off the leaves and stayed toward the back. The people in front of us relayed what was happening up front with Mosheh and the spies."

Danel's bottom was going numb.

"And what did you hear?" the chief asked.

"Once we got used to their accents, we heard how they'd obeyed Mosheh's command to go up through the Negev and into the hill country. They assessed our military strength, and whether we lived in walled towns or not."

The chief frowned.

"They also looked at the land and its produce."

"Sounds like we let them see too much." The chief rubbed his beard as if agitated.

The problem with Canaan was that it was a conglomeration of tiny kingdoms and tribes—Amorites and Hittites, Jebusites, and Ammonites—with even more kingdoms around the borders. The

Gibeonites were part of the broader group of Hivites but often remained aloof from Hivites in other areas. When the spies went through the land, each people group probably assumed the spies were from the neighboring area and thus hadn't perceived them as a threat.

"The spies had brought fruit back with them, including an enormous bunch of grapes that took two men to carry."

Danel whistled under his breath.

Uncle Hammurapi inclined his head toward the chief. "They gave a good report and said, 'We went into the land to which you sent us, and it does indeed flow with milk and honey. But the people who live there are powerful, and the cities are fortified and very large. We even saw descendants of Anak the giant there. The Amalekites live in the Negev, the Hittites, Jebusites and Amorites live in the hill country, and the Canaanites live near the sea and along the Jordan.'"

The chief chuckled. "The spies did their job well. Now if only they will listen to the report and tremble."

"That's when it got interesting," Uncle said. "Two of the spies—men by the names of Kalev and Yehoshua—spoke up. They said, 'We should go up and take possession of the land, for we can certainly do it.'"

"I do not like this mention of taking possession of the land." The chief thumped his knee. "We are already in possession of it."

Surely there was room for more people in the land, but not the enormous numbers that came with Mosheh.

"The other ten spies disagreed with Kalev and Yehoshua. 'We can't attack those people. They're stronger than we are. We seemed like grasshoppers in comparison.' At that point, the people around us began to mutter and speak out against Mosheh, his brother, Aharon, and the two spies who urged the people to war."

Aharon? Danel hadn't heard that name before.

"As the crowd grew angry, I wanted to sneak away but Keret

wanted us to brazen it out. I'm glad we stayed, for that night things got even more interesting. Ten of the spies moved around the groups of people. Whenever they left a group, the group huddled and murmured. We couldn't hear what they were saying, but it was obvious anger was building."

Hammurapi took a deep breath and looked across at Grandfather.

"At dusk, the huge pillar of cloud that hung over their camp turned to a blazing pillar of flame, and the rumble of discontent erupted into fear and despair. The people wept and said to their leaders, 'If only we had died in Egypt! Or in the wilderness during our journey. Our wives and children will be taken as plunder. Let's choose a leader and return to Egypt.'"

But they hadn't. Danel didn't know what happened next, but he knew the Israelites were here, in Canaan.

"We were told Mosheh and Aharon fell prostrate before their god, but Yehoshua and Kalev tore their clothes and rushed through the crowd yelling, 'The land we explored is exceedingly good. If the Lord is pleased with us, he will lead us into that land and will give it to us. Only do not rebel against the Lord. And do not be afraid of the people of the land for their protection is gone. Our Lord is with us. Do not be afraid of them.'"

Danel clenched his jaw. Who did this god think he was, that he could take Canaan for his own people? What had Danel and all the Canaanite tribes and kingdoms ever done to the Israelites to deserve such treatment?

"By this time, the crowd were threatening Mosheh and Yehoshua, and we began to fear for our lives," Uncle Hammurapi said. "Suddenly a blinding light filled a tent in the center of camp and a voice asked Mosheh, 'How long will these people treat me with contempt? How long will they refuse to believe in me? I will strike them down with a plague and destroy them, but I will make you into a nation greater and stronger than they.'"

The chief leaned forward. "Just a moment. Are you saying this god spoke audibly to them?"

Uncle Hammurapi's forehead wrinkled. "That was one of the strange things. We definitely heard his voice. It sounded like thunder—"

"Were you frightened?" the chief asked.

"Yes—" Uncle frowned. "And no." He pursed his lips. "There was something that terrified me. Maybe a feeling of vast power reined in, but the voice also reassured me that this god was not vindictive or capricious. He had a purpose in all he said and did."

"Go on," the chief murmured.

Uncle took another sip of wine. "Mosheh's words were relayed back to us and he answered his god, 'If you send a plague, the Egyptians will hear about it and they will say, "The Lord was not able to bring these people into the land he promised them on oath, so he slaughtered them in the wilderness." In accordance with your great love, forgive the sin of these people, just as you have pardoned them from the time they left Egypt until now.'"

"Hmm," the chief said. "Mosheh was right. We would have said these things. This god obviously changed his mind, for they are still here to be a curse to us two generations later."

Danel was still unsure why the Israelites had not attacked forty years ago. Had the people managed to get their own way and outmaneuver this god?

"We expected the Israelites to submit to their god's demands," Uncle Hammurapi said. "But it didn't quite work out that way. Their god told them, 'Mosheh, I have forgiven them like you asked, but not one of those who saw the miracles I performed in Egypt and the wilderness will ever see the land I promised their ancestors. Everyone above twenty years old will die in the desert except Kalev and Yehoshua. Turn back tomorrow and set out toward the desert along the route to the Red Sea.'"

Danel blinked. This god's reaction seemed a little extreme.

Complaining wasn't such a big deal. Uncle had said he didn't think their god was vindictive, but it certainly sounded as if he was.

Uncle cleared his throat. "Their god still was not finished for he said, 'Your children will be shepherds in the wilderness for forty years, suffering for your unfaithfulness, until the last of your bodies lies in the wilderness. For forty years—one year for each of the forty days you explored the land—you will suffer for your sins and know what it is like to have me against you.'"

"Forty," Grandfather murmured. "Forty years."

Danel leaned back. Everything made sense. Grandfather had been keeping track of the time on the wall of his home so he'd know when the forty-year judgment ended, and know when the Israelites would return to enter Canaan.

The chief rose to his feet and paced the length of the room and back, his forehead furrowed. "There is much to consider, but we will continue in the morning." He clapped his hands to summon a servant. "Prepare a room for our visitor."

Uncle Hammurapi looked up. "Please, your honor, I would prefer to stay with my brother. It has been a long time, too long, since we have seen each other."

So long, in fact, that Danel hadn't even known of this uncle's existence.

CHAPTER TWELVE

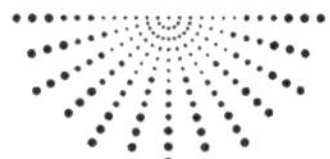

anel walked home while two donkeys, each led by an escort, plodded beside him, carrying the two older men. The chief had cautioned them not to speak to anyone about what they'd heard.

Just as they were about to leave, the chief had pulled Danel aside. "You may tell Yassib what you've heard, but it must be in a place where no one else can hear."

Danel couldn't help his eyebrows rising in surprise.

"Don't think your weapon practices have escaped me. The more fighters we have ready, the better. We're going to need them."

Danel's stomach did a slow flip. War was rushing toward them. Would there be enough time to prepare? Would he survive? Talliya had not given him much hope and Grandfather had predicted complete loss.

"I know you have the bakery to run," the chief said. "We won't need you here tomorrow. Your uncle's presence will be enough."

Danel swallowed the bitter taste of disappointment. For one brief afternoon he'd experienced the excitement of being at the center of things. Danel bowed his head and followed the others home.

His uncle put his hand on Danel's shoulder. "There are still a few more parts of the tale. If you can stay awake, I'll tell you the rest after the others are asleep."

Danel's grin split his face from ear to ear, but he controlled his initial glee. This wasn't some adventure story. Grim and terrible times might be coming.

Today, Grandfather had come back to life. When Grandfather had been younger, he'd always been quick to laugh. He'd tickled Danel until he twisted and squealed. He'd taught Danel and Yassib to fish, and had always been patient and full of good humor when they failed to catch anything, "Next time lads. There's always another day."

In the year of their mutual grief after Danel's father had been killed, Grandfather had disappeared into his own head, reappearing only intermittently. Everything had withered—the laughter, the jokes, the ability to teach others, even the ability to look after himself. Then came the seeming madness, the ranting about coming doom, the forty years. Uncle Hammurapi's arrival was like a key unlocking a treasure hidden deep inside.

"Thank you for coming, Uncle. It means a great deal to us," Danel said.

"My boy, I'm so sorry it has taken me so long." The donkey stumbled and Uncle Hammurapi patted it on the shoulder to calm it.

Danel wondered why they'd never met, but it wasn't right to question someone so much older.

"My father's bakery took me to Kiriath Jearim. Once Father died, I didn't want to continue baking. I'd always been more interested in farming, so I bought the vineyard. Family affairs took over, and I became too busy to leave." Uncle's voice wobbled. "My wife was partially paralyzed for many years. I couldn't leave her." He took a deep breath, and his voice cracked. "She died three moons ago. She was the light of my life and she left me."

Danel's throat constricted. "I am sorry, Uncle."

His uncle placed his hand on Danel's shoulder. "We have many things in common, you and I."

* * *

*D*onatiya and Grandfather had eaten and gone to bed. Danel and his uncle crept downstairs and sat near the ovens, still warm from the coals that remained alight ready to be fanned into flame the next morning.

Danel yawned.

"I know what it is to have to get up early every morning, so I won't keep you long from your bed." Uncle Hammurapi offered a matching yawn. "I had to help my wife every morning before I worked in the vineyard. It gave us a good income, but there was little time for rest."

Or time to visit relatives.

Uncle Hammurapi shifted on his stool. "Your grandfather and I thought the drama was over after the Israelites' god spoke to them, but we couldn't have been more wrong."

Danel raised an eyebrow.

"It was evening, and we were wondering whether we should return to Gibeon. We knew we couldn't stay undiscovered for long in the Israelite camp, not when everyone returned to their tents and we had nowhere to go."

"So what did you do?"

"We were about to go when we heard loud wailing. Soon everyone around us was saying the ten spies who spoke against Mosheh had been struck down."

Danel gasped. "Struck down? You mean they were killed?"

"Killed directly by the Israelite god. We watched their bodies being carried out of the camp and buried."

Fear seeped into Danel and he leaned against the wall behind him. Who was this god? A god who spoke in an audible voice, who demanded absolute allegiance, and who struck down those who opposed him.

"When the people heard of the deaths the following morning they returned to their tents to arm for war."

Danel raised an eyebrow, puzzled. "But weren't they in the desert for forty years?"

"Have patience, son, there is still more to tell."

Danel swallowed his questions.

"In the dark before the dawn the people said to Mosheh, 'We sinned yesterday in refusing to go into Canaan but now we're ready to go up to the land the Lord promised.'"

Danel frowned. If there had been such a battle, why wasn't it known?

"Mosheh said, 'You are disobeying the Lord's command. This will not succeed. Do not go up! The Lord is not with you. You will be defeated by your enemies, because you have turned away from the Lord. He will not be with you, and you will be soundly defeated.'"

"What did the Israelites do?" Danel asked.

Uncle shook his head and gave a gusty sigh. "They assumed they knew best and Mosheh was wrong. The rebels set off toward the hill country. Your grandfather and I allowed ourselves to be swept along. Once we reached the hills, we hid and watched the battle."

"And?"

"And the Israelites were routed and driven toward Hormah." Uncle shook his head. "Many, many Israelites died."

There was silence.

"Early the next day, we watched from far away as the Israelites followed the pillar of cloud and broke camp."

Danel didn't pretend to understand such magical things. "Have you heard anything since?"

"Only rumors." His uncle shook his head. "Rumors I've attempted to verify. That's how I know about the stories of their slavery in Egypt."

"Miraculous if they are true," Danel said.

"Oh, they are true. I spent many years separating truth from embellishments. There was another major miracle as well."

Danel yawned again.

"Perhaps I'll tell you another time."

"No." Danel gripped Uncle Hammurapi's arm. "I couldn't sleep now." And even if he did sleep, his nightmare might return ... as it did every few nights.

"I too need sleep, for your chief will have lots of questions tomorrow and I must be alert." Uncle Hammurapi leaned back against the lintel of the door. "After the tenth plague, Mosheh led his people away from Egypt as fast as possible, for Pharaoh had changed his mind too many times to be trusted."

Uncle Hammurapi cleared his throat. "Pharaoh took time to recover from his grief, but soon he began to castigate himself for allowing his slaves to leave. He summoned his army, and they set off in pursuit of the Israelites. When he caught up with them, they were on the shores of the Red Sea."

Danel drew in a sharp breath.

"It looked like they were trapped, but Mosheh's god opened a path right through the sea." Uncle sounded awed.

Danel whistled. He peered at his uncle in the gloom to see if he was joking. His face looked completely serious.

"The Israelites walked through the sea on dry ground."

"What about the Egyptians?" Danel asked.

"The god of the Israelites blocked the way with the pillar of fire. Once the Israelites were safely across, the pillar of fire lifted. Pharaoh didn't stop to think, and he sent his army in pursuit. The

Israelites' god sent the waters crashing down on the soldiers' heads." Uncle paused for a long moment. "Pharaoh's entire army were drowned. It must have been terrible."

Danel began to understand Grandfather's fear. Grandfather knew what this god was capable of and knew the forty years of judgment had ended.

Uncle Hammurapi also feared for their family, their nation, and all that was familiar. He feared for their very lives. That fear was now seeping into Danel's heart too. If this god who had conquered the mighty Egyptians was coming here, was there any hope?

CHAPTER THIRTEEN

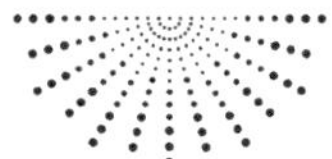

The next morning, Danel had been surprised to see his uncle downstairs at first cockcrow.

"I wanted to see if I could still make bread." He grinned at Danel.

His uncle looked so much like the prosperous landowner that he was, that Danel had almost forgotten his uncle had once worked in the bakery.

With his uncle's help, Danel was able to finish early and head for the grove of trees where he and Yassib did their daily weapons training.

Yassib was holding two bows and quivers. "I don't know how you managed to impress my father, but he insisted you be taught to use the bigger bow."

"Your father knew about our training all along." Danel took the bow out of Yassib's hands and hefted the weight of it.

"I didn't think we'd keep it secret from him for long." Yassib pointed toward the center of Gibeon. "Father is still shut inside the great hall."

Danel didn't know if that was a good sign or a bad sign. Uncle had already been with the chief some time. Was that because he and the chief were coming up with plans to protect their people?

Yassib pointed to a packed straw target he'd placed among a pile of rocks. "See if you can hit that."

Danel would have had no problem with his small hunting bow, but this bow was longer and heavier. He positioned his hands and drew the string back and let it twang, trying to get a feel for the weapon. "First, show me that you can do it."

Yassib placed his feet, notched the arrow, drew the string back to his ear and let the arrow fly. It hit the target close to the center marking. He smirked. "Now see if you can better that."

Danel took his time. His first arrow only just hit the target. His second was much closer to the center. He was getting the feel for the weapon and his years of practice on the smaller bow were paying off. His third shot equaled Yassib's.

"Let's do best of eight," Yassib said.

"I'm always ready for a competition but after that, I need to tell you what happened yesterday with my uncle."

"Your uncle? You've never mentioned an uncle." Yassib's eyes were wide.

"Archery first, talk second," Danel said.

Danel collected all their arrows, and they took turns to shoot. First Yassib was ahead, and then Danel. Yassib's last shot was a fingerbreadth from the center.

Danel shook his arms and moved his neck to release the tension. Then he planted his feet and drew the bow. The arrow released. With a thump, it hit the target equal distance from the center as Yassib's shot.

"Another shot each," Yassib said.

"Some other day," Danel said. "Your father told me to update you on what's happening."

They laid down the bows and sat on the sun-warmed rocks. By the time Danel had finished recounting all he could remember, the shadows were lengthening and the sun was sinking, leaving a pink and gold reminder of itself on the clouds.

Yassib thumped his knee with his hand. "So what are we going to do?"

Danel cocked an eyebrow at him. "What do you mean?"

"Well, someone needs to go and find out what the Israelites are doing."

"Your father has things under control."

"Possibly, but he can't move as quickly as we could if we left at dawn."

Danel stared at Yassib.

"Don't look so shocked. Haven't we always dreamed of being heroes? Well, now's our chance. What better thing could we do than follow the example of your grandfather and uncle?"

Excitement bubbled in the pit of Danel's stomach. Could they do it? Was it possible?

"Forty years ago, your family were spies on behalf of Gibeon. Now it's our turn."

"But—" All the things Danel was responsible for filled his thoughts.

"Don't give me any buts. Your duties will always be there waiting for you, but adventures don't. We either seize the chance or someone else will." Yassib fixed his gaze on him. "If we don't take this opportunity, we will always wish we had. Glory comes to those who grab it."

"I'll have to speak to my uncle," Danel said. Someone needed to watch the bakery, and Grandfather and Donatiya.

"If you do, you risk him saying no," Yassib said.

Tension gripped Danel's shoulders, but it was a risk he was going to have to take. He couldn't leave Donatiya without a protector, and he couldn't close the bakery just as it was beginning to prosper. Maybe they were all doomed, but he wasn't going to give up.

And he had the glimmerings of an idea how to convince his uncle.

* * *

*D*anel swallowed and reminded himself that Uncle Hammurapi wouldn't eat him. If only Danel didn't want to go with Yassib so badly. Yassib would be upset if Uncle said no.

Danel turned to his uncle. "Your story about you and Grandfather was very inspiring. You made a difference to our people. I would like to do the same."

Uncle peered at Danel under his bushy eyebrows. "How do you propose to do that?"

Danel took a deep breath and spoke in a rush. "Yassib and I want to go and see if we can find out anything about the Israelites that would help."

"I can see I'm going to regret reminding you that I am capable of working as a baker." Uncle Hammurapi sounded stern but there was a twinkle in his eye. "How long do you expect to be away?"

Excitement rose in Danel's chest. Was it better to underestimate or overestimate the time?

"I can't imagine it will take less than one moon," Uncle Hammurapi said. "My son would probably be happy if I stay here in Gibeon. It gives him a chance to prove he can run the vineyard without me." Uncle Hammurapi smoothed his beard. "I'll send him a message."

Outside, Donatiya was using the reed broom to sweep the courtyard.

"It will be good for me to spend more time with your grandfather, but make sure you come back to us," Uncle said. "Be safe."

Danel nodded but a flicker of fear mingled with his excitement. He'd been assuming he'd die in battle but that wasn't what Talliya had said. Spying could easily be as dangerous.

* * *

*D*anel and Yassib jogged down the hill and away from Gibeon. The light of a crescent moon provided just enough illumination to avoid the rocks and holes along the path. Dew silvered the long grass, and some animal snuffled in the dark shadows under the trees.

Danel had packed flour and ingredients for flatbread, and dried fruits and nuts. There would be plenty of herbs to forage along the way. He carried their supplies slung across the front of his body, his short bow and quiver across his back. In his right hand, he held a staff. Not only was it a weapon, but it would make climbing hills easier and could be used against snakes or wild boar if necessary.

Yassib, similarly attired, led the way. They hoped to be well on their way by sunrise.

"Mother will let Father know where we've gone," Yassib said.

"Do you think you'll get in trouble?" Danel asked.

"Maybe, but is that a problem?" Yassib grinned broadly. "We're off on adventure, going places we've never been before."

Danel touched the amulet at his waist. Donatiya had been tearful at his departure but she'd have been much worse if she knew about his nightmares or what Talliya had foretold. Yassib might focus on this as an adventure, but Talliya had said she could see death and destruction and total loss in Danel's future. Even carefree adventures could turn deadly.

* * *

*I*t took them four days to reach the Jordan River valley because they went out of their way to avoid towns and hid whenever they saw people. They couldn't risk being robbed or captured. Two strong young men would earn their captors plenty of money at the slave market, and their families would never learn what had happened to them.

They arrived at the last ridge at sunset on the fourth day. Yassib dropped to his belly and crawled to the brow of the ridge. Danel followed. They found some bushes and cautiously raised their heads. Below them was a river, the biggest Danel had ever seen.

"It's in flood," Yassib whispered. "Look, those trees would normally be well clear of the river."

Only the topmost branches of the trees were showing.

"And look at that," Yassib said, pointing well beyond the river.

Danel's eyes widened. The tents of the Israelite multitude spread north and south as far as the eye could see. And in the center of the camp was a tower of cloud rising toward heaven, just like Uncle Hammurapi had said. Danel's mouth dropped open and there was a long silence. He'd never doubted his uncle's tale, but it was quite another thing to see the pillar looming above them with his own eyes.

CHAPTER FOURTEEN

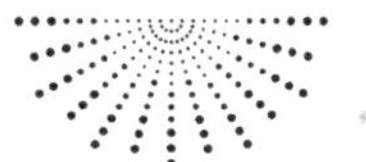

*D*anel was being shaken. He groaned, and Yassib clamped a hand across Danel's mouth.

Danel got up quietly and followed Yassib to their lookout post above the place they'd thought it would be easiest to attempt a river crossing. Below them, two men approached the river from the Canaanite side. They were searching the thickets for something. Danel didn't dare to speak because the men would hear, and they looked like men who knew how to handle themselves in a fight.

"Salmon, can you see a suitable log?" one of the men called. At least that was what Danel thought they said. They had thick accents.

"Come and help," the other called from within the thicket.

With much puffing and panting, the men dragged a log clear of the trees. "It would not do to drown now when we have so much to report."

"Spies," Danel mouthed.

Yassib nodded and they watched as the men dragged the log upstream then launched out across the flooded river. They were pushed downstream but with vigorous kicks they managed to keep the log pointing in the right direction. Before too long, they were climbing the far bank.

Yassib and Danel kept quiet until the men had disappeared in the heat haze in the direction of the Israelite camp.

"I wish we knew where they'd been," Yassib said. "Jericho is the closest city, but it is not the only place nearby. If we knew when they'd set out, we might guess how far they've traveled."

The information wouldn't be much use to Danel, but Yassib might be able to guess—knowing these lands was part of his training. Danel and Yassib had camped in a stand of thick tamarisk trees on the side of the ridge away from the river to keep a constant watch on what was happening, and seeing the two men had relieved the tedium of their task. Danel had gone to the nearest village for food and asked around. The villagers had assured him the river always flooded during harvest time. They believed the Israelites would be stuck on the other side until it receded.

The next morning, Danel was the one to wake Yassib. "The Israelites are on the move. Instead of leaving the river, they are moving toward it."

"But there's no way across." Yassib rubbed sleep from his eyes.

"Well, the pillar of cloud is coming this way."

The pillar of cloud had lifted off the ground and seemed to hover above the people before it moved to the front of the Israelites. Danel's skin prickled with fear as it did every time he looked at the towering cloud. Seeing it transform to flame at night was both mesmerizing and terrifying.

All day, Danel and Yassib took turns watching the Israelites. As each group moved forward, they'd set up their dark-skinned tents with an efficiency that revealed how many times they'd done this before. The braying and baaing of vast herds and flocks carried across the river but there was still no indication of why they'd moved toward the impassable river.

Next morning the Israelites were still there, and the next. Danel and Yassib spent long, boring hours taking turns watching the camp. Nothing special relieved their boredom except when the herds of sheep, goats, donkeys, and camels were watered at the river's edge.

Each day, Yassib set up a fire well away from the ridge. Danel made bread, and they'd roast whatever meat they'd brought down with a bow, a rabbit one day and a small deer another.

"Something seems different today." Yassib said the next morning as he came to switch places with Danel. "People are coming down to the water and washing or collecting water and taking it back to their tents."

Danel shielded his eyes with his hand and looked across the river. Yassib was right.

"Messengers went from tent to tent. Shortly after that, the washing began."

"Do you think it might be a religious ceremony?" Danel asked. Maybe the Israelites' god demanded some sort of ritual purity before people appeared before him.

Yassib shrugged. "It's hard to guess."

Danel took over the watching. If he'd have known their adventure would necessitate so much sitting and waiting, he might not have come. He'd always imagined heroes being in constant action, but perhaps waiting was an unmentioned part of the task.

It would be easy to fall asleep in the soporific heat of the day, but they had to stay alert. They must not miss the moment the Israelites moved elsewhere, although where they would move was a mystery. There'd been no sign of any boatbuilding and there was no other way to cross, for the water ran too deep and flowed too fast. They had found that out when they'd attempted a swim the day after they'd arrived.

Danel rolled onto his stomach and got comfortable. It would be a long, hot day. All around him, the droning of cicadas drilled a hole into his head. He watched as group after group of men came to the water and washed. They poured the water over their heads, hands, and bodies, then carried water back up the rise before disappearing into the vastness of the camp.

As the day dragged on, the activity in the camp only increased. Tension radiated from Danel's jaw and down his neck. He was sure the waiting was over. Something was going to happen soon. Possibly tomorrow. The only question was what?

* * *

A single trumpet sounded, and Danel was instantly awake. He rolled off his cloak and scrambled up to where Yassib was already watching.

They scanned the camp from behind the protection of the bushes. Each family was in the throes of packing up their tents.

Yassib drew in a sharp breath. "Where's the pillar of cloud gone?"

Danel scanned the whole camp. Yassib was right. Sometime in the middle of the night, the pillar had disappeared. What did that mean?

Once the camp was packed up, the people moved apart, leaving a clear space. Danel and Yassib continued to watch. Finally Danel pointed to the far end of the cleared area. A group of men were carrying something.

Danel squinted. "What is it?"

"Some sort of box," Yassib said.

A shaft of sunlight alighted on the box and it flashed.

"Is that gold?" Danel said. "Surely not."

"I don't think it can be anything else. Look at the sheen of it. Bronze doesn't shine that brightly."

The men carrying the box marched toward the river. Everyone they passed drew back, creating a wide passage.

"They must be priests," Yassib said. "They're all wearing the same clothes."

The priests, if that was what they were, continued to march forward.

"They're heading for the river," Danel said. "But what's the point?"

Yassib grabbed his arm. "The priests aren't stopping. If I didn't know better, I'd say those priests are going right into the river."

The priests indeed looked as if they intended to march right into the river. Danel held his breath. As the priests' feet touched the water, the water drew back from their feet and continued to recede as though a burning sun was drying the dampness on a rock. Danel clutched Yassib's arm, the hair on his arms standing upright. What sorcery was this?

They could see the bottom of the once-overflowing river. Even as he and Yassib watched, any remaining little pools disappeared until all that was left was dry ground, as if drought had struck the land in the time it took to blink.

Danel's gaze shifted upriver and his mouth went dry. Upstream there was a wall of water, the entire flow of the river had been brought to an unnatural and horrific halt.

"Remember?" Danel choked. "The Red Sea?"

Yassib's face was pale. "And now we have seen it for ourselves."

The priests continued their march to the center of the river.

On the bank of the river, quite a way downstream, a herald blew a blast on his trumpet and then shouted, "Reuben."

Two men walked forward, carrying a banner. Behind them came flocks and herds and carts. Men and women, young and old. No matter their age, they all looked fit and healthy. Their numbers took a long time to pass before the herald blew his trumpet and yelled, "Gad," and later, "Manasseh."

Danel did not know what the words meant but groups

continued to stream across the river and move out of sight in the direction of Jericho.

The herald blew another blast and continued to yell out the words.

"Judah."

"Issachar."

Each time, men marched forward carrying a banner. Each time, a stream of people and livestock followed.

"I wonder if the words are names. Names of their divisions or tribes or family groups," Yassib said.

"Can't be families. There are too many people in each group," Danel muttered.

They sat and watched as Zebulun, and Simeon passed below them.

"Levi," the herald announced.

"This group looks different," Danel said. Their banner was blue and gold, and all the goods were carried with long poles upon the men's shoulders instead of drawn by carts.

The trumpet blasts and names continued all the time Danel was out of sight preparing their meal below the lookout.

"Ephraim … Benjamin … Dan … Asher … Naphtali."

The names rolled over Danel, and it was a while before he noticed the trumpet and name-calls had ceased. Turning, he saw Yassib beckoning him from the ridge top. Danel crouched low and moved toward Yassib, handing him some food.

Tension coiled in Danel's stomach. He'd thought they were safe until the river receded, but this god had again proved more than able to do the impossible. Their god had conquered the barrier and all of Canaan was now open to the Israelites. Should he and Yassib leave immediately and report, or should they stay and keep watch?

The final group of people were now looking back at the river from the Canaanite side. Twelve men had been called forward to the riverbank. A man, who was definitely too young to be the former leader, Mosheh, called out in a loud voice.

"Each of you is to take up a stone from the riverbed. Twelve stones for our twelve tribes. Twelve stones to serve as a sign among you. In the future, when your children ask you, 'What do these stones mean?' Tell them that the flow of the Jordan was cut off before the ark of the covenant of the Lord. These stones are to be a memorial to the people of Israel forever."

Twelve tribes? That must have been the twelve named groups who crossed the river. If so, the twelve men called forth must be the tribal leaders. The ark of the covenant—was that the golden box? Danel knew the word covenant, for such agreements were common enough, but who had made the covenant and why a golden box?

The twelve men carried long poles into the middle of the river, where the priests were still standing with the golden box. They helped their leader collect twelve large rocks, stacking them in layers until they made a platform in the middle of the river.

Then they repeated the whole task with another twelve rocks. This time, they collected them from the middle of the river and carried them to the riverbank and loaded them onto a cart.

All this time, the wall of water stood upstream, obedient as a docile donkey brought to a standstill by its master's raised hand.

Then the leader called to the priests still standing in the middle of the river with the golden box. "Come up out of the Jordan."

The men straightened their backs, gripping the poles that enabled them to carry the ark, and walked up out of the river. The moment their feet touched the ground there was a rumble and a roar.

Danel had but a moment to register that the wall of water was collapsing before water spray filled the air and a sound like a crack of thunder echoed from the rocks. He touched the amulet at his waist. *Save me!*

Was this how he died? He thought of the fuzzy image he had left of his mother's face, his sister's smile, the warmth of his father's arms, the elasticity of dough in his hands. Then he blinked, and the water spray cleared and the swollen river flowed freely as if nothing had happened.

The priests and their leader moved forward, and the Israelites marched further into Canaan.

Danel held his hands up. They were shaking. He'd heard of miracles, but this was the first time he'd ever seen one. Would Donatiya believe it, let alone anyone else?

CHAPTER FIFTEEN

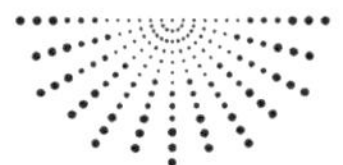

*D*anel and Yassib spent most of the rest of the day scouting out a new lookout post closer to the Israelites. They found a site with clear views, a jumble of rocks, some sheltering trees, and a cave which they checked to make sure it was empty.

"Why are they not moving to surround Jericho if that is their intended target?" Danel asked as they sat hidden from view. "They look like they're properly setting up camp."

Below them, the Israelites were setting up their tents, even using thorn branches to make temporary fencing for the herds.

"You expect me to understand how these foreigners think?" Yassib said. "So far they've been unpredictable."

It would be madness to attack Jericho, for it was surrounded by a high stone wall with many towers and stout gates, and had a large population to defend it. And yet, Jericho had to fall before the Israelites could move further toward Gibeon. Was there yet hope? Danel whispered a prayer to Baal and Astarte.

Even as Danel and Yassib watched, there were two blasts on a trumpet. Almost immediately, the people started streaming toward the center of their camp.

"Now what are they up to?" Yassib rolled over to his stomach to better watch them.

The meeting lasted some time, but the women eventually returned to their tents. It was much later before the men started to return a few at a time. Something was clearly wrong for they were moved hesitantly, as though they were hurting.

Danel raised his eyebrows.

"I'm as confused as you are," Yassib said.

The men were not seen again that day. By the next morning, Yassib was pacing up and down below the ridgeline. "What are these people doing? I thought they were going to start their attack on Canaan but they seem to be dallying around." He spat on the ground. "What would you say if I made a trip to Jericho? I might find out something."

Danel looked down at the Israelites between them and the city. "You'll have to go round the long way, to the far side of the city."

"There's sure to be a back gate," Yassib said. "I'll take my bow and hunt for something to exchange."

Danel nodded. "A change from meat and bread would be good. And we need more flour and salt."

* * *

While Yassib was gone, Danel thought about whether he could do something so that Yassib wouldn't be the only one with news. Could Danel manage to get closer to the Israelite camp? Close enough to overhear something useful?

From their lookout, Danel traced a possible route. There was good tree cover until the ground dipped. Perhaps he'd find a stream at the bottom of the dip and enough vegetation on its banks to approach within a stone's throw of the camp. He blew out a breath.

What if he were caught? He'd need a good excuse to be there. He shrugged. He'd think of something on the way.

The sun was high in the sky when Danel left and considerably lower by the time he'd descended the back side of the hill, found a small valley which led through to the trees, and the stream he'd expected.

He moved like a mouse avoiding an owl, swift and silent under the cover of the bushes, until he heard voices. Laughing female voices. He dropped to his belly and crawled to an outcrop of rocks near the water's edge. He waited to make sure the voices didn't drop into silence or raise an alarm, then peeked through a crack between two boulders. In a waterhole beyond a short cascade of rapids, three girls were standing up to their calves in the water, washing clothes and chattering like a flock of sparrows. He scanned the area but couldn't see a guard. These girls were naive. He wouldn't have let Donatiya wander alone, especially not when every Canaanite would be on high alert.

"Aren't you glad we've found this place of our own," the smallest girl said.

"I'm so tired of Father and our brothers lying around all day and groaning and demanding we fetch them drinks and food."

Danel frowned. Why were the men groaning?

"Their pain hasn't reduced their appetites," said the tallest one with a wry smile.

The third giggled. "You'd think they were dying."

"I don't imagine circumcision was much fun," the tallest one said with a grimace.

Circumcision? Was that why the men had looked to be in pain? Danel had heard of the barbaric custom but didn't know the Israelites practiced it. And on grown men!

"I bet they're cursing our grandparents for not obeying the Lord in this matter," the tallest one said again. "If they'd circumcised all the babies like they were supposed to, they wouldn't be complaining now."

An ant bit Danel's thigh, and he clamped his mouth shut. Now was not the time to slap it or curse. If these girls screamed, there might be someone nearby ready to run to the rescue. Danel was no use to his town dead.

If only he and Yassib had known the Israelite men were all incapacitated. They could have told Jericho, and the whole war might have been over before it began.

"They'll have to stir themselves tomorrow. It's full moon. We will need the Passover lambs killed, no matter how the men feel." The girl giggled as she scrubbed the clothes on a smooth rock.

"I love Passover," the tall girl said. "And hearing Father tell us again why our family left Egypt and followed Elohim to become Israelites."

"I don't like the bit about the blood painted on the doors," said another. "And we're still not fully accepted," said the smallest girl. "That's why I prefer to be out here on our own. I hate the kinds of comments they make about us."

The tall girl gave the younger girl's shoulder a squeeze. "Acceptance will come."

Were these girls not Israelites? Danel couldn't tell, having never met an Israelite. Whoever these girls were, it seemed they and the rest of the Israelites were in no hurry to begin their conquest between the circumcisions and their Passover festival. Uncle had mentioned the last plague and the blood painted on the doors. This festival must commemorate their escape from slavery. They seemed to remember the plagues as a rescue. Danel would bet the Egyptians didn't call it that.

A breeze wafted the scent of some flower toward Danel, and he felt a sneeze coming on. He pinched his nose and put his head down to muffle the sound, but the sneeze still sounded horrifically loud in his ears.

"What was that?" one of the girls said.

"Up there. I saw the bush move behind those rocks," shouted one of the girls, probably the oldest. "Come out, or I'll scream."

Danel wanted to cower down and pretend he wasn't there, but the thought of a girl finding him in such a position made his face flame. "I won't hurt you," he called as he scrambled to his feet.

The taller girl now held a long stick in one hand and a stone in the other. The other two girls hid behind her.

Danel raised his hands to show he had nothing hidden. "I won't hurt you."

"What do you want?" asked the tall girl. "Don't you dare come nearer or I'll, I'll—"

"Smash in your head like a melon," piped up the smallest girl.

The surprise on the oldest girl's face to hear such a violent yet comical threat come from such a little mouth seemed to match his own. For a moment, their eyes met in common amusement.

"I am not here to hurt you." Danel held up his empty hands. "But keep your stone if it makes you feel safe. I'm not sure what good it would do you. My sister always said I'm rather hardheaded."

The girl lowered her arm.

"I just want to talk," Danel said.

"What about?" the tall girl demanded, although her voice was less strained than before.

This girl made him forget all his questions. He thought of several but rejected them as inappropriate to ask at this stage of their acquaintance. He couldn't exactly ask if the Israelites planned to kill everyone in Canaan. So he asked the only question he could think of that sounded innocent.

"Where is Mosheh?"

Her shoulders slumped. "He died just before we came to the Jordan River. Yehoshua is now our leader."

"Was he one of the two spies who urged your people to attack Canaan forty years ago?"

She pursed her lips. "How do you know that?"

He shrugged. "My uncle told me the story."

One of the girls behind the talker whispered something. The talker shook her head. "I think he's safe enough," she whispered. "He doesn't scare me."

Danel wasn't sure whether or not to be pleased to be non-scary. Working in the bakery had strengthened him, but he didn't look like a fighter. Rather weedy, in fact. Weedy but wiry.

"What if I sit down on this side of the stream and you stand on the other?" Danel said. "Then if I scare you, you can whack me with that big rock of yours and finish me off with the stick."

A dimple flashed in the girl's cheek. "Don't think I won't. You may be hardheaded, but I'm sure I could do some good damage to your pretty face."

Danel flushed. The girls used rocks as stepping stones to jump across the stream at the narrow mouth of the swimming hole, and Danel walked slowly to a bigger rock on the near side and sat down, keeping his hands visible so he didn't spook anyone. The two younger girls eyed him warily and hung back.

"You said you weren't fully accepted as an Israelite," Danel said, "What did you mean?"

The talker looked at him for a long moment. Considering whether he was trustworthy, perhaps?

"My grandparents were Egyptians. Grandpa was a papyrus maker." She looked at him. "You do know what that is?"

He nodded. Egyptian papyrus was famed even this far from its source.

"After the tenth plague, Grandpa, his sister, our grandmother, and some of her family set off to follow the Israelites."

Would Danel have been willing to leave his own people to join another? To learn new ways and customs? He did not know. It had never been asked of him.

"They caught up with the Israelites at the Red Sea."

"So your family were there when the sea opened?" Danel asked.

"They said it was an unforgettable experience, even greater than what we saw at the river." She leaned the stick against a rock. "And they experienced all the ways Elohim provided for the Israelites."

Elohim must be the name of her god. Danel raised his head and looked at her. "What do you mean?"

"You don't think this many people have survived by hunting, do you?" She laughed. "Elohim has miraculously provided for us. There is always water. Every morning, we collect a sort of bread from the ground. Even our clothes have not worn out. My grandparents tell us to praise and thank Elohim for his gifts every day."

"They're still alive then?" Danel asked.

"My grandparents weren't yet married the last time Israel was on the borders of Canaan."

"Do you want to taste our food?" one of the younger girls said. "We collect it on the ground every morning, but it gets maggots in it if we leave it overnight."

"Except on the day before Shabbat, when we collect two days' worth without any problem," the other girl said, peeping out from behind the oldest girl.

Danel wrinkled his brow, confused by the new word.

"Shabbat is our day of rest," the oldest girl said. "From sunset on the sixth day to the following sunset. Elohim provides extra food so we don't have to do any work."

"Shabbat is the best day of the week," the oldest girl said. "We all get to rest properly."

It sounded delightful. A whole day off each week.

The middle girl held out something like a small cake of white flakes pressed together. "Taste it. We've had more than enough to last us a lifetime."

Danel stepped over the stones, took the somewhat-squashed cake, and retreated back to his rock. He sniffed the cake. It smelled vaguely of honey. He put it in his mouth. It was like nothing he'd ever tasted. Slightly sweet but with hints of other subtle flavors. It would sell if he made it at the bakery, but could it be replicated? This bread given directly, so they claimed, from their god himself.

Someone whistled and the girls turned to look back toward the camp. "We have to go," said the oldest. "Thank you for not making me use my stick." The tightening of her lips suggested she was about to laugh.

Danel stood and bowed in her direction. "You are quite safe with me."

She looked at him for a long moment. "Maybe." She didn't sound too certain. With a swish of her tunic, the three of them collected their washing and soon disappeared out of sight.

Danel waited a while before taking a circuitous route back to the cave. He'd prepare a meal in case Yassib returned.

CHAPTER SIXTEEN

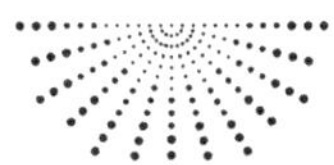

assib arrived back shortly after nightfall, wolfed down his food, and fell asleep. Danel had to curb his desire to know what Yassib had found out from his visit to Jericho and wait.

Danel woke early and scrambled up to the lookout post. Off in the distance, he could hear the bleat of sheep as men sought lambs ready for Passover. The smoke of thousands of fires rose, ready to roast the lamb for tonight's feast. Danel's mouth watered. Then what? Surely the Israelites would start their attacks.

Yassib climbed up beside him, put his hands behind his head, and made himself comfortable. "I had no problems reaching the back gate of Jericho, but the gates were shut tight against the Israelites and I couldn't convince them I wasn't a spy."

"So they are worried about spies?"

"The gatekeeper was obviously a bit lonely because he was happy to talk after a few jokes."

Yassib could charm the birds out of the trees.

"The city believed the two spies visited Jericho and stayed at the home of a woman called Rahab."

"They can't have been good spies if everyone knew about them," Danel said.

Yassib chuckled. "When the soldiers went to her house to demand she give up the spies, she said they'd left and headed for the hills."

"Did you learn anything else?" Danel asked.

"Not directly." Yassib sat up and picked at his teeth with a small twig. "It was obvious the gatekeeper was terrified that the Israelites were coming. His voice shook at any mention of them."

Yassib stared into the distance, his brow furrowed. "There was one strange thing. When I was coming back here, I looked back over my shoulder and was surprised to see a long scarlet cord blowing from one window high on the city wall. I don't know the meaning of that either."

"Maybe we could ask the girls I met yesterday," Danel said, his face warming.

Yassib raised an eyebrow. "You liked at least one of those girls."

Danel punched Yassib's shoulder but said nothing.

"It's like that, is it?" Yassib indicated the Israelite camp. "They don't seem in any hurry."

"They're observing their Passover, some sort of festival," Danel said.

"Funny time to celebrate a festival." Yassib furrowed his brow. "Do you think we could get more information from them?"

Danel's gut twisted. While he'd liked those girls, he needed to remember they were his enemies and he was here as a spy.

"What do we want to know?"

Yassib chewed the twig. "We could ask them if Yehoshua is planning to attack Jericho."

"They're young. Do you think they'd know?"

Yassib shrugged. "It doesn't hurt to ask."

No, but if they revealed information like that, they'd be in trouble. Big trouble. Not that Danel thought they'd reveal too much. The taller girl was smart. She'd remember he was the enemy.

* * *

*T*he girls weren't at the stream the next day. Danel swallowed back his disappointment and made sure to be there even earlier the following day.

The ants bit him mercilessly and he was about to give up when he heard voices and laughter. He felt like cheering when the girls went to the same pool and took off their sandals and paddled.

He waited long enough to check that no one else had come with them, then scrambled to his feet and stood waiting to see if they'd acknowledge his presence and invite him to come closer.

As he'd hoped, the oldest girl said, "Are you going to stand there all day?"

Danel sauntered toward them as casually as he could. "I didn't know if I'd be welcome."

She laughed. "As long as you do nothing that requires me to use my stick, you'll be fine."

Sure enough, the stick was within reach next to the rock she was sitting on. She was courageous but not foolish.

"I'm a baker," he said, flushing. "I've been thinking about that bread you let me taste the other day."

"Manna, we call it." She scooped up a handful of water and had a quick drink. "A strange thing happened. We harvested some wild grain the day we celebrated Passover. The next morning when we went out to gather manna, there was none. We haven't seen it since."

So he'd lost his chance to try and mimic this heavenly food. He'd thought Grandfather might have found it easy to eat. The manna wasn't the only thing to disappear. "The pillar of cloud and fire is gone too."

95

She nodded, glancing to the sky.

"How do you feel about that?" he asked.

She wrinkled her brow. "What do you mean?"

"That cloud has been with you for forty years. Don't you miss it?"

"No, not really. Our family were talking about the disappearance last night. We think it might be Elohim's way of saying, 'Now you know me well enough to listen to me. You don't need a physical guide any longer.' Maybe now we're expected to follow Adonai himself rather than just a cloud." She smiled. "It's a good sign. I think."

Adonai. Was that another name for her god or another god altogether? Danel didn't know what to think because it was all so new. He hesitated, unsure how to ask his many other questions. If he asked her directly about the Israelites' plans, he'd likely scare her off. She'd conclude he was only interested in using her to gain information that might harm her own people. She must know her people were not welcome here. That they were walking into a land that was already fully occupied.

Yassib had been puzzled about the scarlet cord. Maybe she would know something about it. Danel paused. He needed to get this right. He rehearsed what he wanted to say in his mind before speaking.

"There was a scarlet cord hanging from the wall outside Jericho."

She shrugged. "I have seen it, but I don't know what it means. Adonai doesn't tell us much up front. He expects us to trust him and follow."

It was all so different from the Canaanite gods. This god seemed to want a connection with his followers.

"When you talk about your god there is admiration, even love, in your voice," Danel said. "I don't understand it. He seems warlike, even ruthless, to me."

She sat down on a rock. "My grandparents still remember what it was like to worship the gods of Egypt. They often tell us how Adonai rescued the Israelites from Egypt and how mercy always accompanied judgment. Grandpa Kheti and Grandma Nophret and Grandpa's father listened to the warnings and were able to save much of their livestock." She sighed. "But sadly, most of the family refused to listen and lost their lives in the final plague. Only my cousin, who was just a young child, survived the final plague. That was only because my great-grandfather sacrificed his own life to make it possible."

"I'd like to hear the full story someday," Danel said, even though he doubted he'd ever have the opportunity.

"Grandpa and Grandma both chose to follow Adonai out of Egypt because they saw the love and mercy within his justice."

"Yes." The middle girl looked up from where she'd been paddling. "There are always two ways to respond to Adonai's commands. We can obey and be blessed, or we can disobey and live with the consequences."

Danel tossed a pebble into the water. "Why does Adonai get to tell you what to do?"

"Because he knows what is best for us," the youngest girl said.

"But how do you know that?" Danel persisted.

"Adonai knows everything." The oldest girl nibbled her lip. "I've learned to trust him. Every time I've gone my own way, I've regretted it. I find that when I obey, then my heart is at peace."

Peace. Danel wished he had peace. He still repeatedly dreamed his original nightmare about the crows and death. Since consulting Talliya, he also had nightmares about her tent and her terror. Peace. There was no peace for Danel.

A white-throated kingfisher dived into the water and came up with a wriggling silver fish.

"Didn't you say Yehoshua has seen the commander of the army of the Lord?" the middle girl asked.

"What do you mean, the commander of the Lord's army?" Danel asked.

"I'm not sure anyone knows. Yehoshua was walking near the walls of Jericho when he saw a man standing in front of him with a sword in his hand. He walked closer to the man and asked, 'Are you for us or for our enemies?' The man replied, 'Neither, but as commander of the Lord's army I have now come.'" She paused and drew in a sharp breath as though seeing the scene before her own eyes. "Yehoshua fell face down on the ground and asked, 'What message does my Lord have for his servant?' The commander said, 'Take off your sandals, for the place you are standing is holy ground.'"

Danel wrinkled his brow. He'd expected the messenger to give Yehoshua some sort of instructions, not talk about holy ground. Whatever that meant.

She looked sad. "Then the commander of the Lord's army gave Yehoshua instructions for what he was to do next."

He gave a wry smile. "Which you're not going to tell me?"

She shook her head. "It's not safe to trust anybody. I don't even know your name, let alone who you are or where you come from."

And he couldn't tell her those things either. "I'm sorry. Like you, there are things I cannot tell you."

"Then I guess it's goodbye." Her voice cracked.

He nodded and turned to go.

"May Elohim guide your steps and bring you peace," she murmured behind him.

He stopped. She'd blessed him, this girl on the verge of becoming a woman. What would make her do such a thing, to someone she must know was an enemy? Not an enemy by choice, but simply because they were on opposite sides of a war neither had chosen.

Danel swallowed the lump in his throat and headed in the opposite direction from where he needed to go. She had not revealed much but she had confirmed something would soon happen. He and Yassib would have to stay, glean all they could about Israel's battle tactics, and see what Israel planned to do next.

If Jericho was the target, how were the Israelites going to fight a battle when Jericho's walls were high and strong and the gates firmly battened shut?

CHAPTER SEVENTEEN

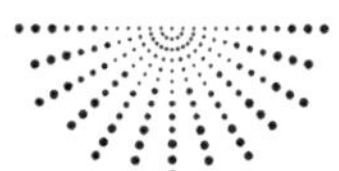

here was a scrabbling noise outside the cave. Danel grabbed his staff, ready to protect himself.

Yassib stuck his head into the cave. "Wake up sleepyhead. Something's happening."

Danel grabbed some bread and a handful of raisins, and followed Yassib up to the looking post. The dawn sun was just cresting the hills and shining on the distant walls of Jericho.

Armed men were coming out of the tents of the Israelite camp. Both excitement and anxiety tingled down the back of Danel's neck. Now they'd get a chance to see how the Israelites functioned as an army. Clumps of women and children were gathered in the entrance of each tent. Many briefly hugged their menfolk, watching as they walked to the edges of the camp closest to Jericho.

"Look, there's the golden box." Yassib pointed.

As the priests carrying the ark reached the outskirts of the camp, a man, presumably Yehoshua, issued orders. The army formed into position. An advance guard assembled at the front, then a row of seven trumpeters, the priests carrying the ark, and finally the rest of the army.

"Where do you think they got their spears and swords?" Yassib asked. Swords were rare and expensive.

Danel put his head to one side. "Perhaps from Sihon and Og's defeated army. Or from the Egyptians who drowned in the Red Sea." If it was possible for some to still have swords on their bodies. It might have to remain a mystery.

The trumpeters sounded a blast and kept blowing their trumpets as the army set off in orderly rows.

"I'd have expected them to try and starve out the city," Yassib said. "Why announce themselves?"

"Perhaps they hope to entice those in Jericho to come out?" Danel said, puzzled.

"The men of Jericho would never be that foolish," Yassib said.

The trumpets continued to sound. Instead of heading straight for the city, the army turned parallel to the wall and far enough away to be out of bowshot. They then proceeded to walk in silence following those blowing the trumpets and carrying the ark. It looked as though battle was far from their thoughts.

Eventually the Israelites disappeared around the far curve of the wall. The trumpets faded until Danel could barely hear them.

Danel was getting thirsty by the time they heard the trumpet again. The women of the camp were still standing and waiting. Slowly the army completed a loop of the walls, then walked back into camp.

"What do you think that was about?" Danel asked.

"I have no idea," Yassib said. "But watching and waiting is why we are here."

"I never expected spying to include so much sitting around. Not to mention being bitten by every insect in the country," Danel muttered.

"Me neither, but at least we're still alive."

They wasted hours watching the Israelites collect water, harvest edible plants, and herd their animals. It was boring, boring, boring.

The next morning Danel woke Yassib. Again they watched the army follow the trumpeters, walking around the city in silence. The third day was the same, as was the fourth. By the sixth day, Danel and Yassib's supplies were running low and they were more puzzled than ever. Whatever this crazy plan was about, it didn't seem to be achieving anything except that each day there were more and more watchers on the walls of Jericho. Danel imagined that many of them would be jeering at the Israelites from the security of their high walls.

Day seven started in just the same way as the others. Just as Yassib and Danel turned to go back to their cave in disgust at another wasted day, Danel nudged Yassib.

"Stop! They're going around a second time."

Yassib flopped down on his stomach. The ram's horn trumpets were still blowing, and soon the Israelites had disappeared on a second loop of the city.

"What more can be achieved with a second walk around the city? All that will happen is they'll get sunburned," Danel said. "We need to get closer. How long do you think it would take to get there?" He pointed to a high point much closer to Jericho.

"Longer than we expect. We could follow the back of the ridge and use the trees for cover." Yassib indicated the route.

Danel and Yassib moved quickly, not worrying about concealment. Any person in the area would be watching the army, not worrying about two people who seemed to know where they were going. Every so often Danel climbed to the ridgeline to see what the army was doing. Still walking laps.

Danel found a stream and wet a piece of cloth to place over his head. The army weren't the only ones getting sunburned.

By the time the army had started the sixth lap, still with the trumpets blowing and the men marching in silence, Danel and Yassib had reached the new lookout.

Still the marching continued. It was both eerie and weird and it defied all Yassib said he'd learned about military tactics, but it was also impressive. The men on the walls of Jericho must be watching with the same bewilderment as Danel. The sixth lap had finished and the Israelites started on another.

The seventh lap seemed the same as all the others and indeed it was the same until they neared the end. Then the ark stopped. The men stopped marching, and there was a long silence.

The trumpets blew one long blast. Yehoshua was clearly visible off to one side, and a gentle wind was blowing in just the right direction for them to hear his command.

"Shout! For the Lord has given you the city!"

Danel held his breath. What good would a shout do? Maybe it was merely to rally the men, so bravado overtook fear. But even so it would be a huge waste of lives to simply throw themselves at the city walls.

"The city and all that is in it are to be devoted to the Lord," Joshua shouted. "Only spare Rahab ..." The wind obscured several words. "... she sheltered our spies."

Yehoshua continued. "All the silver, gold, bronze, and iron are sacred to the Lord and must go into his treasury."

Danel looked at Yassib in astonishment. Not take loot? Armies always took loot. It was one of the reasons they fought.

Before Danel had time to think more on it, there was a shout as every man in the army raised their voices together. The shout reverberated off Jericho's walls and startled birds into flight. It was impressive, it was long, it was loud, but as a strategy it seemed weak. A shout could not scare men to death.

They waited. Waited to see what this army would do next.

There was a gigantic cracking sound. Danel gasped, eyes wide.

Yassib clutched Danel's arm, his fingernails digging in. "Look at the tower!"

An enormous crack opened in the wall under the main tower, then another. Yassib gave another gasp as a new crack ran diagonally down the wall. Soon the cracks were spreading and joining. The walls groaned as though in agony.

Fear rose up to choke Danel as the first tower leaned further and further to the side before it collapsed with an ear-shattering grating and crashing. A giant cloud of dust mushroomed up and prevented them seeing the next collapse, for that must be what was happening as the cracks and crashes continued.

"Why?" Yassib asked. "I don't understand." He shook his head. "There was no earthquake, so why have the walls collapsed?"

Danel held up his hand and stared at it. It was shaking like his grandfather's so often did. There was no explanation for what had happened, except that this god had done another miracle. A miracle greater than opening the way across the Jordan.

The Jordan hadn't been an impassable barrier to this people. The mighty walls of Jericho weren't either. What was to stop this army reaching Gibeon? Danel squeezed his eyes shut. Donatiya. Grandfather. What hope did anyone have against such a god?

Danel opened his eyes. The worst of the dust had cleared and it was obvious the entire wall had collapsed. Only one little section stood like a broken tooth alone amidst the rubble.

With a roar, the Israelite army charged toward the rubble. As they reached the wall, they spread out like a river bursting its banks and flooding into all the cracks and crevices. Horror clutched at Danel and made it hard to breathe. He shook his head back and forth, still finding it hard to believe his eyes. There wouldn't be any resistance, there couldn't be. If any in Jericho had survived being crushed, they'd be too shocked to lift a sword.

Sunlight glittered off raised swords and Danel turned away, the sourness of vomit rising in his throat. It didn't take much imagination to replace Jericho with Gibeon. To see his people shattered and crushed and wailing, unable to protect themselves from the disaster unleashed upon them.

Yassib was still watching, scanning the scene in front of them.

His eyes ceased moving and stared intently at one spot. "You remember I said there was a scarlet cord hanging from one of the houses on the wall?"

Danel nodded, too weary to look.

"Well, that house is the only one still standing."

Danel peered through the dust. Yassib was right. The standing bit of wall still had an intact house at the top, and there was a scarlet cord hanging from its window. Could this be the house of the woman Yehoshua had mentioned? The woman who had sheltered and hidden the two spies they'd seen crossing the river?

Yassib tugged on Danel's arm and directed his focus toward Yehoshua, recognizable because of the trumpeter and banner-bearer at his side. He was speaking with two men, who set off toward the still-standing bit of wall. When they reached it, one of the men grasped the cord and swung it. A pale blur of a face appeared at the window and the men gestured to the person in the window before one of them commenced to climb.

The man moved slowly up the wall until he disappeared at the top. Someone from within must have helped him, but it was too far away to see. Before long there was more movement at the window.

A smaller body, presumably a child or small woman, was lowered down the wall. Once the person reached the bottom of the wall, they were untied and the cord was pulled back up and inside. More people were lowered. Once on the ground, they huddled close together.

A series of bundles were lowered and then more people.

"The house must have been packed," Danel said.

"If she was offered rescue, then she'd tell her family. They all appear to know each other," Yassib said.

The people were still standing close together and several had an arm around the next person.

"Here comes the soldier," Yassib said.

Danel looked back up to the window where the soldier, still

wearing his helmet, was perched on the windowsill. He lowered himself, hand over hand, down the cord. When he reached the ground, he drew out something, reached as high up the cord as possible and cut it off. He coiled the rope and handed it to a woman who stood a little apart from the rest. Could she be Rahab?

The little group of refugees were soon on their way back to the Israelite camp, escorted by a couple of younger soldiers.

Danel turned to Yassib. "Do we need to see anymore?"

There could be no honor in this massacre of people who could not defend themselves.

Yassib shook his head. "We can see all we need to from our original lookout."

At a distance, the sounds of war would be overridden by the caroling of birds, the caress of a breeze, and the warmth of the sun. At a distance, it would be easy to pretend this massacre wasn't happening to people not unlike the Hivites. People who only this morning had eaten, secure in their fortress, secure in their belief in its impregnability.

If Uncle Hammurapi was right, this was the fate that awaited all within the borders of Canaan. Danel swallowed the sour taste in his mouth. If the Israelites had been like any other people the Hivites would have had a chance. But if Elohim kept fighting for the Israelites, who could possibly stand against them?

As Grandfather had kept saying, they were all doomed. Donatiya and Grandfather, Yassib and his family, and all the people of Gibeon and the surrounding towns. Was this the doom Talliya had predicted, or would Danel's end be even worse?

CHAPTER EIGHTEEN

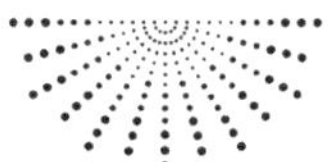

Fingers of light penetrated their cave. Danel's eyes stung from a lack of sleep which had been caused by chaotic nightmares, a mixture of his original nightmare, Talliya's predictions, Donatiya's pleading eyes, and the crashing of Jericho's walls.

Beside Danel, Yassib snored. After returning to their original lookout, they'd choked down some old bread in silence. Danel hadn't wanted to eat and it had tasted like dust, but they had to keep up their strength if they were to be of use to Gibeon. The silence had stretched between them. Danel had wanted to speak but didn't know how to start when he didn't want to talk about the horror of what they'd witnessed. He could not help seeing Gibeon in place of Jericho.

Finally Yassib had spoken. "What should we do? Return to Gibeon or wait?"

They'd eventually decided to wait until the Israelites moved toward their next conquest. That could give them hints as to Yehoshua's plans. If the Israelites headed north or south, rather than west, Gibeon might have more time. Time to come up with a plan. A plan Danel doubted would be any use, but they would—

must—try. They couldn't just lie there and accept annihilation. If Danel was to die, he would die fighting for his family and people.

Yassib snorted, jerked, and opened his eyes wide. Confusion and then fear clouded his eyes. He groaned. "What a horrible night."

"Nightmares?" Danel asked.

Yassib nodded. "Have you been to see what's happening?"

"Just about to." Not that Danel expected the Israelites to move today.

Yassib sniffed. "Is that smoke?"

Danel crawled out of the cave. The sun was much higher than he'd expected and the smoke was much heavier outside. He peered into the cave. "I'll go and see."

From the lookout, the source of the smoke was obvious. Dark ants of men scurried to and fro over the rubble of Jericho. Flames licked at the stones.

Yassib scrambled up beside Danel and they watched groups of men working together to carry bundles toward their camp. The closest men stumbled and the bundle fell on the ground spewing its contents. Gold! The rest of the bundles must contain the precious metals that were to go into Elohim's treasury.

Group by group, the men passed in front of the lookout and disappeared into the depths of the Israelite camp.

* * *

Three days later, smoke still lingered in the air. All the waiting was wearing their tempers thin.

"Can you go and shoot something to eat? I'll go and collect some fruit along by the stream," Danel suggested. He'd observed some fruit and herbs there. And maybe the girls would be at the stream. Although if any of them had hinted they'd met a stranger, their parents wouldn't allow them out of sight.

Danel prepared some bread dough ready for later, took a bag to carry anything he found, and picked up his bow. The times were too dangerous to leave it behind.

It didn't take Danel long to reach the stream. Sure enough, he found fruit and herbs. He followed the stream to the series of deeper pools, hid himself in some thick bushes, and checked that he had an escape route.

The sun moved higher and higher in the sky. Danel licked his lips and wished he'd thought to bring a waterskin. The sound of the stream was driving him crazy with thirst.

Somewhere close by a cicada chirruped into action, its call increasing in volume until the sun became too hot and it subsided into silence.

A bird flew down to the nearby rock and had a drink and a scratch amongst the gravel. Danel wiped the sweat off his face and watched the bird as it hopped in and out of the watery coolness.

His thirst grew and he listened for the sound of anyone coming. Not hearing anything he cautiously ventured out. He found a pool and scooped water in his hand. Thirst assuaged, he listened again and hearing nothing, plunged into the pool. He sighed at the refreshing coolness.

"You again," said a voice full of surprise and something else he couldn't identify. Perhaps she'd assumed he was from Jericho and would never see him again.

Danel sucked in a breath and paddled in place. For a moment he'd lost his caution and hadn't heard the girls arrive. She was standing there, grim-faced, with the two younger girls behind her and a few items of clothing ready for washing.

He swam a few strokes to the opposite side of the pool and got out of the pool, shaking the water out of his hair.

He cautiously looked around to see if anyone else might be in the vicinity.

"Don't worry. You're safe," she said.

For now, but not for long if her people had their way. Still, he tried to lighten the tension between them. "I'm not sure you're dangerous."

"Maybe. Maybe not. I'm pretty handy with a slingshot." She pulled one out from among the pile of clothes.

"Prove it," he said without thinking.

"You want me to shoot you?" She raised an eyebrow.

"I'd prefer you didn't. Just choose a target." He paused. "Other than myself."

She handed the clothing to the other girls and stooped to pick up some small rocks. Setting one in the sling, she aimed and fired at the rock next to him. The stone whistled by his foot and hit exactly where she'd aimed, sending a chip of rock flying. Better the rock than him.

She was a good shot. The Danel of before the battle would have been delighted to compete with her, but not now, not today, perhaps never. That thought further darkened his mood.

"Do you have brothers?" he asked.

"How did you know?" she asked, eyes narrowed.

"I thought it likely, given you're carrying a slingshot."

"They did teach me, and I liked it enough to keep practicing."

It would be a good contest, if they ever got the chance. Danel had practiced a lot as a child and had always done well with games that involved aim.

There was a slither, a scream, and a splash from the far side of the pool where the younger girls had been half washing the clothes and half splashing each other.

"My sister can't swim," the tall girl screamed, running towards the water.

The child was struggling, gulping water, and about to go under. Without thinking, Danel ran to the edge of the deeper water and dived in. Coming up, he swam a few strokes and grabbed the child's hair. She struggled and hit his nose. A stinging pain brought tears to his eyes.

"Don't struggle. I've got you."

From the riverbank, the middle sister repeated his words. "Don't worry. You're safe."

Danel murmured to the struggling girl in the voice he used with sick goats. "That's right, relax."

The child gave a whimper but allowed Danel to pull her toward the bank. The tall girl waded in and pulled her sister into a hug and kept her there while the younger girl sobbed. She patted her younger sister's back. "You got a fright, but you're safe."

Danel wrung the water out of his hair and clothes for the second time. He turned to look at the girls as they came out of the water. The oldest one's head covering had slipped backwards. There was a long pale streak of hair among the dark strands.

She flushed and tugged her head scarf back into place. "It's a family characteristic."

He liked it but he wasn't going to comment.

"Thank you," she said. "None of us can swim. There wasn't exactly enough water in the desert."

His face warmed at the thanks.

She looked at him. "What's your name? I can't keep thinking of you as the man at the stream."

He hesitated. Under normal circumstances he'd have been happy to tell this girl his name and his town and his family, but not now. Not in this time of war, when her people wanted to wipe out his.

He had thought about what he'd say if this question came up. "Keret," he said, hoping Grandfather would forgive him.

"And mine is Rivkah," she said. "It means to bind or be bound. My parents say it's because I bound them together and we are all bound to Elohim."

It suited her.

She led her sister to a rock and sat both of them down. Now she'd asked a question he'd see if she'd answer one of his own.

"Did you watch the battle?"

Her eyes clouded and she shook her head. "My parents wouldn't allow us."

He was glad. The thought of such a girl seeing all that death and destruction bothered him.

She glanced over to where the middle girl was washing the clothes.

Take your time with the washing. He had so many questions clamoring for attention and now Rivkah was talking, she might give him some answers.

"I'd like to know about the family that was rescued from Jericho."

"Rahab's family you mean?"

He nodded as he sat himself down on the nearest rock.

"She's an incredible woman," Rivkah said.

"So you've met her?" Danel asked.

"I have. Grandfather Kheti sent my grandmother along to welcome her and offer any help. He knows it's never easy to be an outsider. Grandma Nophret asked me to come too." She flushed. "I'd never met someone like Rahab before."

"A Canaanite, you mean?" She'd met him but maybe she didn't think of Danel as a Canaanite.

She blushed. "No, someone in her line of work."

There was only one kind of work that would make Rivkah so uncomfortable. Danel had never been near the temple area where women who served the gods as prostitutes lived. His father had explained that most of the women who lived there were destitute or had been abducted and forced to serve in the temple. Danel's stomach tightened at the memory that it could also have been Donatiya's fate if they hadn't thought of a way to save her.

"And was she what you expected?" he asked.

"Not at all," Rivkah said, sounding surprised. "She didn't seem too much different to anyone else. There was a weariness, even a wariness, and a sort of sadness but that would be expected. After all, everything has changed for her."

She sat in silence for a few moments. "Rahab knew only a miracle would save her family. When she saw the spies she grabbed her chance."

"How did she recognize them?" Danel asked.

"She was on the lookout for strangers who were looking at the defenses. Once she identified them she invited them to stay with her and when the soldiers came looking for them, she hid them under a pile of flax stalks on her roof."

"They weren't much good as spies if both Rahab and the king knew of them."

The corner of Rivkah's mouth quirked. "I guess not. Rahab told the soldiers the men had left at dusk before the city gate was closed. The soldiers pursued the spies to the fords of the Jordan but couldn't find them."

"And how did the spies escape?" Danel said.

"Rahab lowered the men out her window and down the wall using the red rope. But before the men left Rahab said, 'I know your God has given you this land. All who live here are already melting in fear, for we've heard how your God dried up the water of the Red Sea and the defeat of Sihon and Og. Your God is God in heaven above and on the earth below. Please swear to me by the Lord that you will show kindness to my family, because I have shown kindness to you. Give me a sure sign that you will spare the lives of my father and mother, my brothers, and sisters, and all who belong to them—and that you will save us from death.'"

Rivkah smiled, a smile of such joy that Danel had to look away.

"You see, Rahab placed her faith in Elohim and he rescued her."

"Faith," Danel repeated the unknown word, although already he was beginning to see its meaning.

"Faith enough to protect our spies, so she could appeal for safety for her family," Rivkah said. "The spies told her to leave the scarlet cord hanging from the window as a sign. They warned her not to tell anyone, and that her family must all gather in Rahab's house."

"She kept her word then," Danel said. "For we saw the scarlet cord and the family being lowered from the window."

Rivkah raised her eyebrow and Danel grimaced. "We watched the battle but were puzzled by what happened afterwards. The men took no plunder except the precious metals which were taken into the tent where you keep the ark."

"The tent is called the Tabernacle and it is where our God lives." She frowned. "No, that's not quite right because he is present everywhere, but the Tabernacle represents him in a special way."

"Present everywhere?" Danel found that confusing. The Canaanites made offerings to their gods in their temples, or on the high hills, or under special trees or rocks. Places where the gods lived.

"Our God is spirit," Rivkah said. "That allows him to be present in all places at once." She pointed to the heavens and then to the earth. "There is nowhere we can escape him. He knows everything and can read our thoughts."

That sounded worrying. There were thoughts and deeds that Danel preferred were not known. Grandfather would certainly be hurt if he knew how often Danel wished he didn't have the burden of his grandfather's care. Danel's face heated. He loved Grandfather, but between the exhaustion of managing his erratic behavior, the loneliness Danel felt without his parents, and the frustration of having his grandfather present yet absent, he had to admit there were times he wondered if it would hurt less if his grandfather had simply died.

"The army took no plunder because God gave us exact instructions about what to do. We are not to keep the plunder or even the livestock for ourselves. Everything is to be dedicated to him."

Danel had begun to think this god was different to the Canaanite gods but this greed sounded familiar. The Canaanite gods were nothing if not demanding. Not only animals but children as well. Bile rose in his throat.

"Mama said not to be too long," Rivkah's sister called, wringing out the last piece of clothing.

Rivkah gave an apologetic smile and got to her feet. It was no use trying to ask questions about which city the Israelites would target next. She probably didn't know. Even if she did, she'd never reveal it. He would just have to keep watching and if the army turned toward Gibeon, he and Yassib would have to reach home before the Israelites arrived.

CHAPTER NINETEEN

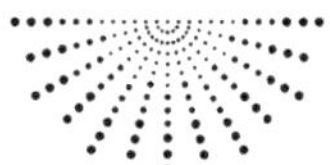

assib arrived back well before sunset with a plump rabbit. Danel's mouth watered as he lit the fire. Though still careful about smoke, he wasn't too worried as the Israelites had not given any indication that they were hunting individual Canaanites.

"I took much longer than I intended," Yassib said as he deftly skinned the rabbit. "On the way back I was delayed when I saw a group of men heading west. They'd obviously come from the Israelite camp."

"Where do you think they might be going?"

Yassib paused in his task. "I'm presuming they'll stick with towns. It might be Bethel. I believe that's in the right direction."

Danel had heard of Bethel but he'd never been there. Few Hivites traveled nowadays. There were too many thieves, too many willing to kill for whatever was hidden in your bags. And Canaan was certainly not safe for women. Danel had heard horror stories of kidnapping, rape, forced marriage, and slave-taking. Groups of bandits from the different cities preyed on each other and strove for dominance.

Danel's father had said that Gibeon used to be the same but things had improved when Yassib's father had become chief.

Danel leaned down and blew steadily on the tiny flame, feeding it with twigs. "How long did you watch them?"

"Until they were out of sight." Yassib pulled the innards out of the rabbit. "It occurred to me that it might be easier to see them when they come back."

"The problem is how to hear their report. The most likely place will be right in the center of the camp."

Danel scratched his head. "What about if we follow Grandfather and Uncle's lead and simply keep quiet and mingle with the Israelites?"

Yassib poured some water over his hands to clean them. "You'd need to have a way to make sure no one saw us entering the camp."

"What if we were carrying a bow and some birds, as though we'd been hunting?" Danel said.

"That might work, but I'm worried about small things that make us seem foreign," Yassib said.

"Our hair is different. I've noticed that a lot of their men tie their hair back out of the way with a leather tie. Don't you have something like that tied to the end of your bow?"

Danel nodded.

"And they wash more," Yassib said with a chuckle. "There's a stream over the next hill where we could wash."

Some spy action would be good but Danel's still felt anxious. "What do we do if we're discovered?"

Yassib shrugged. "Duck into the nearest tent and pretend it's ours? I'm sure we'll think of something."

"Perhaps only one of us should go," Danel said. "If something goes wrong, one of us needs to be able to warn our people." He indicated Yassib's knife. "Shall we spin for it?"

Yassib took his knife out of the case around his waist, found a flat rock, and gave it a vigorous spin. It spun rapidly several times before slowing down. "Come on," Yassib muttered. "Point at me."

Danel wished it would too but the blade seemed determined to choose him. It slowed to a standstill and he tried to look pleased about it. He couldn't back out now, not with disappointment written all over Yassib's face.

"I'll take first watch for the spies returning. You go and pretty yourself up." Yassib punched Danel's shoulder.

* * *

After catching some quail and washing, Danel took the next watch.

He woke with a start. His neck had a crick in it and the shadows were lengthening at the lookout. Fine spy he made. All he had to do was watch, yet he'd fallen asleep on the job. He should have walked around rather than lain in the warm sun.

Danel turned and looked over the Israelite camp and his gut did a slow flip. A group of men was moving rapidly toward the center of the camp, presumably the returning spies heading to report to Yehoshua. Danel groaned. Now he'd have to confess to Yassib that he'd fallen asleep and missed his chance to go and hear the report. Danel got to his knees and crawled backwards down from the lookout. Danel's failure would give Yassib plenty of opportunity to crow that a baker couldn't hope to match a soldier's training.

* * *

The sound of marching feet woke Danel at daybreak. Still feeling the sting of yesterday's failure, he didn't pause to grab anything but climbed to the lookout. As usual, Yassib had been faster. Danel lay down next to him and peered down at the camp.

Men, fully armed, were marching west. They were swinging their arms confidently. Their confidence wasn't unexpected considering that Jericho had been defeated without a single Israelite casualty.

"Quick. Count them," Yassib said.

The soldiers were tightly bunched together but Danel did his best. Every time he reached one hundred, he picked up a leaf. Yassib seemed to be counting too and even if their count was slightly different it would give them an estimate. One thing was already clear—Yehoshua wasn't sending the entire army.

Eventually the sound of marching receded into the distance.

"How many leaves do you have?" Yassib asked.

Danel counted twice to make sure he was correct. "Twenty-eight, but I missed some."

"Close enough to three thousand." Yassib frowned. "They can't be attacking Bethel. Too few men."

"Are we going to follow them or wait for them to return?" Danel asked.

Yassib gnawed his lip. "There's not much point following. If we wait, we'll know soon enough."

* * *

*D*anel and Yassib were returning from foraging for edibles when Yassib dragged him to the ground.

Danel hit his elbow and turned toward Yassib to tell him off. Yassib held a finger to his lips and pointed toward the trees on the far side of the clearing. Danel narrowed his eyes. Two soldiers were limping past, dragging a body with them.

More men were weaving in and out the trees. Some had blood on their clothes, others were badly gashed, or held their arms at awkward angles. There were more bodies. Every soldier looked weary and distressed. Had the impossible happened? Had the

Israelites lost a battle? And if so, did that mean there was hope for Gibeon?

Danel and Yassib waited until most of the soldiers passed before they returned to their lookout. From their vantage point they could see a line of bodies laid outside the camp. The injured soldiers were slumped on the ground nearby and mourners were gathering. Another body was brought in and laid down and a woman gave a piercing scream and rushed forward, throwing herself on the body.

"How many bodies can you see?" Danel asked.

"Twenty-two so far, but look back up the hill. There's another being carried by four soldiers," Yassib said.

The shadows lengthened and the heat leeched out of the day. A man who might have been Yehoshua came and stood, body rigid, and watched the bodies being brought in until there were thirty-six. Thirty-six bodies, each surrounded by their grieving family members. When the last had been brought in, the leader, almost certainly Yehoshua, tore his clothes before hurrying back into the depths of the camp.

Was this it then? Would the Israelites give up now that they'd suffered a defeat? Danel sighed. He was ready to go home, but they couldn't return until they knew what Yehoshua intended to do next.

CHAPTER TWENTY

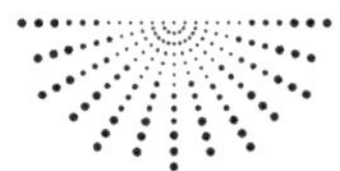

*D*anel called out softly so that Rivkah would not be afraid. Her back was to him as she collected water in a pot. She gasped and turned her face toward him. It was streaked with tears.

His chest tightened. "What's wrong?"

"Thirty-six dead." Tears welled again and she swiped them away with her hand. "The Lord told Yehoshua that we lost the battle at Ai—"

He noted the name to tell Yassib.

"—because someone in Israel has sinned. They have violated the Lord's command not to take anything from Jericho." She sniffed again. "All those men died because someone disobeyed."

Danel sat down on a rock. "It's natural for soldiers to take plunder."

"You don't understand." She rubbed her face, smearing mud across her cheek. "Elohim always gives clear instructions, and he expects us to follow them."

Danel gestured to his own face to indicate where she'd smeared mud. She flushed and scooped up a handful of water and washed her cheeks. "Is that better?"

He nodded, although she'd looked cute with the muddy streak.

"There have been many, many times since my grandparents left Egypt that they've had to learn to follow Elohim's instructions. It started with little things like the manna. Six days of the week we were to collect it every morning. When people tried to gather and save more manna than they needed, it would go maggoty by next morning. Yet in preparation for our day of rest we could collect twice the amount and there wasn't a maggot in sight." She looked across at him. "Don't look so skeptical. Yahveh once provided meat in the middle of the desert for everybody and he produced water multiple times, even out of a rock. He is a God of miracles."

Danel couldn't deny it. He'd already witnessed two major miracles. There was no other explanation for the river crossing and the crumbling of Jericho's walls.

"There were many times in the wilderness when people complained or didn't obey. Each time, there were consequences."

"What kinds of consequences?"

"Not long ago, the Lord enabled us to defeat the king of Arad, who lived in the Negev. He'd captured some of our people. Mosheh made a vow that if the Lord would deliver this king into our hands, we'd destroy them."

Danel hadn't heard of this victory.

"We'd only just seen the Lord deliver us from Arad when many started to complain against the Lord. 'Why have you brought us up out of Egypt to die in the desert? There is no bread! There is no water! And we detest this miserable food!'"

Rivkah mimicked the whining tone of the complainers perfectly, and a laugh threatened to burst out of him. The first laugh he'd felt since the battle.

"The Lord sent venomous snakes to bite us and many people died."

Danel's eyebrows rose. "That sounds a little extreme. If I was bitten by a snake every time I complained, I'd have been dead long ago."

"Unfortunately it wasn't the first time our people had complained. Father says Adonai's people must be thankful rather than complaining. Complaining shows we are not trusting the Lord."

And a thankful person was much easier to live with than a complainer.

"Obviously you didn't all die," Danel said.

"No, but only because the Lord had mercy. Mosheh prayed for us and the Lord told Mosheh to make a statue of a snake in bronze. He was told to put it up on a pole and anyone who was bitten could look up at the statue and they would be healed."

Danel stared at her. "That statue would be worth a king's treasure. There is no cure for a snake bite."

Rivkah frowned. "I don't think the bronze snake itself had any power. People were saved when they obeyed the Lord's word."

They were both silent for a while.

"I still don't understand why your gods insisted that no plunder be taken from Jericho. The livestock was extremely valuable," Danel said.

"Why do you say gods? We only worship one," Rivkah said, forehead furrowed.

"You speak of Adonai and Elohim," Danel answered.

Rivkah frowned. "I see where you got the wrong idea. We have many names for our god. Adonai meaning Lord, Elohim, Yahveh. I also call him Creator. Each name reveals something about him." She paused. "Back to your question about why Elohim said we were to take no plunder. I asked my parents and grandparents about that. We wondered if it might be something to do with first fruits."

"First fruits?" Now Danel was even more confused.

"Forty years ago, the Lord appeared to Mosheh on Mount Sinai and gave us ten commandments to help us live joyfully as Yahveh's people. He also gave us other guidelines. One of them was the command that when we have our own land and orchards, we must always bring the first portion to the Lord to thank him for the harvest."

"A kind of harvest festival?" Canaan had harvest festivals, but they included much drunkenness and revelry. Even with Danel's limited knowledge he guessed that this god would not approve of such behavior. Danel had always avoided the festivals, for Father had said, "Much beer and wine befuddles your head and makes you do things you will later be ashamed of." Danel had wondered if Father was talking from his own experience or from observation of others, but had never summoned the courage to ask.

"It's not only harvest. The Lord also wants us to offer the first offspring of our livestock and to dedicate the first son as well."

"You mean sacrifice your firstborn?" Danel asked, eyes wide.

Rivkah gasped and her hand flew to her mouth. "Never! The Lord would never require human sacrifice."

This god was better than any other god Danel had ever heard of. Child sacrifice was a horrible part of life in Canaan. He'd inadvertently stumbled on one such festival as a young boy. Father had pulled Danel's head against his chest and covered Danel's ears but his father hadn't been fast enough. Danel had never forgotten the terrified look on the face of the little girl waiting to be sacrificed or the screams of her parents.

"There is a system where the firstborn son is redeemed by giving a perfect lamb in his place."

"So poor families suffer more?" he asked.

"Oh no. The Lord allows them to give doves or pigeons."

This god seemed to think of everything.

"So putting all the precious metals in your god's treasury was also a sort of first fruits?"

She nodded. "That's our guess. The killing of the livestock was also a kind of sacrifice."

"Does that mean that you might be able to keep plunder from other places?"

She shrugged. "It may be so, the Lord has always been generous."

It was easy for her to say. She was far away from the battles. She would probably never see the slaughter. To her, the battles were more like a checklist of conquests. But what about the soldiers who had to do the killing? What would be the impact on them? Watching the battle of Jericho had made Danel feel sick. Of course he couldn't say anything to Yassib. As a chief's son, Yassib had been trained for battle since he could walk. Maybe chief's sons were born with an extra amount of courage.

People being conquered sounded alright, but "conquered" glossed over the fact that people—men, women, and children— were being killed. Killing meant a horror of blood and fear and pain. And the people that the Israelites were killing were Canaanites. Sure, there were many people around with different ancestry to the Gibeonites but they weren't that different. They were also born, worked, married, and had children, just like his own family.

"Why?" Danel burst out. "Why are the Israelites killing the Canaanites?"

She looked at him and blinked back tears. "I also find that very hard to understand. Only yesterday I asked Grandfather the same question."

"And?"

"And he told me about Avraham, the ancestor of all the Israelites."

Avraham seemed to be the key to understanding the history of the Israelites.

"He was seventy-five when the Lord spoke to him in Babylon saying, 'Go from your country, your people, and your father's household to the land I will show you.'" Her voice had taken on a singsong quality, as though this was a refrain she'd heard and repeated many times before. "'I will make you into a great nation, and I will bless you; I will make your name great, and you will be a blessing. I will bless those who bless you, and whoever curses you, I will curse; and all peoples on earth will be blessed through you.'"

"Obviously Avraham obeyed this message from your god and left everything he was familiar with to come here."

"My grandparents sometimes talk about how hard it was to leave Egypt, learn a new language and culture, and wander around the desert for forty years with no permanent home of their own."

And now the Israelites were looking to make this land their permanent home, whether Danel and the people already here agreed or not.

"Avraham never owned more than one field in Canaan because the Lord told him that the sin of the Amorites had not yet reached its full measure."

Danel frowned.

"Grandfather said it meant the people living in Canaan still had time to repent before judgment would fall." She flushed. "Avraham's descendants would have to wait another four hundred years and they'd be slaves in Egypt, until the Lord rescued them from there."

And now the time was up. Danel had never thought of the Canaanites as particularly evil. Things were simply the way they were. Yet Grandfather had often bemoaned about how things used to be better. That the priests were more money-hungry and demanding, that it wasn't safe for anyone to travel unless accompanied by an armed band of men. Perhaps, like a live frog placed in a pot of cold water over a fire to heat, Danel hadn't noticed the water warming because he knew no different. Was he worried about Donatiya growing up in Canaan? He was, and he would love things to be different for his children.

"So is it only the Amorites and other Canaanites that are to be conquered?" He asked the question quietly, avoiding words like "annihilated" or "wiped out." He didn't even know why he was asking the question, but it somehow seemed important.

She was silent for a long while. "Yes." Her tone was sad. "Sihon and Og were offered payment for our passing through their land. If they had allowed us to pass through, they'd all be alive today. They attacked us and forced us to respond." She shook her head. "All those men, women, and children didn't need to die."

Why was it that some people fought first rather than being prudent? Yassib and his family were the fight-first kind of people but Uncle Hammurapi was different. He used his head.

Rivkah looked down at her water jar. "Oh, I must go. Everyone is waiting to wash."

"What's special about today?" Danel rose to his feet.

"Yehoshua has commanded us all to purify ourselves, for tomorrow the Lord wants us all to appear before him. He will reveal who has sinned."

"How?" Danel asked.

"That's up to him. He can see into men's hearts." She picked up her water jar and hoisted it onto her head. Steadying it with one hand, she walked back toward the Israelite camp.

Danel wasn't sure what he felt about a god who could see into men's hearts. The Canaanite gods didn't have that power. When he prayed at the temple, he had to start by saying, "This is Danel, grandson of Keret, from the bakery next to the huge fig tree." Then he could present his petitions with the confidence that the gods at least knew who they needed to answer, that is if they'd bother to answer or notice him at all.

CHAPTER TWENTY-ONE

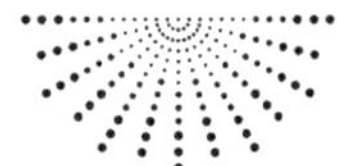

Danel kept his head down and stayed toward the back as the crowd of Israelites gathered around the special tent they called the Tabernacle. He and Yassib had decided it was worth the risk to be closer to the action but they were in separate parts of the crowd to decrease their chances of being discovered. They'd each wrapped a head covering loosely round their head as a disguise, and hoped people would assume it was sun protection.

"Yesterday," Yehoshua called to the crowd. "You saw me tear my clothes and fall face down on the ground before the ark of the Lord."

Danel was too far away to hear Yehoshua, but he spoke one line at a time so that his words could be accurately relayed to everyone. Although the language was similar to Danel's, there were still unusual words. Words he now understood better because of his conversations with Rivkah.

"I and the elders of Israel sprinkled dust on our heads and remained on our faces before the Lord until evening," Yehoshua said.

There was a pause before the next line. "I said to the Lord, 'Why did you bring our people across the Jordan if you simply meant to deliver us into the hands of the Amorites?'"

The pauses gave Danel space to absorb the message of each line.

"If only we had been content to stay on the other side of the Jordan! What can I say, now Israel has been routed by its enemies? The Canaanites and the other people of the country will hear about this and they will surround us and wipe out our name from the earth. Lord, what then will you do for the sake of your great name?'"

Hope had indeed seeped into Danel's heart yesterday. These people weren't unbeatable. Grandfather and Donatiya and the people of Gibeon might yet live.

"As I poured out my heart to the Lord, I never imagined that one of us might be at fault."

The man relaying the messages spoke with much emotion, as though he felt Yehoshua's pain and discouragement.

"But the Lord said to me, 'Stand up! What are you doing down on your face? Israel has sinned. They have violated my commands. They have taken some of the devoted things.'"

In front of Danel, someone asked, "Who sinned?"

"Yes," said another. "Tell us who."

The message continued, "'That is why the Israelites cannot stand against their enemies. I, the Lord, will not be with you anymore unless you destroy whoever among you is devoted to destruction.'"

A murmur started at the front and built group by group toward Danel. Someone clutched his arm. "What will we do if the Lord does not go with us?"

The sense of fear filled the air. Their fear was not like Danel's, the fear of death or annihilation or a wasted life, instead, they feared their god would abandon them. What other people group had their god in their midst as the Israelites did?

"This is why you consecrated yourselves last night, for the Lord will show us who has taken the devoted things."

Danel hunched his shoulders. Did this god know he and Yassib were here? Would he expose them to a mob who were already simmering with fear? Perhaps even anger?

The messages continued to be relayed. "You cannot stand against your enemies until you remove this stain from among you."

All around Danel people were looking at each other then glancing away, unable to discern who was a friend and who should be shunned. Danel stood as a stranger in their midst. Was Yassib, over there by the big tree, feeling the same accusations as Danel did?

The messenger turned pale and Danel held his breath. "Whoever is caught with the devoted things shall be destroyed by fire, along with all that belongs to him."

Burned! Danel's gasp was swallowed by the collective gasp around him. So Rivkah's god did not consider this theft a small thing. Danel stared at his feet. Was the chaos and evil of Canaan because too many things had been left unpunished? Bandits and cheats and kidnappers were not brought to justice, so those things increased. Girls like Donatiya could never be left alone. She accepted that because she had to, but how different Donatiya's life would be if she could safely go to the river on her own, to enjoy the water and the beauty. Did this god take sin seriously because unchecked sin wrecks everyone's lives?

"Now the leaders of the twelve tribes must come forward and present themselves tribe by tribe in front of the Lord."

There was movement somewhere near the front and a long pause. The people around him held their breaths and then he saw people in front turn and mouth something. Soon the whisper reached him, "Judah, it's the tribe of Judah."

The crowd's eyes were wide with shock. Danel remembered this tribe crossing the Jordan. If he remembered correctly, it had been the largest group. Perhaps it was a tribe of special significance.

"Now have the leaders of the clans of Judah come forward." The messenger's voice rang out like a trumpet. Off to Danel's right, a man started pushing his way toward the front. There was another moving forward from behind him on the left.

They stood waiting. A fly buzzed around his face and Danel shooed it away. Someone called out a name and once again the verdict was passed back. "It's the Zerahites."

The names meant nothing to Danel, but it seemed that Yehoshua was the leader under Elohim. Then the elders, including a leader for each of the twelve tribes. Then clan heads under each tribe.

"The heads of each family among the Zerahites must come forward," the messenger relayed.

More men pushed their way forward, not looking to the right or the left where thousands of pairs of eyes drilled holes into their backs.

More waiting until the whispers came, "Zimri. It is Zimri's family." The messenger looked around. Perhaps he knew the family of Zimri. Then he called out, "All the men of the family of Zimri must present themselves before the Lord."

Danel shivered. If this god could truly read people's hearts, then one person was now terrified that the finger of judgment would soon point at him.

"Karmi, someone in Karmi's family," relayed the messenger.

Tension twisted Danel's gut and his chest tightened.

At last the word came. "It is Achan. Achan has done this terrible thing."

The crowd around Danel sighed and then surged forward as everyone tried to see the man. Somewhere nearby, someone was weeping.

"Step back," the messenger called. "Don't crush one another. I will convey Yehoshua's words." He cupped his hand around his ear.

"These are the words of Yehoshua to Achan, son of Karmi, son of Zimri, the son of Zerah, of the tribe of Judah. 'My son, give glory to the Lord, the God of Israel, and honor him. Tell me what you have done. Do not hide it from me.'"

Danel leaned forward, ready for Achan's response.

"Achan has said, 'It is true! I have sinned against the Lord, the God of Israel. This is what I have done. When I saw a beautiful robe from Babylon among the plunder, two hundred shekels of silver, and a bar of gold weighing fifty shekels, I coveted them and took them. They are hidden in the ground inside my tent, with the silver underneath.'"

Danel raised his eyebrows. Gold like that would mean a life without care. A protection from the winds of ill-luck that blew randomly during a person's life. If Danel had that much gold, he could hire someone to care for Grandfather, he could buy all the land he wanted, and he could offer the best of dowries for Donatiya.

That much gold and silver would have been a serious temptation. The only thing that would have prevented it was trust that Israel's god knew what he was doing when he forbade it and a confidence that this god would look after people no matter what ill fortune struck. Rivkah believed this about her god. But how did one know?

A group of men pushed their way through the crowd and disappeared way over to the left. The crowd stood silent, united in grief. Danel would have liked to leave and return to the sanctuary of their cave but everyone was standing still. It would be too dangerous. Danel looked around for Yassib. Yassib was moving slowly toward Danel. Perhaps he too thought they should leave. The longer they stayed, the higher the chance of discovery.

"They're coming back," someone called from behind him.

Danel turned and watched as three men walked past them carrying a gold bar, silver, and a folded robe. Donkeys, cattle, and sheep were also led forward.

Yassib arrived at Danel's side and they watched in silence as the animals passed, followed by a rolled-up tent on the shoulders of two well-muscled men, and finally a group which must be Achan's family. The woman managed to look both defiant and terrified at the same time but the younger adults were pale and walked with their eyes downcast. Achan could not have buried those things without the other family members knowing. Danel swallowed. Tension crackled in the air. Did the Israelites know something he didn't?

Once the family had moved past them, the people around him began to inch toward where Yehoshua stood. Danel and Yassib could not move against the flow. They too were pushed forward but could not see what happened. They only heard the sighs and moans of the crowd and murmurs about Achan's family who were stoned first. At least Danel had not needed to see the judgment being meted out. Later, he smelled the smoke of burning.

As the crowd dispersed and Danel turned to go, he could see the pile of stones that had been laid on the site where Achan's family and possessions had been burned as a terrible reminder of this day.

Rivkah's god wanted people to trust him and to obey without question. But could this god be trusted to look after those who trusted and obeyed him? Was this god really good and loving, or only powerful?

CHAPTER TWENTY-TWO

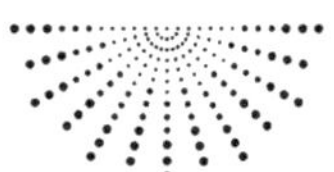

"When do you think we should return home?" Danel asked Yassib that evening.

Yassib stroked his wispy attempts at a beard. "If Yehoshua has a victory further west, then we must go and warn our people."

Danel's shoulders slumped. "What use is a warning against a people whose god fights for them?"

"First things first. Yehoshua won't risk another defeat because he knows every defeat gives the people of Canaan hope," Yassib said. "They'll march out with far more than three thousand troops and they can't hide the preparations for that many men. We'll follow."

So tomorrow would be more watching and more waiting. Boring, but necessary. Disappointment twisted Danel's gut. He'd have liked to talk to Rivkah again, but Yassib would consider that a waste of time—and possibly dangerous. Danel had assured Yassib that Rivkah didn't even know his real name. It had been hard to lie, but what else could he do? A spy who lacks discretion is no spy at all. He wished the days were normal and he and Rivkah could have been friends. His neck warmed. More than friends would have been better, but that was impossible.

Her people were intent on wiping his off the face of the earth, and he saw no way to escape. He tried not to think too much about it. Perhaps Yassib's optimism had rubbed off a little. Yassib was so certain they could work something out. He loved to remind Danel of Gibeon's strength and his father's ability to form alliances. Danel wanted to share Yassib's belief, his optimism, his hope. Yet Egypt had been many times more powerful than any of the peoples of Canaan, and the Israelites' god had trampled them into the ground.

Hope? There was none. They may as well go home and resign themselves to their fate. After all, hadn't the fortune teller said she only saw great loss in Danel's future? She'd refused to say what Danel would lose, but surely the greatest loss of all would be his life?

Danel touched the amulet round his waist.

"I didn't think you were the kind of guy to rely on an amulet," Yassib said.

Danel's face heated and he shrugged. "I'm not usually, but these are dangerous days. I wear it just in case it helps."

"I'll stick to relying on myself," Yassib said.

It was all very well for Yassib, but he didn't have other lives solely dependant on him.

From the lookout, it was obvious the Israelites were mustering. The blacksmiths were busily sharpening swords all day. Targets were set up for those with bows, and extra arrows were made from among the willows along the edge of the stream.

The women scurried to and fro, gathering food. Once he imagined he saw someone who walked like Rivkah. He sighed. Did she think of him too?

When the sun was highest in the sky, Yassib relieved him at the lookout.

"We need to be ready to move," Yassib said after watching for a while.

Danel scuttled down away from the ridgeline before he stood upright and went back to their cave. He'd use the remainder of their barley flour to make flatbread. That'd be easier to carry. He'd also seen some ripe grapes on a vine climbing a nearby tree. With a bit of scrambling, he should be able to reach them. He'd look for nuts as well. Anything that could be easily carried. His gut quivered. Soon this unstoppable conquest would move on, deeper into Canaanite lands.

* * *

*D*anel and Yassib ate at the lookout so they wouldn't miss anything in the camp below. While foraging for fruit and nuts, Danel had come across two nests of quail eggs, so he'd scrambled them to go with their bread and some wild vegetables he'd found.

The sun dropped in a blaze of golden glory. Almost immediately, torches were lit in the camp below them. A trumpet blasted twice, and shadowy figures of men armed for battle could be seen moving from all directions toward the central gathering area. It looked like Yassib's prediction was right. The army would move during the hours of darkness.

"Are you ready to go?" Yassib asked.

Danel nodded. "I've divided the food between us."

"Good, because I still don't know if we should remain together."

Goosebumps ran up Danel's arms. He didn't want to admit that he'd prefer not to be alone in the dark. There might be a decent moon tonight, but it was hard to distinguish between shadows and the spirits he'd always been taught wandered at night, seeking to devour the unwary.

A group of torches broke off from the main group. Once clear of the camp, the torches were extinguished and the men stood still. What were they waiting for? Why had the army divided? The majority seemed to be staying put for the night.

"Their eyes need to adjust to the lower level of light," Yassib said as though reading Danel's mind.

"How many do you think?" Danel asked.

"Thousands, many thousands," Yassib said. "Time to go."

Danel reached for the gear that he'd brought to the lookout. He slung his bow and quiver across his back and the food across his front. If they were in danger, he could easily let the food drop to the ground and be ready to use his bow. Lastly, Danel took his staff in his right hand and they headed west, keeping the brow of the hill between them and the what seemed to be an advance party of Yehoshua's army, since there'd been no sign of Yehoshua and there were more armed men still in the camp.

Overhead, the half-moon and a myriad of stars provided enough light so they wouldn't trip. They moved swiftly, stepping from rock to rock or on hard ground, avoiding twigs.

The ridge ended and Yassib held up his hand. "Listen!"

Somewhere off to their right sounded the march of feet and the rattle and creak of armed men on the move. Wherever they were going, there was no need for secrecy—at least, not yet. The Israelites crossed the flat area in front of Yassib and Danel. On the far side of the flat area was a creek, and there were many exclamations as the men entered the water. Several slipped and landed with a splash.

The sound of the marching men faded, but still Yassib stood.

A breeze blew toward them. Danel rubbed his arms.

"I don't think there are any stragglers." Yassib moved cautiously across a stretch without cover and into the bushes along the creek. It didn't take long to find the ford and Danel slipped off his sandals and hitched up his tunic. It was cool enough tonight without having to walk in wet clothes or footwear.

They crossed without any problem. On the far side, the way narrowed as they began to climb toward the hill country. They walked further apart and with more caution. If this group of soldiers had been sent ahead, then maybe they would get in position on the far side of their target and wait in hiding for the main force. He and Yassib must be careful. An army planning to remain hidden would be extra alert and deal swiftly with anyone who threatened their plans.

Ahead of Danel, Yassib moved with the grace of an animal tracking its prey. Sometimes Danel had considered Yassib's training a waste of time, a luxury for someone who didn't have to work for a living. But out here, it was obvious Yassib knew how to move quickly and silently through the countryside. Danel tried to copy his gliding steps.

The army was moving surprisingly quickly for such a large group, but that made it safer for Danel and Yassib as the men had less time to look behind. It also suggested the army needed to be in position before morning.

Yassib halted beside a pool of water. They quenched their thirst and partially filled their waterskins. They might not have access to water later.

"We can slow down a little," Yassib said. "They're almost certainly going back to wherever they were defeated."

"To try again, you mean?"

"They have to. They can't leave a city that has beaten them off and they can't leave anyone alive to warn any neighboring cities." Yassib looked at Danel, his face serious. "We must not get caught. If one of us is captured, the other must immediately head for home."

Danel knew what Yassib was going to say before he opened his mouth.

"I'll go first to the far side of the valley. You stick on this side. Wait until I'm out of sight before moving."

Danel nodded, not trusting himself to speak in case the quiver of fear in his belly revealed itself in his voice.

Yassib grasped Danel's arm in farewell and set off.

There was a loud screech overhead, and Danel clutched at the amulet. He took a deep breath. Only an owl hunting for prey, rather like he had to do. He left the shelter of the rock and headed for the line of trees which stretched along the base of the rocky hills, carefully placing one foot in front of the other. If there were trees, there'd probably be water.

* * *

It had taken Danel most of the night to reach the end of the upwardly sloping valley. There now seemed no option than to climb to a much higher ridge. The moon had risen and glimmered above the cliffs, and he wiped the sweat off his forehead with the back of his hand. He would never tell Yassib how many times he'd dived for cover, sure the spirits had found him. He'd nearly wept with relief when the howl he'd hidden himself from turned out to be a wolf trotting along, minding its own business. There were many times that long night when he'd wished to be sitting by his own fire, working in the bakery, or sleeping comfortably under the stars on his own rooftop. But he reminded himself that he'd wanted to prove himself, and shoved all thoughts of home away.

With a final scramble, Danel reached the top of the pass. He remembered not to stick his head above the ridgeline and dropped to his belly to see the lay of the land, the rising sun warming his back. He crawled toward the lip of the ridge, keeping his shoulder next to a large rock so he'd be hidden in its shadow and making sure there was a bush in front of him.

The strengthening light revealed a wide flat plain. On the far side, a walled town, smaller than Gibeon but still a decent size, shone pale in the first rays of the sun. Was this the Ai that Rivkah had mentioned?

His eyes scanned to each side. Not so far away, maybe a few miles, there was a second, bigger town. Bethel perhaps. Yassib had mentioned that it was in this direction.

Danel continued his scrutiny. There was no sign of the Israelite soldiers but there was really only one place they could be—in the densely wooded gully between the two towns.

Where would Yassib be? Danel slowly turned his head. There were several highpoints with clusters of rocks along the ridgeline. Yassib would most likely be on one of those. Places where he could see the action, but with an escape route that would allow him to head further west to home. As he looked right Danel thought he could be trapped there. So left it was for him. If Yassib was at the first clump of rocks, Danel would move to the second.

Danel wriggled back off the ridge and set off for the first clump of rocks.

CHAPTER TWENTY-THREE

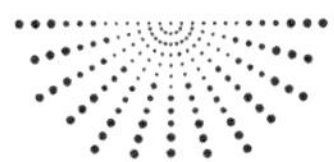

It was late afternoon the following day, and Danel was glad Yassib had beaten him to the first clump of rocks, for Danel had found a tiny spring at the second. As the day had heated up, the cool of the spring had relieved his thirst. It had been a long day.

The townsfolk of Ai, if that was indeed what the town was, went about the usual business of taking their herds outside the walls. Merchants arrived with their wares. There must be a market inside Ai's walls.

Danel briefly considered warning the town, but there was no reason they'd believe someone his age, especially a stranger. He was more likely to be imprisoned than believed. His own people must be his priority.

The hidden men hadn't been discovered so far, but neither had Yehoshua arrived. Had something gone wrong? If Danel found the day long, how much worse it must be for the hidden men. They'd have to lie totally still all day. No fires, no talking, no getting up to relieve themselves.

The sun was just past its highest point when a trumpet sounded.

Danel turned to look back at the ridge as the first row of soldiers topped it, making no attempt to conceal themselves. As soldiers continued to come up onto the plateau, there was a startled bleating of sheep nearer at hand. Turning, Danel saw a group of shepherds dashing for the safety of the town walls, leaving their sheep to scatter in all directions.

Shortly afterwards, there was a blast of horns. The group of merchants left Ai and set off as fast as possible towards the further town. Behind them, Ai's gates slammed shut.

Meanwhile, Yehoshua's army spread out to the north of the town with the valley between them and the wall. They made fires and prepared meals.

Danel's leg cramped, and he grunted as he massaged it. A walk would have been wonderful, but it wasn't possible. Not with the Israelite army filling the valley.

Danel curled up in his cloak and tried not to be envious of the army with their fires. He contented himself with the thought that the hidden part of the army must be as miserable as himself.

After dark, a large bonfire was lit on the town wall and torches appeared along the wall. The men of Ai alternately showed or covered the torches and were answered by lights on the wall of the farther town. It made sense the two towns would use signals as a means of communication.

Eventually the messages ceased, and Danel did his best to get comfortable and doze.

* * *

Creak. G-grind.

Danel woke with a start and peered across the valley. The main gate of Ai was opening. There was the merest hint of the dawn in the sky, but the men of Ai were streaming out from the protection of the city walls. Perhaps their recent victory had made them overconfident.

Once out the main gate, the men of Ai aligned themselves in battle formation. Danel switched his gaze to the Israelite camp. It was as busy as an anthill, with people dousing fires and grabbing their weapons.

Danel rubbed his arms to get warm then turned to gather his things, stretching and moving his legs in case he had to suddenly move away from his hiding place. There was a flicker of movement at the first cluster of rocks. Yassib was awake and watching too. He'd be thirsty by now, as neither of them had expected to have to hide for two nights.

The troops from Ai were now out of the gates, thousands of them, stamping their feet. Danel could feel their impatience to get on with the fight and clear away this enemy who had dared to bother them again. This time the men of Ai would want to inflict far more casualties than a mere thirty-six. They'd want to deal with the Israelites once and for all.

Little did the people of Ai know that their earlier defeat had nothing to do with physical weakness. If the Israelites' god was once again with them, the whole population of Ai should tremble.

A man on a horse paraded along in front of the town's troops, presumably yelling instructions although the words were only a faint garble to Danel.

Had their god given Yehoshua the plans for the battle as he had at Jericho?

The Israelites were much closer to Danel. They braced themselves, waiting for the charge from the men of Ai.

Danel held his breath. The man on the horse turned to face the Israelites, horse prancing. Finally the man raised his arm. With a mighty roar of voices, the men of Ai ran forward, past the horse, eager for the fray.

The pounding of feet matched the pounding of Danel's heart. Now the people of Ai would see something.

The Israelites held their ground, bodies tense and ready for action, and weapons held up. Danel's body tensed too, ready for the clash to come. But instead of fighting, the Israelites turned tail and fled before Ai's army.

What? Danel shook his head to clear it. What had happened? The Israelites were scattering in all directions, running with no attempt at fighting.

Hope soared in Danel's heart. Was Yassib right after all? Was Israel's victory not guaranteed? Perhaps their god was still angry with them.

Danel peered at the closest men, running a mere spear's throw from his hiding place. There was no sign of panic at all. In fact, they looked like their main goal was to run and keep away from the army they'd come to fight.

Danel frowned as he looked back toward the city. He looked up toward the more distant town. Its gate also stood open, and its men were running down into the valley to join the rout. Or was it? Both gates were now open and both towns were empty of their fighting men. Danel swiveled his head, searching for Yehoshua. It wasn't easy in the chaos of the valley. He looked for someone who wasn't moving.

There was Yehoshua, safely away from the commotion, standing on a high rock. As Danel watched, Yehoshua lifted a javelin above his head. Danel glanced toward where he believed the rest of the Israelite army had been hidden to the west of Ai. Sure enough, the hidden men were now emerging from among the dense trees and scrambling out of the deep gully. The men of the two Canaanite armies hadn't seen them, for they were caught up in the pursuit of the fleeing Israelites.

Some of the ambush party headed towards the more distant town, but most headed down to Ai.

The ambush party entered Ai through the open gate. Danel had no way of seeing or hearing what was happening in Ai, but it was not long before he noticed a puff of smoke and then another. Soon fires were burning in different parts of the city.

There was a sudden cry of shock and horror, a cry of pain and loss. The Canaanites had stopped pursuing the Israelites and were staring back at their towns. Some started to run back. The Israelites stopped running, turned, and attacked the opposing armies with a mighty clash of metal and wood.

The Israelites closest to Danel worked together to wipe out one group of soldiers then moved toward another group. It was hard to know where to look, for there was action everywhere. Bethel was now burning too. Some of the ambushers left the towns and came out to fight, and the men of Ai and Bethel were crushed between two forces.

"Psst!"

Danel nearly jumped out of his skin. He swung around. Yassib was standing nearby, gesturing for Danel to come. He grabbed his bow and other belongings and backed out of the hollow, making sure that neither of the armies could see him. Keeping low, he ran toward Yassib.

"Good thing I wasn't the enemy. You'd have been dead." Yassib mimicked drawing his bow, then gestured back to where he'd been hidden. "The fight was getting too close for my comfort. I didn't want to be mistaken for a man of Ai."

Neither did Danel. Not with the way this fight was going.

"We need to be much further away," Yassib said. "Ready to head in the direction of home once the battle is finished."

Yassib led the way, moving from one form of cover to another. As the sounds of battle lessened, they moved more quickly, finally standing upright, and running away to the southwest.

"I'd like to see what happens," Danel said when he judged they were far enough away.

Yassib held up his hand for silence.

A bird called, but Danel didn't think Yassib was listening for birds.

"There's a stream this way," Yassib said.

Yassib drank his fill, and they filled their waterskins.

"I plan to watch, but we can't risk being caught up in the battle," Yassib said. "From this direction, we have a clear line to home. We need to find a hill that gives us a view."

"Will that one do?" Danel said, pointing.

Yassib nodded. "Probably."

They toiled their way up the backside of the hill and arrived at the top, panting. The valley near Ai was spread out before them, and the battle was still in progress. Ai was now fully ablaze. They couldn't see Bethel, as it was hidden by a fold in the hill, but there was smoke coming from that direction too.

The battlefield was covered in bodies. Danel's heart sank.

"Look," Yassib said, pointing.

The town was obscured by a cloud of dust.

"The wall has collapsed," Yassib said. "We've seen enough. Our people must be warned. These people pose no ordinary danger."

Not ordinary at all. If the Israelites remained faithful to their god, they were unbeatable.

CHAPTER TWENTY-FOUR

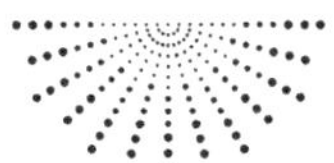

"**W**ill they listen?" Danel panted as he and Yassib paused for rest on the second to last ridge before home. It was the question that had been bothering him since they'd left Ai. They hadn't been sent out as official spies, and they were young in a culture that prized the wisdom of the older generation. Yassib had told Danel that many of the council were men who valued their own opinions. Danel took that to mean the men were pig-headed.

"It depends how scared they are. At the moment, the Israelites are seen as far away and pose no real threat to Gibeon." Yassib leaped over a small boulder as they started off again. "After all, there are many towns between us and them. Towns that the Israelites will have to conquer before they reach us."

The two of them skirted the town before Gibeon, cutting through the newly harvested olive groves.

Danel concentrated on not tripping over the rocks in the field they were crossing. "I'm worried Gibeon will think they're too big and powerful to be defeated."

"Then we must tell them about Jericho." Yassib's voice rang with intensity. "Ai seemed more of a conventional victory with a human plan, but Jericho obviously was not."

Danel jumped across a small stream. "That's just it. What if we don't get the opportunity to tell our story?"

Yassib punched Danel's shoulder. "You're always a flour-store-half-empty kind of guy. You see the problems, the weaknesses." He shook his head. "Whereas I always see that the flour-store-is-half-full and consider all the possibilities."

That was certainly one of the differences between them, but Yassib was also confident, tall, handsome, and courageous. Danel was a fade-into-the-crowd kind of guy. The kind of guy that no one remembered his name. He was simply "the baker."

"Don't look so gloomy," Yassib said. "Let's look at our strengths rather than our weaknesses."

"I can't see many strengths," Danel said. "Apart from the obvious —that you're the chief's son. You might not be the oldest, but you seem to be a favorite."

"That's because of my mother rather than me," Yassib said. "But you have to change the way you think. You have strengths."

Danel spat out a mouthful of dust. "Such as?"

"Well, I won't give you a swelled head by telling you now, but in this case, we have strengths other spies don't. I doubt anyone else has seen the series of connected events from the river crossing to the battles." Yassib's voice rose. "And you've actually talked to Israelites. No one else has done that, not even me."

"Yes, but they were only girls."

Yassib hooted. "Don't let Rivkah hear you say that. You won her trust and she told you a lot. She helped you see the motivations behind why the Israelites have come and why they fight."

There was a bitter taste in Danel's mouth. Yes, he had won Rivkah's trust, but he intended to use it against her people. He didn't want his people slaughtered any more than she would, and he'd do his utmost to save them. Yet it felt like he was betraying her.

"If we work together," Yassib continued, "We can use our combined strengths to gain a hearing. You also have an advantage in that your family has already been helpful to Father. He seemed to respect your uncle."

They toiled up the final rise. There was Gibeon. Home. A lump rose in Danel's throat. The stone walls glowed in the late afternoon sun looking strong, secure, and prosperous. Gibeon would be a prize for any conqueror. Somehow, he and Yassib must make the people of Gibeon understand the danger, the urgency, and that conventional battle strategies would not work.

At the gate of the city, Yassib clasped Danel's arm. "Don't worry too much. I will ask for an audience with Father. If he agrees, I'll send someone to find you."

Danel nodded. The thought of having to stand up in front of all the leaders terrified him, but he'd do it because he had to make them understand. Had to make them listen for everyone's sake.

Yassib set off toward his home with a spring in his step.

Danel turned toward the bakery, walking through the winding streets. When he arrived, he pushed open the gate and walked into the courtyard. There was nobody to be seen, but inside he could hear the thump, thump, thump of bread being kneaded. He let out the breath he'd been holding with a whoosh. Grandfather was still here. If he was kneading bread, then Uncle and Donatiya must also be around.

Danel walked across the courtyard. The fig tree had been harvested and the fruit was drying on racks laid in every sunny spot. Guilt oozed into his belly. Someone had been working hard while he'd been away.

He reached the bakery and peered into the doorway. Grandfather stood sideways to him, and he was humming. The sound was happy and relaxed, so different from the sense of urgency in Danel's gut.

"Danel! Danel!" Donatiya flung herself at him.

A lump clogged his throat as he hugged her back. This was why he and Yassib must succeed, for Donatiya and all others like her. She had no inkling of the approaching storm that threatened to end her world.

CHAPTER TWENTY-FIVE

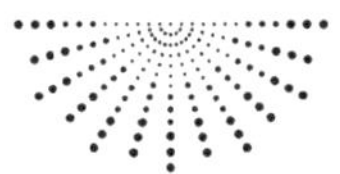

"So the wanderer has returned?" Danel's uncle said.

Danel looked up to gauge if his uncle was pleased to see him or annoyed he'd been gone longer than initially planned.

"Come and talk." Uncle Hammurapi turned toward the courtyard bench. "Donatiya, I'm sure your brother would love some figs and goat's milk." He peered at Danel. "He looks like he needs feeding."

The afternoon shadows were long, but there was still a patch of sunshine on the far side.

"Your sister has been worrying." Uncle seated himself with a creak.

"I was afraid of that," Danel said.

Uncle stifled a yawn. "I'm glad you're back. Running your bakery was a little too much hard work, although it was good to discover I hadn't lost all my skills. Thank you for giving me a job to do. I was getting in the way back at the vineyard. When a parent hands over a vineyard, they shouldn't keep meddling." He looked sheepish. "Being here has given me space to think, and your sister has kept me on track. She reminds me of your mother. She'll be running your business before too long."

"Donatiya will be delighted to hear you say that. Did you know my mother well?"

Uncle shook his head. "I allowed myself to get too busy with my own concerns. I regret that now." He laid a hand on Danel's shoulder. "I'm sorry I didn't come sooner. Perhaps your grandfather's deterioration might have been slower if he'd had a friend to talk to." Uncle sighed. "Since I've been here and talking to him every day about our past, he seems to have improved."

Danel leaned forward. "Do you think he might get better?"

Uncle shook his head. "No, but the deterioration seems to slow if we stick to his routines and include him in everything we do." Uncle sat up straight. "No more chitchat. I need to hear about what you saw. I'm sure there was plenty of hanging around, hard ground, and not enough to eat, but we can skip those parts."

Danel nodded. "That describes it well."

"Do you want to wait for the others?" Uncle asked.

Danel shook his head. "Donatiya doesn't need to hear the details of war."

Uncle sighed. "She might soon be forced to know far more than she wants to."

Fear washed over Danel again. For a few moments he'd been able to rest in the security of being back in a familiar setting with loved ones, but his uncle was right. There were far more urgent matters. He took a deep breath, "Yassib is going to ask for a hearing from his father but I need your help on how to tell my story. What to focus on."

"We'll work at it together." Uncle leaned back against the wall behind him.

Donatiya came out, carrying the milk and figs for both of them.

Uncle thanked her as he took what she offered.

"Can't stay," Donatiya said. "Still working on the last batch of dough, but I do want to hear your news."

"I'll tell you during our evening meal. I need Uncle's help for what to tell the chief." If the chief ever wanted to hear what he and Yassib had discovered.

She rubbed her hands on her apron. "I'll get Grandfather washed up and prepare the meal."

"Thank you, Donatiya. Uncle has been telling me what a splendid help you were while I was away."

She flushed and returned to the kitchen. Uncle hadn't said if he was staying longer. If he did, Danel was going to take Donatiya to pick wildflowers, something she'd once mentioned she wished she had the time to do.

* * *

The tantalizing smell of fried onions filled the air as Danel told his tale. He spoke of the Israelites crossing the River Jordan and the defeat of Jericho. His uncle asked occasional astute questions but mostly let Danel talk.

Danel finished his tale with the Israelites' initial defeat at Ai, followed by their victory.

His uncle turned to him. "So what have you learned?"

Danel had been thinking about this on the long trip home.

"This will not be a normal series of battles." Danel paused to gather his thoughts. "The Israelites are not going to stop until they've conquered the entire Canaanite region. They've been promised this land by their god, and they have a strong sense of purpose."

"Yes," Uncle said. "And much as we'd like them to, they will not be content with the land they already have. They've been promised all these lands and they intend to take them, especially when they know Elohim is using them as a means of judgment on our people."

153

Danel blew out a long breath. It was a relief to have Uncle here, someone who not only believed Danel's tale but understood the implications.

"And as long as the Israelites obey their god completely, their god will be with them and fight for them." Danel shook his head. "It's the miracles the chief will find hard to believe. Yassib and I saw them, and we still found them hard to believe. How could walking around a city every day and a loud shout knock down the walls?"

"That's the battle you need to concentrate on when you speak to the chief. It is the one that best demonstrates their god's power. I will come with you and remind them of the ten plagues in Egypt, and we'll both pray they listen."

Pray to whom? The people of Jericho would have been praying to some of the same gods Danel had been taught to pray to, but what good had that done? Danel had always made the morning offering of incense to Astarte and Baal, but lately he'd seen much that made him rethink.

The gods of Canaan craved sacrifice, including human sacrifice, but what did they give in return? Certainly not joy, and joy was what he'd seen on Rivkah's face whenever she recounted the tales of Elohim. Yet Elohim was the Israelites' god. To be a Canaanite was to worship Baal and Astarte. Could a Hivite even worship the Israelites' god? And if it was possible, would it mean he was a traitor to his own people?

CHAPTER TWENTY-SIX

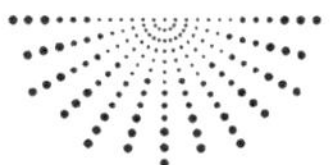

"Come on, Grandfather." Danel gently tugged on his grandfather's arm. "You know you've enjoyed your walk each day. It's only a little further."

Grandpa halted and stamped his foot. "Fortieth year!"

"Yes, I know. Yassib has asked for an audience, but the chief still hasn't sent for us." Danel sighed. "Our age counts against us."

Besides which, the chief had other pressures. Raiders had kidnapped a group of girls who'd been drying figs outside the walls. Men had been sent out north, south, east, and west.

Danel led his grandfather one shuffling step and then another to the rock at the top of a small hillock.

Below them, guards were now stationed around the olive groves where the drying racks were positioned toward the sun. The chief was making sure no more girls were kidnapped. Danel shivered. If the girls weren't found, they'd end up as temple courtesans, a name that sounded glamorous but concealed a terrible future. Or they'd be sacrificed to the gods as substitutes. The thinking was that one girl was much like another, so why sacrifice your own children when you could kidnap someone else's. Bile rose in Danel's throat and shame washed over him. These were the people he lived among. He had busied himself at the bakery, burying his head in a flour jar, but did that absolve him from guilt? He had never stood up against evil. He simply closed his eyes to it.

"Danel! Danel!" Yassib yelled.

Danel looked down the path to where Yassib was waving and yelling.

"He wants you to come! He wants you to come!"

Grandfather was startled by the shout and began to slide down off the rock on which he was perched. Danel grabbed him and then helped him stand.

Yassib slid to a stop. "I've been looking for you everywhere. Father has called the leaders from Kiriath Jearim, Beeroth, and Kephirah and wants you to come with me to speak to them. He wants us there as soon as possible."

* * *

Danel wiped his sweaty palms on his tunic. This council of chiefs and warriors were never going to listen. They were hard men, men whose eyes now bored into his head as though trying to frighten him enough that he'd leave. But too much was at stake to let fear conquer now. This was no game. This was Danel's life, and Grandfather's life, and Donatiya's life. It was the life of every man here, even if they didn't yet know it.

"Now you're here, tell us what you saw," the chief said. "Then we will decide what to do."

There was more than one scornful laugh from some of the men. Uncle had been reassuring on the walk between the city gate and the chief's hall. Telling him not to worry about the other men and to look only at the chief and tell him what he and Yassib had actually seen.

Danel looked at his uncle, who locked eyes with Danel and gave a slow nod. Danel took a deep breath. This might be the most important conversation he ever had. "You know that Israel defeated both Og and Sihon and then encamped on the far side of the Jordan."

Danel closed his eyes and pictured the scene. The rocky hills and the flooded Jordan below their lookout. "When we saw the flooded river, we nearly came home. It was obvious it couldn't be easily crossed and certainly not with women, children, goods, and livestock."

"And yet they managed to cross? By what means?" asked one of the men in the front row.

"By a miracle," Danel said. "The water stood up like a wall above the crossing and the tens of thousands crossed on dry land. We watched them all. It took the whole day."

There was a hum of conversation and finally one man called out. "But this is unheard of."

Danel's uncle stood. "That is not true. Israel's god did this forty years ago at the Red Sea. Pharaoh's army pursued them along the dry path in the sea, and all the men drowned. Some of you must have heard of this happening."

"And who are you?" asked the man.

"Peace," the chief said. "I have invited Hammurapi from Kiriath Jearim to be here. Forty years ago, he and Danel's grandfather spied on the Israelites as they camped on the borders of our lands."

The man snorted. "So these people have been here before. Why are they back again after having given up all those years ago?"

"Forty years ago, the Israelites turned back to the south because they rebelled against their god," Uncle said. "Their god told them that since they didn't trust him, he would not fight for them. Some of the Israelites went to battle anyway, but they were soundly defeated."

"Who is to say that won't happen again?" the man said, sitting down.

"Perhaps," Uncle said, "but I think crossing the Jordan River is meant to remind them of crossing the Red Sea and to prove that Yehoshua is the proper successor to Mosheh himself."

Uncle sat down again. Having Uncle here gave Danel confidence that he and Yassib might be believed.

"Danel, continue your account," the chief said from his raised seat on the platform in the center of the hall.

The long delay waiting for this audience had been frustrating, but one advantage was that Danel had told his story to Uncle and Donatiya several times. Each telling had honed the account. He'd learned how to stick to the main points and what to emphasize. Now as he told his story yet again, the men in the room sat wide-eyed as he recounted the astonishing war strategy Israel had used at Jericho.

"On the seventh day, the Israelite army walked seven times around Jericho. At the end of the final circuit the trumpets blew and the soldiers gave a mighty shout and—"

"And?" three of the men said together.

"And the walls of the city collapsed. The Israelite army rushed in and annihilated every man, woman, and child. Only one woman and her family were saved, because she'd earlier sheltered the Israelite spies."

There was a long silence. Finally, one gray-bearded man spoke up. "Perhaps this means the Israelites can't fight. They need their god to do the work for them."

"We are fighters." Another man spoke up. "We can muster thousands and ally ourselves with tens of thousands more. Talliya has already promised us victory."

Danel's heart sank. He doubted Talliya had dared to do anything but promise victory, not for the amount she was being paid. These men lived and breathed strategy and fighting. They didn't understand that the Israelites' god was totally outside their experience.

"Sihon and Og were strong like you," Uncle said. "And look what happened to them. Their towns are destroyed or empty and their people are no more."

The man thumped his fist into his palm. "We are stronger than them, and have had more warning and preparation time."

"Are you more powerful than Pharaoh and the Egyptians?" Uncle asked. He barely raised his voice but each of his words came with a punch.

"It wasn't a fair fight," the man insisted.

"The Israelites' god fights for them," Uncle said. "He is very clear in his purposes."

"Enlighten us," the chief interjected.

"On the surface, he appears to be giving his chosen people their own land," Uncle said. "Thus fulfilling the promises he gave to their ancestor Avraham."

The chief leaned forward with a frown. "What do you mean, on the surface?"

Danel too had noticed his uncle's careful use of words.

"I say on the surface because I believe there is a deeper purpose, but I am not yet clear what it is. What is clear is that this god never behaves in an arbitrary way. In Egypt, Elohim sent plague after plague, but each one came or went based on his word and each one achieved Elohim's plan."

"Such as?" the chief said with a glare toward a group of men who were fidgeting.

"Prior to the plagues, the Israelites were a group of slaves who were struggling to survive day by day. They were not unified. By the tenth plague, they were bound together and functioning as a single people."

Uncle had had forty years to ponder on these things.

"But the man who bound them together is gone," the chief said. "The question is whether this Yehoshua is as good a leader as Mosheh." The chief turned to Danel. "What do you think?"

Danel swallowed. He felt like a rabbit surrounded by hungry eagles.

"The people followed him across the Jordan and seemed to accept his authority."

The chief stroked his beard. "Tell us about the battle at Ai."

Uncle Hammurapi had made Danel review this story several times, emphasizing that he'd be speaking to soldiers, to men who wanted to know how the battle worked.

Recounting the Israelites defeat at Ai did not take long.

"So they're not invincible?" said a younger leader.

"It gave us hope for a while too," Danel said. "But we soon found out it was a false hope. The loss was not due to their strength or lack thereof."

The men murmured among themselves.

Once they'd quieted, Danel told them about Achan and how he and his family had been stoned and then they and everything they owned were burned.

"They'd stone a man for simply taking some of the plunder?" the chief asked, incredulity in his tone.

Danel gulped. How could he make things clear without mentioning Rivkah or confusing the matter with too long an explanation?

"I don't really understand why, but it seems the Israelites must obey all their god says exactly. If he says no plunder, he means it. Certainly, the Israelites were taking plunder at Ai."

"I thought they were defeated at Ai," said a man in the back row rubbing his head.

"They were defeated the first time. Let me tell you what happened after Achan was stoned." Using some objects that Danel had prepared and his uncle had remembered to bring along, Danel placed the first loaf of bread. "This represents the walled town of Ai. Bethel is further up the hill." Danel had confirmed the town's names with his uncle, who was much more well-traveled than he was.

Danel placed another loaf and then proceeded to add objects representing the soldiers in hiding in the gully and camping on the plain. The men in the room leaned forward, their gaze directed onto the simple loaves and stones.

"So they are using military tactics," the head of Gibeon's forces said.

"Yes," Danel said. "But I don't think they're coming up with them. I think their god is somehow speaking directly to Yehoshua."

"Directly?" the chief said.

Danel nodded. He and Yassib had seen no evidence of any divination ceremonies or any other person who was the equivalent of the diviner, Talliya.

The main doors of the hall opened. The chief's steward came to the chief's side and whispered something in his ear.

Danel's mouth went dry. Was there news of some sort? In all these days of waiting, he'd lived in dread that Yehoshua would be on the move again, that they had run out of time.

The chief stood up and everyone else jumped up, for it was impolite to sit while the chief stood. Danel's heart sank. Was that it?

"We will take a break," the chief said. "It is not good for such active men as you to sit around for so long. We will meet again after our meal."

Danel looked across at his uncle. He wasn't sure if the break was a good thing or not. These men didn't seem able to think in terms of anything but fighting.

CHAPTER TWENTY-SEVEN

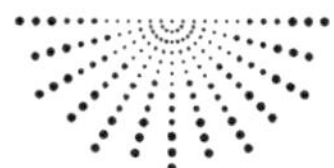

The fire in the center of the chief's hall flickered and sent dark shadows dancing on the walls. Danel shivered. The shadows reminded him of that disastrous visit to Talliya. He didn't want to think about her prophecy. Didn't want to think that the predicted losses might include his life. Certainly, the woman had been frightened of something.

Everyone waited for the chief to sit down, then huddled close to the fire. At this time, most people would normally be heading for bed.

"I have been thinking about possibilities, about how our people and towns are to be saved. In our hearts we want to fight, but others of equal strength have tried that and failed." The chief looked at the head of his army. "We can flee far, far away. That might save our lives."

"But it would destroy our honor," an old man said.

"And it would mean the loss of all our crops, fields, and homes," the chief continued. "Another possibility is using divination to curse these people."

Uncle cleared his throat.

The chief raised an eyebrow. "Are you sickening or do you have something to say?"

"Divination has already been tried." Uncle looked around the room. "Has anyone heard of the recent alliance between the Moabites and Midianites?"

Many shook their heads.

The chief growled. "Obviously our spy service isn't as good as I thought."

And how had Uncle heard of these things? Perhaps someone had visited him while Danel was away.

"The Moabites had good reason to keep things quiet," Uncle said. "They were humiliated by the entire incident."

"It sounds like you better inform us." the chief held his hands toward the fire.

"The Moabites were terrified when they heard how the Israelites defeated Sihon and Og, so they sent messengers to the Midianites, saying 'This horde is going to lick up everything around us, as an ox licks up the grass of the field.'"

Danel swallowed. It was a good description of what he and Yassib had seen.

"They agreed to work together, and Balak sent some Moabite and Midianite elders with much gold to bring Balaam, son of Beor, from over near the Euphrates River."

The chief whistled.

Danel looked at the other men. Some seemed to know the name but the rest were as mystified as he was.

"Balaam is even more powerful than Talliya," the chief said. "Those he blesses are blessed and those he curses are cursed. If Balak sent messengers to Balaam, then he was truly worried, for the man costs a fortune." He gestured toward Danel's uncle. "Go on. What happened next?"

"Balaam refused to come."

The chief leaned forward. "Refused?"

"So Balak sent more men, with more treasures. They said to Balaam, 'Come and put a curse on these people, because Balak says they are too powerful for him. Perhaps if they are cursed, then Balak will be able to defeat them and drive them out of the land.' But Balaam kept saying he could not come to curse a people whose god had determined to bless."

A murmur spread around the group but the chief held up his hand. "There is more, I think."

Uncle nodded. "Eventually Balaam agreed to accompany the Moabites back to their land, but still insisted he would only be able to say what god told him to."

"Which god was he referring to?" the chief asked.

"That's the odd thing. He seemed to be referring to the god of the Israelites. How he knew their god and how Balaam communicated with him, I do not know."

"Continue," the chief said.

"Balak took Balaam to various points overlooking the hordes of Israelites, who were camped on the plains of Moab. Many sacrifices were offered, but at each place Balaam blessed the Israelites rather than cursing them."

The chief snorted. "I begin to see why we have not heard this tale."

"Most of the blessings were fairly conventional, but one I think was important." Uncle closed his eyes. "Let's see how much I can remember. 'God is not human that he should lie, nor a human being that he should change his mind,'" he recited in a singsong voice. "'Does he speak and then not act? Does he promise and not fulfill? I, Balaam, have received a command to bless; for their god has blessed, and I cannot change it. For no misfortune is seen in Israel, for their god is with them.'"

There was a long silence in the hall.

"So that's it," the chief said. "If Balaam did not have the power to prophesy against these people, then no other diviner does." He sighed. "Does anyone have any other ideas?"

"The Moabite tale doesn't quite end there."

The chief raised his head. "Go on."

"Moabite and Midianite women went into the camp and seduced the men of Israel."

Two of the men hooted and made several ribald comments before the chief regained control of his men. "Is that what you're suggesting we try?"

Uncle shook his head. "No, it wasn't a solution. The Israelites did engage in revelry with the women and did follow them to worship the gods of Moab, but the Israelites' god sent a plague that killed twenty-five thousand of them."

"That sounds like a solution," one of the younger men said. "Can we make their god angry enough that he wipes them out for us?"

There was laughter and several loud inappropriate comments. The chief held up his hands for quiet. "Much as I'd wish we had time for joking, we do not have that luxury. We have already heard that fighting is of no use, and divination is no use." He ticked both off on his fingers. "What other solutions do we have?"

Think, Danel, think. There had to be something that could be done to rescue them all from certain death.

Yassib's quote. What was it? A warrior had many weapons besides bows, swords, and pikes. They'd rescued Donatiya from the slavers using a trick. Could that be the solution?

"A trick," Danel said.

Every head in the room turned toward him, including Yassib's.

Danel took a deep breath. "We have to trick them."

The chief fixed a hard speculative gaze on Danel. "Trick? What sort of trick did you have in mind?"

Danel's face heated. "Surely we can come up with something between us. Yehoshua is a new leader. A new leader succeeding

Mosheh—not an easy man to follow. It would only be natural if he felt a little insecure and wanted to prove himself. He might not have learned the wisdom our chiefs have." Danel inclined his head toward the chiefs of Gibeon, Kiriath Jearim, Beeroth, and Kephirah. "And Achan proves Yehoshua does not yet have complete obedience among the Israelites."

"There might be murmurings of rebellion below the surface." The chief stroked his beard. "Other leaders who think they should have been chosen as Mosheh's successor."

Now that the chief was talking Danel could not interrupt.

"Yehoshua has also had some major victories. If we're lucky, he might become overconfident." The chief looked across at Danel. "Do you think this is possible?"

Danel could not claim to know Yehoshua, but he'd heard the awe in Rivkah's voice when she talked of Mosheh. What man would want to be constantly compared to the great rescuer and lawgiver?

Danel nodded. "Somehow we have to get Yehoshua to act without asking his god or anyone else for advice."

The chief chuckled. "I like the way you think. Let's meet again tomorrow, after the sun has passed its highpoint. We won't make the mistake we hope Yehoshua will make. There is much wisdom in conferring together. Together, I believe we can come up with a workable ruse that will save our people."

Uncle laid his hand on Danel's shoulder and squeezed. A warmth filled Danel's belly. The chief sounded confident that they could come up with a plan to deceive the enemy but in half a day? Danel tensed his jaw. Half a day would be a challenge.

CHAPTER TWENTY-EIGHT

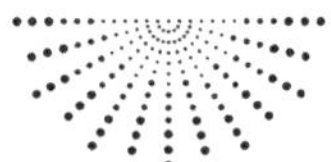

anel, Grandfather, Uncle, and Donatiya took their places around the tablecloth spread out on the ground. Danel handed his grandfather the first flatbread and Grandfather tore it in pieces and handed it to each family member. It was a role that Grandfather, as head of the household, had performed as long as Danel could remember.

Donatiya had mixed the goat curds with herbs from the courtyard garden, and there were also onions pickled in vinegar.

"I still haven't come up with a single idea," Danel said.

Uncle sighed. "Neither have I. Maybe we should just throw out any idea and see if that triggers another better thought."

It was worth a try, for kneading dough, which usually helped Danel think, had achieved nothing. Neither had a night's sleep or a morning walk.

"Maybe we could trick them into thinking we're more powerful than they think we are," Danel said.

"Or that other people are going to fight with us," Uncle said.

"Or that we're protected by some sort of curse that is activated when we're attacked." That had worked with the bandits who had tried to kidnap Donatiya.

They kept tossing ideas around. Danel sighed. He didn't think any of their ideas would work.

"Didn't Rivkah say something about Sihon and Og being fools because they didn't need to fight the Israelites?" Donatiya asked in a small voice.

Danel wrinkled his brow.

"That Sihon and Og could have given the Israelites a welcome, and the Israelites would simply have walked through their land and paid them for anything they used," she continued.

"Yes, that's right." Danel still wasn't sure what Donatiya was getting at.

"Does that mean the Israelites' god has only told them to conquer the peoples within the bounds of the land promised to Avraham?"

Uncle squinted at Donatiya. "It sounds like you've been listening to some of our conversations."

She ripped some of the bread in front of her. "It annoys me that I'm left out because I'm still considered a child. If the Israelites are coming to wipe us out, I want to have a part in trying to save our people."

"We're sorry for being overprotective," Uncle said. "But keep talking. What you're saying is important."

Donatiya put her head to one side. "So is it that people within Canaan are to be wiped out, and people outside to be left alone?"

Danel frowned. He remembered Rivkah's sadness at the needless deaths of Sihon and Og's people.

"I think Donatiya is right," Uncle said. "The Israelites' god has promised his people specific lands, and we're right in the middle of them. It doesn't include the land of the Edomites or other people related to them."

What a pity that they couldn't claim kinship with the Israelites.

Donatiya clapped her hands together. "Somehow we have to trick the Israelites into thinking we live outside the boundaries of their promised lands."

Danel whistled. "You're brilliant. Perhaps we can say we've come because we've heard of their fame—"

"—and we want to make a peace treaty with them," Uncle added.

There was a long pause.

Danel put his hand on Donatiya's shoulder. "I do believe you've solved our problem."

Donatiya's grin lit up her face in a way Danel hadn't seen for too long.

"But how do we make them think we've come from faraway lands?" Danel's voice rose as he caught Donatiya's excitement.

Uncle held up his hands. "Just slow down and let me catch up with all you young people." He picked up a cup of wine and sipped it slowly.

Donatiya kept opening her mouth then closing it again. Danel understood her impatience, but they needed Uncle. He was wise and would see ramifications Danel and Donatiya were blind to.

Uncle looked up. "The first thing, Donatiya, is that we must never mention that this was your idea."

Her face fell.

Danel grasped her hand. "The town leaders think ideas are best if they come up with them themselves. They respect people like Uncle."

"If the leaders have any inkling that this idea comes from a child —" Uncle said.

"The problem isn't just that I'm young, but that I'm a girl. Men don't listen to women." Donatiya said in a huff.

"Men can be fools." Uncle winked at her. "We need to cloak your plan in my voice. That will be yet another trick."

Donatiya grinned at the thought.

"We mustn't speak too early," Uncle said. "Instead, we let the other men give their ideas, then present this plan at just the right time."

Danel's mind had been working furiously trying to answer his own question. "I think I've worked out how to trick the Israelites into thinking we've come from far away."

"Tell us," Uncle said.

So he did.

"Let's not make the mistake of presenting the complete plan to the council," Uncle said once Danel had finished talking. "They are much more likely to adopt this plan if they think the idea is their own."

Danel laughed. "Most of them would prefer to fight rather than resort to a ruse."

"Exactly. They're chiefs and warriors, outspoken men of action." Uncle Hammurapi slapped his knee. "Yes, the more they think the plan is their own idea, the better."

Danel hoped Uncle was right.

CHAPTER TWENTY-NINE

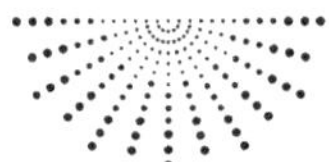

The chief looked around the group. "I know danger seems far away at the moment, but it is only three days at a fast march to where the Israelites are camped."

Inside the hall, several flies buzzed in the stuffy heat. Sweat trickled between Danel's shoulder blades.

"I think we should fight," one man shouted, and there was an immediate chorus of support.

"It's better to die with a sword in our hand than to give up," yelled another.

"We are not suggesting giving up," the chief said.

"Then what are you suggesting?" one of the leaders from Kephirah asked.

The chief held up his hand. "It is not a question of what we'd prefer. We'd all prefer to fight, but we have already established that fighting will not work."

The chiefs of Kephirah, Beeroth and Kiriath Jearim nodded.

Danel exchanged a look with Yassib and relaxed. Their report had been believed.

"Now, let's hear your trickiest ruses," the chief said.

There was a long silence. The man next to Danel, tapped a finger on the floor.

"Could we somehow pretend to be more powerful than we are?" asked one man.

"Or form an alliance with all the Canaanites in the land," said another.

"That won't work. We can't even work together to prevent kidnappings," another said.

There were murmurs of agreement.

"And we don't have enough time," said one of the men from Kiriath Jearim.

"Keep the ideas coming." The chief's voice held a note of tension.

Danel forced his muscles to relax. Uncle would present Donatiya's idea when he thought the timing was right. It was no use Danel getting all uptight and ruining their chance.

The ideas continued to come, slowly at first, then more quickly as the men gained confidence that they wouldn't be laughed at. It disappointed Danel to hear that most ideas were still linked with military strategy, including drawing off sections of the Israelites and wiping them out group by group. Didn't these men realize they didn't have forty years to gradually whittle away at the Israelites?

Through all the suggestions, Danel's uncle remained quiet.

At last, the suggestions trickled to a halt.

"Is that all?" the chief asked. "Has no one come up with anything more?"

The chief couldn't conceal the anxiety in his voice. If these were the only suggestions, the Hivites were doomed.

Come on, Uncle. Now!

"We need to get them to make a peace treaty with us," Uncle said.

All eyes turned toward Danel's uncle.

The chief rubbed his eyebrow. "I don't know why they would agree to one."

"Mosheh was their leader for forty years and was highly respected," Uncle said. "Now they have Yehoshua. The Israelites will be watching him to see if he measures up to his famous predecessor. At the first mistake, there will be other leaders ready to jump into action."

Clever Uncle. The chiefs experienced this reality every day. The former leader of Beeroth had been ousted by a younger leader, and one of the earlier leaders of Kiriath Jearim had been murdered. He'd brought in unpopular taxes and alienated all those who'd supported the previous chief.

"The Israelites might have won some battles, but they are not considered a nation," Danel's uncle continued. "Kings like Sihon and Og thought of them as a gaggle of slaves. The Israelites crave respect." Uncle looked around at the assembled leaders. "A delegation arriving to make peace with them implies not only that they are a nation, but that they are also worthy of respect."

Danel held his breath. Donatiya's idea was by far the best of all the suggestions, but would these men see it?

"But why would they agree to a peace treaty when they can just fight us and take our land?" the chief asked.

"Remember how the Israelites offered money to the people east of the Jordan." Uncle asked looking round the men. "They could have lived if they had not attacked the Israelites."

"What are you trying to say?" the chief of Kephirah asked.

Uncle unfolded a piece of cloth. "This cloth represents the lands we occupy between the Jordan and the Red Sea. The Israelites have been promised all those lands, but they have not been promised the lands here to the north." He tapped the ground beyond the top of the cloth. "We must pretend we have traveled far from the north to make a treaty."

"Pretend we're from outside the lands to be conquered." The chief stroked his beard.

"Ha! Very clever," the chief of Kephirah said.

Come on. Come on, chiefs and warriors. Start adding your ideas.

"This plan relies on Yehoshua not checking our story," came a voice from the back. "What can we do to ensure he acts quickly without consulting others or his god?"

Again there was a pause. Danel held his tongue. The more ideas that came from the group, the better.

"Flattery can befuddle a man's mind," the man next to Danel said.

Did the leader speak from experience?

"What kind of flattery?" asked the chief of Beeroth.

"Perhaps tell Yehoshua we've heard of his fame and what a fantastic military leader he is," the man said.

"And that although we live far away to the north, we've heard of what happened in Egypt," added another.

Danel tried not to let excitement show on his face. The plan was working.

"Thus giving them the respect they crave," said the head of Gibeon's army.

"No," the chief's voice cut cold through the growing excitement. "No. That treaty would be worthless the moment their army worked out our ruse. Yes, they may sign our treaty but what would compel them to keep it?"

All eyes were on Uncle, but for once he was struggling to find the words. Israel's history with covenants was a lot to explain. The energy shifted in the room. Several men muttered their opposition. Danel's mouth was dry. The attention Uncle had gained was slipping away.

"They won't betray their god!" Danel shouted.

All attention snapped to Danel, and his gut cramped.

"Their god punishes all disobedience. Yassib and I saw this

with our own eyes, when we stood in their camp. When only one man violated a covenant with their god, he was stoned and his body burned. If they swear the treaty in the name of their god, they will not break it. If they do, their own god will turn against them."

Danel waited for the chief to throw him out. Instead, the chief turned to Yassib. "Is this true?"

"Yes, Father. I believe they'd keep the oath."

The chief nodded, eyes brightening.

"I doubt they'll believe us if we merely say we come from far away," the head of Gibeon's army said. "How do we trick them into thinking we have indeed traveled a long way?"

There was a long pause before Yassib spoke. "Old shoes, cracked and worn thin."

"Clothes that are threadbare and dusty," said another.

Danel listened with a racing heart. The plan was back on track.

"Exhausted animals," another man said. "I have some donkeys we can use, but we'll have to wear them out before the start of the journey."

"Clothes, shoes, donkeys," the chief ticked the items off on his fingers. "What else?"

The chief of Kiriath Jearim leaned forward. "The provisions need to be old too."

"I can supply moldy bread," Danel said.

Another man offered old wineskins and stale dried fruit.

"Who shall we send?" the chief asked. "We need elders. People who would be sent to represent our people. People worthy of forging a treaty. But they must also be able to convince the Israelites that they have indeed come from far away. They must be able to lie and make it sound like they speak the absolute truth." The chief frowned and looked around the hall. Sometimes his gaze moved quickly and other times it lingered. "It is also a dangerous role. We need enough men that it is a delegation, not too many and not too few. Five or six, perhaps. Men who will not be afraid if the ruse is discovered."

The chief turned to Hammurapi. "You should be one, I think. You have a presence about you and can think quickly. Danel can go as your aide."

"Might I not be recognized?" Danel asked, heart in mouth.

"I think we must risk it," the chief said. "Think about how to cover your face."

"I'll go, Father," Yassib said.

The chief pursed his lips. "I know you are eager to serve but it will increase the risk to have both of you. You must stay behind."

Yassib nodded reluctantly, and Danel caught Yassib's eye to show he understood Yassib's disappointment.

The chief turned to the others. "Who will go as part of a retinue to support Hammurapi and Danel? I think we need another three elders and some servants."

The chief's steward stepped forward. "Perhaps myself and my son can be of service."

The chief pursed his lips. "Yes, I think you would both be suitable. Let's have one more man from Kiriath Jearim to accompany Hammurapi, and the rest from Beeroth and Kephirah. Yes, eight should be suitable. Four elders with authority and four attendants."

The delegates from each town talked together and after some to-ing and fro-ing put forward their proposed candidates, all of whom were endorsed by the whole group.

"When do you think you can be ready?" the chief asked.

Danel waited for the other suppliers of provisions and donkeys to answer and then said, "I'll have plenty of stale bread ready in four days and it will be truly moldy by the time they arrive."

"I hope you don't expect us to eat it," the steward's son said with a grimace.

"Never fear. I'll provide the best bread the bakery has to offer for your daily food," Danel said.

"We'll hold you to that," Uncle answered. "I am not looking forward to sleeping on the ground for all those nights.

"It will add authenticity," the steward said.

"That's what I'm afraid of," Uncle said.

The chief clapped his hands. "I know you're all excited about this plan and ready to go home, but we must all swear an oath before you leave. The lives of our people depend on the success of this trick. We will not get a second chance. Much as we'd prefer to fight, it seems our combined strength is not enough to fight the the god of the Israelites." He looked sternly at each man in the hall. "No word must leak out. You must not speak of it to your wife, or your lover, or your children. If I see you drunk, I will lock you up myself."

Danel gulped. Donatiya was going to be mad, but she'd just have to wait until the men returned.

"Hold up your hands and we will swear our oaths," the chief said as he stood and raised his own fist. "Repeat after me."

The men stood around the chief in several rows.

"We swear," the chief said.

"We swear," everyone repeated.

"To keep our mouths sealed shut."

Danel and the others repeated the oath line by line and finished with, "On pain of death."

There was a long silence. Danel's blood pounded in his neck. This was dangerous and their futures—all their futures—rested on their success. If they didn't succeed, his family would be blamed. Although perhaps that didn't matter if they were all to die anyway.

CHAPTER THIRTY

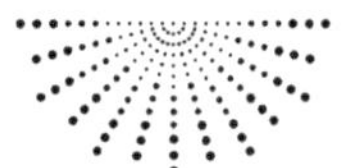

"Halt! Who goes there?" A voice cut through the mid-morning haze.

Heart pounding, Danel stood still.

"Don't touch your weapons," Uncle said out of the corner of his mouth. "Raise your empty hands above your head."

Sweat broke out on Danel's forehead but he didn't pause to wipe it off. If this was an Israelite outpost, they needed to appear peaceable. If the men weren't Israelites? Then they were in trouble. The problem was they had no way of knowing who was delivering the command.

"Come out slowly where we can see you," the voice continued.

Please, please, please, let them be Israelites. Danel didn't know who he was praying to—any god who'd listen and answer. Hands raised, he followed his uncle and the other members of the delegation out into the open. Would this be the moment Talliya had predicted? The moment when arrows thudded into his body? The moment when all was lost?

Danel's heartbeat thudded in his ears, and he squared his shoulders. If he was to die, he would die with his head held high.

Die as a Hivite should die. Mouth dry, Danel stepped into the clearing and forced his face in what he hoped was a look of innocence and calm friendliness. By his calculations, they were close to Gilgal and the Israelite camp. These should be the people they were seeking.

"Stop right there," another voice said. "Spread out."

Danel and the others obeyed, hands still in the air.

"Now, slowly, very slowly, pull out all your weapons and throw them on the ground in front of you."

Danel took a deep breath and cautiously reached behind for his bow.

"No tricks, or I'll command the archers to drop you right where you stand."

Danel unslung his bow and quiver, and gently tossed them where they'd been instructed. A few more bows and knives followed. Back in Gibeon, there'd been much discussion about how many weapons they'd bring. Enough for hunting and cutting up any meat. Enough to protect them in dangerous times, but not so many that they looked like a war party.

"Hands on heads," the voice said again.

Danel obeyed and saw the others follow the command too. Perhaps it was good that Yassib hadn't come. He'd have struggled to put down his weapons without protest.

A man stepped out of the shadows cast by the closest trees, and then another, and another. Danel counted five men but there might be more behind them. Each held a bow with an arrow at the ready.

"Now talk," the leader said. "What do you want?"

"We want to talk to your leader, Mosheh," Uncle Hammurapi said, his voice as calm as though he was chatting to a neighbor at the local well.

Night after night on their trip north then south again, Uncle Hammurapi had made them practice their story. All of them had agreed Uncle would be the main spokesman and that they must not reveal they already knew Yehoshua was the new leader. People from the north would still be ignorant of that fact.

"Mosheh is no longer with us. Why would you want to speak to Yehoshua?" the man asked.

Danel breathed out with a rush. They'd found the Israelites.

"We have come from far to the north to speak with your leader. Please send a messenger with our request," Uncle said with great dignity.

The soldiers moved off to the side and spoke in low voices. Danel took a few steadying breaths. *Please, please, please let us be taken into the camp.* Danel no longer prayed to Baal or Astarte and he didn't dare to bring himself to Elohim's notice, but he hoped there was some other god out there who could hear him.

The soldiers returned. "We will send word to our leader Yehoshua and see what he says. First we will bind you, for these are perilous days and we can trust no one."

Wise man. Danel's hands were tied to the next man's and they were looped around a broad tree with their backs propped against the trunk. It would be a long and uncomfortable wait.

Danel heard the messenger leave. Three of the Israelites stood around the tree, alert and ready for any sudden moves from Danel and his fellow Hivites.

Soon, Danel could hear snuffles and snores. Had some of their delegation managed to doze off? He couldn't. The rope chafed his wrist.

Most of their trip had been uneventful. They'd crept out of Gibeon in pairs, under cover of dark. Once over the first ridge, they'd linked up and headed north, avoiding towns, and only traveling when they could do so unseen. Once far enough north, they'd changed their tactics, allowing brief stops in villages, so Yehoshua would find proof of their progress from the north if he checked.

Then they'd grown overconfident and stumbled into a campsite. They'd been fortunate, because the group of Jebusite shepherds had told them an unexpected tale of a vast movement of the Israelite camp further to the west. The shepherds had followed at a distance and seen the Israelites climb Mount Ebal and Gerizim. The shepherds had sent two men up each mountain. Although the shepherds had missed the earlier ceremonies and sacrifices, they'd been in time to hear half the group shout words of cursing and half shout words of blessing.

Such covenant ceremonies were not unknown. The blessings were promises for those who kept the covenant, and the curses were what would happen if the covenant wasn't kept. Covenants were usually between nations, but the shepherds said this one must have been with the god of the Israelites for there were curses for making an idol, dishonoring their father or mother, or withholding justice from a foreigner, the fatherless, or a widow.

Danel had been encouraged. It was as he had told Gibeon's council. The Israelites had renewed their covenant with their god. As a god who saw everything, they would not dare to break it.

Now if only the Israelites could be induced to enter into a covenant with the Hivites.

* * *

There was the sound of horses' hooves, and Danel licked his dry lips. He must have fallen asleep, for the sun was now well past the midpoint.

He would be willing to give up the secrets of one of his bread recipes to anyone who would give him a drink of water.

The leader strode toward their tree. "I apologize for our excess caution. Yehoshua has sent for you."

The Israelites untied the Hivites and helped the older men to their feet. Danel stretched his stiff muscles and wriggled his shoulders. They were reunited with their donkeys, and had a long drink and a hurried meal before setting off.

As they reached the outskirts of the Israelite camp, Danel was pleased to see they were approaching from the far side, away from where he'd met Rivkah at the stream. He'd be highly unlikely to see her. More importantly, he was unlikely to be recognized by anyone else who might have seen him on the day Achan was stoned. Being a hot day, it made sense to have his head and part of his face covered.

As they were led through the camp, many of the Israelites came to the entrance of their tents to watch. Danel kept his head down and his hand on the bridle of one of the donkeys, donkeys that indeed looked like they'd traveled huge distances because their owner had made them work non-stop while the preparations for this trip had been made.

As they approached the center of the camp, Danel couldn't help raising his head to look at the Israelite place of worship. He'd only just caught a glimpse of the protective barrier around the special tent when he found himself looking into the wide, startled eyes of Rivkah.

Danel felt sick to the pit of his stomach. He hadn't expected to see Rivkah, and he hadn't expected her to recognize him, but he also hadn't reckoned on everyone's curiosity. As they were probably the first outsiders to enter the Israelite camp he should have known they'd draw attention.

Danel shouldn't have come. His head had known this, even if in his heart he wanted to be a hero. The risk was too great. Rivkah might not know his real name or where he had come from, but if she spoke to the right people, her words might raise a little doubt. And a little doubt would be all that was needed for Yehoshua to investigate their story more carefully and discover that no one had seen this delegation past a certain point to the north.

Danel swallowed the bile in his throat and pulled the donkey's bridle. *Please, please, please don't let her say anything.* It was all Danel could do not to start running forward to finish their business before Rivkah convinced anyone to listen to her, but haste would also ruin their chances. Rivkah turned and pushed her way through the crowd. Where was she going and who would she talk to? Danel wiped his clammy hands on his tunic and followed his uncle.

They were led toward a large tent with a dull red banner on the top. As they approached, a man came out of the tent, eyes blinking as they adjusted to the setting rays of the sun.

Uncle Hammurapi bowed and said, "Greetings from our king and people near the banks of the great Euphrates."

Yehoshua inclined his head. "You have come a vast distance then. Why would you travel so far south?"

Danel's role was to be a servant for his uncle, and a servant he would be. The donkey stamped its hoof and a cloud of flies rose in the air. Danel stroked the donkey's neck to keep it calm.

"Your servants have come from a very distant country because of the fame of the Lord your God," Uncle Hammurapi said. "For we have heard reports of him—all he did in Egypt, and all he did to the two kings of the Amorites east of the Jordan—Sihon king of Heshbon, and Og king of Bashan, who reigned in Ashtaroth. Our elders said to us, 'Take provisions for your journey; go and meet them and say to them, "We are your servants; make a treaty with us."'"

Uncle Hammurapi had the perfect voice to lead the delegation, deep and sonorous, the kind of voice that sounded like it was telling the truth even when it wasn't. A voice that suggested respectability and dependability. A voice to be believed.

Let him be believed. Let us be saved.

Yehoshua raised an eyebrow. "A peace treaty? How do we know you are not tricking us? That you have not come from somewhere much closer?"

Danel's chest was tight. These were the critical moments. He continued to stroke the donkey's neck. It calmed Danel as much as the donkey.

"We are sorry to have come to you in such a state, not befitting your nation's greatness. These clothes and sandals you see were new when we set out." Uncle Hammurapi raised his foot to point at the sole. "You can see how worn the soles are. I'll have to get a new pair when I return home." Uncle turned and indicated the wine-skins dangling from the donkeys. "Our wine was poured into new skins when we left, and our bread was fresh. It is no longer edible."

Yehoshua turned and spoke to several of his fellow leaders. "I apologize if we seem to disbelieve you, but we would like to see your packs." They moved toward the donkeys.

"I can respect a man who takes such care." Uncle stepped back to allow the Israelites easy access.

Was that a slight flush Danel could see on Yehoshua's face? Maybe Uncle was right and Yehoshua was insecure in his new role.

A child cried inside Yehoshua's tent, the cry of a child impatient to eat. Yehoshua glanced back at the tent, as though reassuring someone inside that he wouldn't be much longer.

Danel moved to stand in front of the donkey as the Israelites burrowed into the bundles on each donkeys' back. They laid every-thing out on the ground, took sips of the wine, and sniffed the bread.

Danel flicked his gaze to the people standing well back. There was no sign of Rivkah. *Hurry, Yehoshua.*

The child was now whining. Everyone within hearing shifted their feet, all too anxious to be away from the insistent sound.

One of the leaders examined each donkey then walked back to Yehoshua. They held a murmured conversation which Danel couldn't hear above the fretful cries of the first child and now a second.

"Look at the donkeys," one voice broke out. "They have clearly traveled a long way."

When Danel got home, he would tell the donkeys' owner of the success of the workout he'd given the animals. But would it be enough?

The leaders were still conversing. Behind them, a young woman came to the entrance of Yehoshua's tent, bouncing a still-crying child on her hip. Yehoshua mouthed something toward the young woman, perhaps letting her know they were nearly done.

Let Yehoshua forget to consult the one he should be consulting.

Danel would never have chosen late afternoon to present their case, but it was proving to be the perfect time. A time when everyone, even children—or perhaps they were grandchildren—were tired and ready to eat and rest. Not a time for making a well-considered decision.

Yehoshua said something to a younger leader, and he set off at a run toward the Tabernacle compound. Danel held his breath. What was happening now? He forced himself to relax. To not show the anxiety swirling in his stomach. To hide the fear knotting his neck at the thought of Rivkah. Was she even now speaking to someone of real influence? Someone who would believe her, and have the courage to approach Yehoshua? Someone whose words would destroy all hope of a treaty?

The young man reappeared from behind the barrier clutching two scrolls. Approaching Yehoshua, he held them out. Yehoshua unrolled them and instructed a scribe to write.

Danel was too far away to hear what was being said, but there could be no mistake about what was happening when his uncle and Yehoshua made their marks.

One copy was handed to Uncle Hammurapi, and Yehoshua retained the other. Joy rose in Danel's throat, but Uncle had warned them not to show an excess of emotion. They were not safe until they arrived home. Even then, they might not be safe. For if Danel was wrong and the Israelites did not honor this treaty obtained by trickery, it would not be long before the consequences fell on all their heads.

CHAPTER THIRTY-ONE

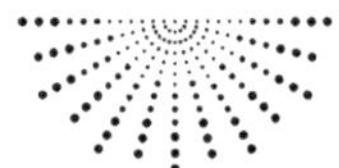

Back at Gibeon

There was one trumpet blast, then another.

"The gates. Close the gates!" someone yelled.

Heart pounding, Danel looked across at his uncle. They'd only been back in Gibeon a few days, for they'd had to travel north after leaving Gilgal, before heading west then south to reach home.

"Go and find out what's happening," Uncle said. "I'll stay here and keep an eye on things."

Danel dashed into the street. Others were also heading for the walls. He took off down a narrow alley that would bring him more quickly to the side gate where there'd be less of a crush.

A line of soldiers stood at the top of the wall, arrows ready. Danel climbed the stairs and, with a bit of wriggling through the crowd already there, found himself a spot. A large group of heavily armed men were descending the hill, heading straight toward the town.

"Does anyone know who they are?" Danel asked the nearest soldier.

"No one knows," the soldier said. "There have been rumors of an alliance of Canaanites preparing to attack the Israelites."

"Or it might be angry Israelites," another soldier added.

"Madder than enraged hornets," said the first.

When the delegation had returned, the chief had told the towns-folk about the treaty. Yet nothing was being left to chance, for the men of the town continued daily weapons practice. Danel now felt confident with the bigger bow.

Danel watched as the approaching soldiers marched down the hill and came to a well-disciplined halt just beyond arrow-shot distance. They too must be nervous about their welcome. Two men moved slightly closer to Gibeon's walls, still keeping a safe distance.

One of them took a deep breath. "We want to speak to your ruler," he shouted.

If Danel stood on tiptoes and turned slightly he could just see the front section of the wall. There was movement, and the men pressed against the walls to allow the muscular figure of the chief and his spokesman to move to the front.

The spokesman cupped his hands around his mouth. "Who wants to speak with the chief?"

"Yehoshua, son of Nun, leader of the Israelites, the people of the great Adonai, Creator of heaven and earth," called the spokesman outside the walls.

The soldiers around Danel muttered to themselves.

"Creator of heaven and earth, did you hear that?"

"I'm not sure Baal would agree."

"Or Astarte, or any of the gods of these lands. Those Israelites will have to learn more respect."

There were nods of assent among the soldiers nearby.

Danel kept his mouth shut. These men had not seen the walls of Jericho crumble. The people of Jericho would have made many offerings, but their gods had not protected Jericho. It probably wouldn't help to point out that the famed gods of Egypt hadn't stood a chance either. If the people of Kephirah, Beeroth, Kiriath Jearim, and Gibeon were allowed to live, they might all be learning much of the Israelite god.

"What guarantees do you give for our safety if we come out to talk?" called the Gibeonite spokesman.

"On the basis of our treaty and the honor of Adonai and his servant, Yehoshua," the Israelite spokesman called back.

It was still a risk to open the gates. Danel believed Yehoshua was honorable, but could he control the Israelites? A hostage situation would dramatically change the whole situation.

The chief held a consultation with several men around him. Then he issued some orders and assigned messengers to set off in various directions.

Much as Danel would have liked to stay, he must get home. It was highly likely Uncle Hammurapi would be one of the men chosen. He doubted the chief would risk his own life.

Danel headed down the stairs and jogged home, arriving at the same time as the messenger. Pushing his way into the courtyard, Danel called his uncle and then watched as the message was delivered.

"I'll have to wash and change out of my work clothes," Uncle said. He headed toward the inner room. "Danel, see if you can find out who else is in the delegation."

When questioned, the messenger said he hadn't heard all the names but he did mention some names of the men who'd been in the original delegation. "Oh, yes, and the chief's son, Yassib, is to go."

Lucky Yassib. The chief was wily. He wasn't endangering himself or his likely heirs but still sent a family member and others he could trust.

Uncle hurried back into the courtyard, his hair and beard slicked down and all traces of flour gone. He looked like what he was, the prosperous owner of a vineyard.

"I might be a while," Uncle said as he followed the messenger. "Say a prayer for us."

Uncle had never requested prayer before. He must be more nervous than he looked. Danel wasn't even sure who his uncle prayed to. He certainly had never used incense to pray at the family altar. Not that Danel had been praying at the family altar recently either. The altar lay cold and disused. Donatiya had asked him about it, but he'd muttered something vague and she hadn't pushed him any further. It was hard to worship gods he considered corrupt and even evil. They did nothing to stop the kidnapping and sacrificing of girls. Girls like Donatiya. Girls who were full of life, creative ideas, and loads of potential.

So if his own gods were powerless, to whom should he pray for his uncle's safety?

Uncle had asked Danel to pray, and Danel would do his best. Danel went up to the rooftop and raised his hands. "God, I don't really know which god I'm praying to, but if you see me on this rooftop, if you're listening, please keep Uncle safe. He means a lot to us. And great god of the Israelites, if you listen to people like me, please let us live. Dead bodies cannot worship you. I don't understand why you want to wipe us all out, but if you let us live, I'll try to understand."

He had no idea how to end his prayer. "Thank you that your servant Yehoshua seems to be a man of integrity. Help him to honor his promises. And god, if you are there, I would love to see Rivkah again. Sorry for asking, but I figure if you're god, then you can see my heart anyway. That's all."

Danel put his arms down with a sigh of relief. He was still alive. No lightning bolt had shot out of the sky.

The creak of the main gate opening signaled the delegation was leaving the city. Danel thought he might as well get Donatiya and Grandpa and set to work himself. If they were busy, they'd have less time to worry about what might be happening outside the gates.

Less time to fear that the Israelites might consider themselves justified to repay the Hivites' trick with one of their own.

CHAPTER THIRTY-TWO

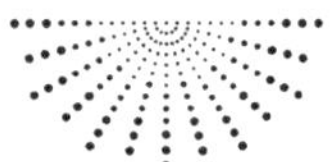

*D*anel stood at the main city gateway and watched as it was opened. The delegation was returning and that must be a good sign. Already the tension that had gripped his body since his uncle left was oozing out of him. There'd been no retaliatory tricks, no hostage taking. The men of the delegation were relaxed and smiling.

Danel pushed his way forward, getting as close to where his uncle would pass as possible. The delegation would have to report to the chief first.

Uncle Hammurapi clasped Danel's hand in passing and leaned in. "Tell Donatiya to prepare a celebratory meal," he whispered.

Danel would be delighted to do so. Donatiya deserved to know the full details of what had been happening and Uncle should now be free to tell her.

* * *

he smell of roasting quail filled the house by the time Uncle opened the gate.

"I'll be ready to serve after he's washed up." Donatiya removed the birds from the oven.

Uncle was carrying a large bundle wrapped in cloth.

"What's that?" Danel asked.

"If you go and get an old man a drink and gather the others in the inner room, I'll show you," Uncle said.

"Sounds mysterious," Danel said. "Shall I tell Donatiya to put the food in there too?"

Uncle nodded and went to wash. It wasn't long until they were all seated. The sunshine filtered through the latticework at the window and a wasp buzzed around the room before settling somewhere.

"Gift or story first?" Uncle asked.

Danel knew what Donatiya would say before she opened her mouth. Gifts, apart from a few wildflowers, were not something she had encountered before. He must make sure that he gave her some, for she deserved more than one for all her hard work.

"Gift it is," Uncle said with a laugh.

It was good to hear laughter after so long under the shadow of the Israelite threat.

"How did you know it was for you, Donatiya?" Uncle asked.

She beamed at him. "Is it? I thought it would be for all of us."

"We'd look funny wearing it," Uncle said, handing her the bundle.

Her forehead wrinkled, but she took the package and untied it. "The cloth it is wrapped in is gift enough."

The cloth was finely woven with some sort of colored thread running through it. Donatiya put it up to her face and rubbed her cheek across its softness before folding it carefully and laying it aside. Then she unfolded the clothing inside one at a time. Three tunics in different colors and fabrics. She stroked each before reverently refolding them and then looked up at her uncle. "I don't understand."

"They're not from me, although they were my suggestion," he said. "After our return from Gilgal, the chief thanked me privately. He said most of the other men had forgotten who'd suggested the plan, but he hadn't." Uncle smiled at Donatiya. "I simply said that though I'd love to claim that the plan was my idea, it hadn't originated with me."

Donatiya looked up at Uncle, eyes shining. "Did he believe you when you told him whose idea it was?"

"He took a little persuading, but eventually he asked what you'd like as a gift from a grateful people."

"And you suggested the clothing?" Danel said.

"I did, and that is likely all you'll receive. He won't publicly admit that a girl saved Gibeon. The army would still prefer that victory came from the power of their might rather than a mere ruse."

Donatiya knelt and leaned over to kiss her uncle on his forehead. "Thank you. It's a beautiful present and will last me for many years. I won't wear the best one but the plainest one I need right now."

Now she mentioned it, Danel could see Donatiya's work tunic was wearing thin at various spots and getting too tight. He must pay more attention to her needs. Donatiya would save the finest cloth for her wedding. Danel would start buying other things in preparation for the same event, as their parents would have done if they were still there.

Donatiya smoothed out the last crinkle in her gift. "Let me serve the dinner. Then can you tell us what Yehoshua said?"

"You have all earned the right to know what is going on," Uncle said, "But you must not speak of these things elsewhere. Let the chief tell us what he wants us to know. Do you agree to these conditions?"

They all nodded, though Grandfather's nod was slower. Danel didn't know how much he understood, yet he and Uncle were so much a part of this whole story.

Once the meal was served and they'd all eaten their fill, Uncle took a cushion and leaned against the wall. "It only took Yehoshua three days to work out they'd been tricked. He sent some fast scouts to check where we'd said we'd come from and discovered the point at which we'd suddenly appeared and begun the journey south toward Gilgal. Someone they asked must have recognized us, because they told the Israelites we were Hivites from this area."

Danel would have hoped the Canaanites might have protected their own. Obviously not. There'd always be someone willing to talk for the right price.

"Thank goodness they didn't check before the treaty was signed," Danel said.

"Yes. The journey was always going to be the weakness in our plan. If we'd have had more time, we could have traveled much further north to the area we claimed to come from," Uncle said.

"Do you think the other Canaanites know about our treaty with the Israelites?" Danel asked.

"If they don't, they soon will," Uncle said. "And they might not be too happy about it."

Danel swallowed and made sure not to look at Donatiya. She didn't need to be worried about something that might never happen. It was dangerous to be the Israelites' enemy, but being their friend might bring new dangers.

"The army outside our walls set out as soon as they knew where we were from. It only took them three days to get here."

Donatiya gripped Danel's hand and he squeezed hers back. How he wished that he could promise her that everything would be alright, but in all truth he could not do so. They might have a treaty, and the Israelites might be willing to honor it up to this point, but what would they do if other people attacked Gibeon? And even if Gibeon was saved, there was still Talliya's prophecy to be faced. There were no guarantees Danel would live to see things work out.

"Yehoshua said many of the Israelites grumbled against him for not coming to wipe us out. But he told them, 'We have given them our oath by the Lord, the God of Israel, and we cannot touch them now.'"

"Thank goodness he is a man who keeps his word," Donatiya said.

"What did Yehoshua say about the trick?" Danel asked.

"He asked why we had tricked them," Uncle said. "And we told him, 'Your servants were clearly told how the Lord your God had commanded his servant Mosheh to give you the whole land and to wipe out all its inhabitants from before you. So we feared for our lives because of you, and that is why we did this.' Then we told him we were in his hands, for him to do what seemed good and right."

Donatiya leaned forward. "What did Yehoshua say?"

"Yehoshua told us that we are now cursed and that we must serve the Israelites as woodcutters and water carriers for the house of God."

Danel stared at his uncle. "But I'm a baker."

"Don't panic yet," Uncle said. "Yehoshua may just have been trying to placate his own people, because he immediately asked us a big favor."

Danel cocked an eyebrow. "A favor?"

"Remember what you told us about the special food that their god provided for them for the forty years in the desert?"

"They called it manna," Danel said. "Their god also made sure their clothes never wore out."

"I would have liked that," Donatiya said, hugging her new clothes to her chest.

"Yes," Uncle said. "But can you think of the practical consequences of their god's provision?"

Danel shook his head.

"I hadn't either," Uncle said, "But Yehoshua pointed out to us the negative side to all that time in the desert without baking, cooking, making clothes, and growing their own food."

"Sounds delightful to me," Donatiya said.

Uncle chuckled. "I can see why you might think that. Remember, everyone who was over twenty when they rebelled on the borders of our lands forty years ago died in the desert, all except Yehoshua and Kalev. That means almost no one remembers how to bake, make clothes, or grow crops."

Danel stroked his bristly chin. "I can see how that would be a problem."

"Yehoshua wants us to train their people in practical skills. The chief is going to consider how it's possible and send me back to speak to Yehoshua tomorrow."

"How many people are they talking about?" Danel asked.

"I don't think they've thought that far ahead yet," Uncle said. "The chief is going to meet with some of the leaders and work out how many our towns can accommodate. I already said we could take a few here. I thought you'd be grateful for the help."

"We would indeed," Danel said. Any apprentices could probably stay with the widow next door in exchange for help around the house.

"I've been charged to walk down our street and see who would both appreciate help and be willing to teach some of these skills," Uncle said.

"And do you know when they will come?" Danel asked.

"I guess when both sides agree," Uncle said. "The chief said you could come with me to talk with Yehoshua tomorrow, as breadmaking was particularly mentioned and he immediately thought of you. If things work out, I'll then head back to Kiriath Jearim. I will need to help the Israelites settle in at the vineyard."

Danel's throat narrowed. He would miss Uncle. Miss his help in the bakery, miss his practical wisdom, miss how his presence made life seem somehow lighter.

"You know you'll always be welcome here," Danel said.

Uncle nodded. "I do. Being here has shown me my usefulness doesn't have to end just because the vineyard now belongs to my son."

"But will the vineyard still belong to your son and the bakery to us?" Danel asked.

"I don't think anybody knows how this is going to work. Officially we have our lives, but now we have become servants to the Israelites. But while we train them, we are the bosses. It won't work otherwise." Uncle put a hand on Danel's shoulder. "Just live each day one at a time, and don't let tomorrow's burdens weigh you down."

Uncle looked around at them all. "You're a good team, and you should soon have some more hands to help."

Danel took a deep breath. Life was about to change, probably forever, but he'd do his best to see them thrive.

CHAPTER THIRTY-THREE

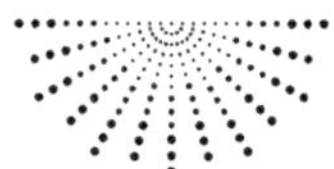

The sun was already past its high point the next day when Danel and his uncle went out through the main gate. Danel and Donatiya had made their bread and sold it while Uncle walked along the street, looking for any families who were willing to apprentice an Israelite or provide accommodation.

Ahead of them were the Israelite tents with a ring of guards alert to any approaching danger. Glancing around at the other men accompanying them, Danel recognized a tailor, other bakers, and several farmers.

As they approached the Israelite camp, the guards clumped together and one of them called out at the central tent. The Hivites waited at a distance, and Yehoshua eventually emerged from his tent and came toward them.

"Welcome," Yehoshua said to Danel's uncle. "Have you thought about my suggestion?"

"We have. These men with me represent farmers, bakers, weavers, and tailors. Each of them know how many Israelites they can accommodate and train."

Yehoshua gestured to someone behind him who came forward

with a clay tablet and scratched the numbers on it as the Gibeonites made their statements.

Danel's uncle spoke up. "We have sent messengers out to Beeroth, Kephirah, and Kiriath Jearim to ask if they are willing to take apprentices and how many. The messengers should be back tomorrow."

"We will wait then," Yehoshua said. "I would like to talk with your chief once again."

Uncle raised an eyebrow.

"I must make sure that our people are well looked after," Yehoshua said. "They are not slaves. I want this to be both mutual help and mutual learning. You know about these lands and the seasons and climate and how to live here."

Yehoshua was tactful enough not to say that everything in these lands would one day belong to the Israelites. It still made Danel's heart ache to remember that the people in these four towns might be the only ones to survive the arrival of the Israelites.

A young man came toward the group, and Danel couldn't help a little gasp escaping. Amidst the darkness of the man's hair was a streak of much paler hair. Rivkah had said that this was a family trait. Could this man be Rivkah's brother or a cousin? Mouth dry, Danel hoped for a chance to speak to him.

"Do you have something to ask, Zeb?" Yehoshua asked.

"I do," Zeb said. "I want to know if some of us can stay here and get started."

"We will see," Yehoshua said.

Yehoshua was careful. Leaving a few Israelites in Gibeon could be dangerous. Any Hivites angry about the conditions that had been laid upon them could take that out on any Israelites in their midst. Some of the townsfolk were angry because they hadn't been told about the trick until it had been successful. Uncle had said there would now be a series of community meetings to inform people what was happening and why.

* * *

"Ready to go, Danel?" Uncle poked his head through the doorway of their home at the bakery. He'd been to the chief's hall and back.

"Have all the towns replied?" Danel asked.

Danel had heard a group of men on donkeys arrive in the late morning and another two groups later in the day.

Uncle nodded. "We have all the offers of accommodation and a list of which families are willing to teach the Israelites."

Those were the wise families. The ones who saw this as a chance to escape becoming woodcutters and water carriers. The ones who wanted to be valued, like Danel, for the skills their families had acquired over many generations.

Danel slicked down his hair with water and followed his uncle toward the main gate.

"All the chiefs are going this time," Uncle said. "They're beginning to trust Yehoshua. They must get to know him personally if they are to gain advantages for our people."

The chiefs would also want to make their own judgments of this man who was going to have such a great an impact on Canaan.

The group gathered at the gate was impressive. Each chief was seated on a pale-colored donkey and had brought their own bodyguard with their standard flying on a long pole.

"Yassib's not here," Danel said.

"The chief has some of his oldest sons accompanying him. When he asked me to accompany him, I requested that you be included as well. You won't be saying anything, but keep your eyes and ears open."

There was only one person Danel wanted to speak with, but would he get the chance? Yehoshua had called the youth Zeb—an odd sort of name, but maybe it was short for something.

Before they went out the gate, Danel watched as the chief issued instructions to his soldiers.

"What's he doing?" Danel asked his uncle in an undertone.

"Being cautious," Uncle said. "Making sure we're protected in case this is a ruse."

Danel gave a low whistle. He didn't think the Israelites would back out, but he might be wrong. It now made sense why he hadn't seen the chief's two oldest sons, and why the bodyguards included the best troops. If this was a trap, then the chief planned for them to be able to defend themselves until the troops inside the city reached them.

A trumpet blared from the city wall. The first line of guards marched out the open gate in a row, followed by the chief of Kephirah and his retinue. There was a line of soldiers along each side, so the chiefs were surrounded by guards, each one with a polished sword and wearing a leather breastplate polished with oil. Would they be accepted as ceremonial guards?

Danel believed Yehoshua was an honorable man, but men could be influenced and there must be Israelites who desired revenge for the way they'd been deceived. Danel took a deep breath and followed his uncle out of the gate.

Yehoshua and his scribe were waiting for them at a large rock, with a few guards at his back. All looked safe but Danel saw their guards' eyes sweeping the area for danger. The soldiers fanned out and stood braced for action.

Each representative and their attendant moved forward. Danel's heart pounded, but he followed behind his uncle as they all walked toward the rock.

"I notice your caution, and understand it," Yehoshua said. "But Yehovah, our God, does not lie or go back on his word, and neither will we." Yehoshua looked at the chiefs. "Thank you for your trust in coming to meet me. I want your guarantee that my people will not be harmed. If they are, then our treaty will be null and void."

"What do you mean by 'harmed'?" the chief asked. "The word seems open to interpretation."

"I see your point." Yehoshua tugged his beard. "Obviously not a burned finger or tripping over a rock." He smoothed his beard. "Perhaps the wording should be killed or intentionally harmed." He looked up at the chief. "Does that wording work for you?"

"Would you allow us some time to discuss it?" the chief asked.

"Of course," Yehoshua said.

The four chiefs and the attendants moved to a point out of earshot of the Israelites and proceeded to analyze the words Yehoshua was proposing.

Danel paid little attention, for he had no right to contribute his thoughts in such company. Agreements were for leaders. Instead, he watched the Israelites. Yehoshua was also in consultation with his scribe and a few others. They soon finished talking and Zeb, the pale streak of his hair glowing in the sun, approached Yehoshua. How could Danel get a chance to speak with him? It was likely that the Israelites would return to Gilgal once this treaty was signed. Much as Danel would like to find Rivkah, he couldn't leave the bakery, especially as his uncle was planning to return home to prepare his son for the imminent arrival of some Israelite apprentices.

Yet it was possible that Rivkah might not be happy to see him for although they'd gotten along well over near Gilgal, he hadn't been able to be honest about who he was. She was just as likely to slap his face and never want to speak with him again.

"We're agreed then?" the chief asked the group.

"Yes, but we will have to make sure our people know we are all endangered if any harm comes to the Israelites," the chief of Beeroth said. "It would be too easy for someone to allow anger or frustration to boil over."

Danel straightened his shoulders and followed the chiefs back to Yehoshua.

Yehoshua stood. "Now all your chiefs are here, I would like to read the treaty aloud." He signaled for his scribe, and the man came forward and picked up the Israelite copy of the treaty. He cleared his throat.

"This treaty is made between the Israelites, the descendants of Avraham, Yitzchaq, and Yaakov with the Hivites, based in the towns of Gibeon, Kiriath Jearim, Beeroth, and Kephirah, in the year the Israelites crossed the Jordan River and entered the land of Canaan."

The scribe took a break and then continued in his ringing voice. "Both sides agree that our peoples will remain at peace. This treaty is declared on oath before Yehovah, Creator of all and the One who sees into men's hearts and judges all thoughts and actions."

Uncle had told Danel that initially the other delegates had wanted the names of their gods on the treaty, but Yehoshua had been immovable on that point. His god would not share anything with gods they didn't believe existed. The Hivites had backed down, since they considered the seals and the wording of the actual treaty more important than the heavenly witnesses.

"Below the main treaty are the seals of Yehoshua and Eleazar, the high priest of Yahveh, and the seals of each of the four chiefs of your towns, which your delegates used on your behalf."

Each side bowed to the other and exchanged words of agreement. Finally Gibeon's chief gestured to the messengers from each of the other towns. "Now, let Yehoshua's scribe note down the numbers of Israelites you can train and the various crafts."

The men came forward and each gave the numbers they could train and accommodate. When they were finished, Yehoshua said, "Some of our young men are keen to get started. Would Gibeon be ready to take twenty right away?"

Danel held his breath. Would Zeb be one of them? And if so, would Danel be able to find a chance to talk to him?

The chief turned to Danel. "Your uncle assured me that you could handle two. Is that right?"

"Yes, the widow next door is happy to have some stay with her, and several families are willing to take someone in to learn to spin, weave, and make clothing," Danel said.

"Good lad," the chief said.

Yehoshua turned to Zeb, who was still standing nearby. "Call the others."

The others? Excitement swirled in Danel's stomach. It sounded like Zeb would be one of the group. Would he want to come to the bakery or at least stay nearby?

Young men clutching small bundles emerged from various tents and walked toward Danel and his uncle. Some of the young men smiled, others gnawed their lips, or gripped their bundles too tightly. What must they be feeling? Leaving their people to be surrounded by strangers? Strangers who might be more than a little hostile?

CHAPTER THIRTY-FOUR

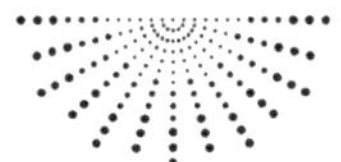

$\mathcal{A}$ cool breeze blew across Danel's rooftop, bringing the scent of damp earth. An owl hooted in the darkness, and the moon danced fitfully between clouds. Danel grinned into the darkness. Zeb and his friend Simeon were settled with the widow next door and would come over in the morning to learn the whole process of bread making.

The chief had asked Uncle to delay returning to his family and oversee the settling of the newcomers. Uncle had divided the Israelites into three groups—those who preferred indoor work, those who preferred to be outdoors, and those who didn't mind either way. Danel had watched with bated breath and been pleased to see Zeb join the group which didn't have any preference. Uncle had then listed the kinds of jobs available and the skills needed, and matched each person. Danel hadn't left things to chance. He'd asked Zeb if he'd be interested in coming to the bakery. Zeb had said he'd be happy to and asked if his friend Simeon could join him.

The two young men were now sleeping on the widow's rooftop. Or maybe they were awake, like Danel, wondering what the future would hold. Danel rolled over onto his side. Would it be a night without nightmares? Danel sighed. Only half his nights were free of nightmares.

Uncle was snoring. He would leave in the morning to return to Kiriath Jearim with the chief and his retinue. There would be a lot of work to do to prepare for the flood of new workers. Uncle said there were several empty houses that could be repaired, as whole families might come. Might Rivkah's family move here? Danel wasn't sure if that would be a good or a bad thing. If Rivkah was angry at him, Danel didn't want her here. He'd prefer to remember their conversations as they'd been. One of the first times he'd ever talked to a girl his own age.

* * *

Uncle Hammurapi placed his hands on Danel's shoulders and looked into his face. "Blessings on you, my boy."

Danel cleared his throat. Uncle leaving was hard. It had been a relief and comfort to have him around. "Please come again."

"And soon." Donatiya threw her arms around Uncle.

Uncle turned and hugged her back. "I plan to come back and see how you're all getting on."

The gate into the courtyard opened and Zeb peered in. "We're early, but we wanted to see if we could offer a blessing for your uncle's trip."

"You can do more than that," Uncle said. "You can teach me how to pray to your god."

Danel's eyes widened.

"I've been trying to pray to him ever since we saw the pillar of fire and heard Adonai talk to his people," Uncle said. "I couldn't deny that Adonai was real. Knowing that showed me the local gods were either false or too weak to matter."

Danel understood. Seeing Adonai's power at the Jordan and Jericho had completed the undermining of Danel's trust in the gods too. He wasn't sure if they were false, but they certainly permitted much evil in their names.

Zeb came forward, followed by Simeon. "I've never taught anyone to pray before. I can't remember being taught because my parents and grandparents simply prayed every day."

"Don't be nervous," Uncle said. "In this matter, you know more than I do. I've done my best but I'm never sure I'm doing it right."

"I'm not sure it is about doing it correctly," Zeb said. "Grandmother always says Yahveh looks at the heart."

"That's a relief," Uncle said. "Canaanite prayers are based on ritual."

"And our prayers won't be answered if we get it wrong," Danel said.

Donatiya looked a little uncomfortable at all this talk, but perhaps it was just that she was young, the only girl, and unsure in the presence of two strangers. Danel held out his hand and drew her in toward his side.

"Most of us pray while standing," Zeb said. "Sometimes I raise my hands, but I've seen people praying kneeling with their face on the ground. Whatever shows respect." He flushed. "Should I pray for you as you travel? Then you can hear what I say?"

"That would be helpful." Uncle lay down his bundle of food and clothing.

Zeb raised his hands, bent at the elbow and palms up, and looked up to the sky. "Great Yahveh, maker of heaven and earth, and Creator of all good things. You save, you redeem, you purify. Thank you for your daily care. For health, and food. Thank you for this city and that Simeon and I can learn skills to help our people."

Was Uncle as surprised by this prayer as Danel was? It was full of praise and thanks. It lifted his spirits just to hear it.

"We praise you that you welcome all who are willing to trust and follow you."

All? Could Danel really follow Adonai for himself? And how did one follow a god like Adonai?

"Today Danel's uncle is going back to his home. Keep him safe on the journey. Please guide him and give him wisdom for any decisions he must make. For the sake of your holy name." Zeb lowered his hands.

"Thank you for your prayers." Uncle smiled. "Please continue to pray for me. The days are evil, and I worry about my family."

"I will commit myself to pray for you until we meet again," Zeb said. "That you will stand firm and shine Yahveh's light into dark places."

"Why do you use Elohim and Adonai and Yahveh almost interchangeably?" Uncle asked.

"Yahveh was the name that the Creator revealed to Mosheh. It means something like 'Before everything existed I was there.'"

"Like he's eternal?" Donatiya asked quietly.

"Something like that," Zeb said.

"Our gods are visible," Danel said. "And you used to have the pillar of fire, but what do you worship when you are far from home and there are no statues or altar?"

"The pillar of fire wasn't to be worshiped," Zeb said. "It was a reminder of Yahveh's presence with us and a way to guide us on the next stage of our journey."

"It filled me with awe when I saw it," Uncle said. "I imagine some people worshiped it."

"Possibly," Zeb said. "We've had that trouble before, before I was born. Soon after the Israelites crossed the Red Sea, they reached Mount Sinai. Yahveh showed his power by terrifying shows of thunder, lightning, and fire on the top of the mountain. He allowed Mosheh and Yehoshua to climb the mountain and talk with him. Mosheh was given ten commandments." Zeb paused, as though aware that all these things were new to Danel and his family.

"The commandments are rules to live by. Yahveh said, 'I am the

Lord your God, who brought you out of Egypt, out of the land of slavery. You shall have no other gods before me. You shall not make for yourself an image in the form of anything in heaven above or on the earth beneath or in the waters below. You shall not bow down to them or worship them.'"

Zeb spoke his god's words with such reverence that goosebumps appeared on Danel's arm. It still amazed him that this god communicated directly with the Israelites.

"Yahveh was clear that we must not use any kind of image to represent him, but even while Mosheh and Yehoshua were with Yahveh, our people sinned," Zeb said. "Mosheh was up the mountain so long that our people feared he might have died and they'd be leaderless. They begged Mosheh's brother Aharon to make gods for them. Aharon used gold and made an image like a golden calf and told our people, 'Here is your god that brought you out of Egypt.'"

"Why a golden calf?" Danel asked. Danel had often seen sacrificial bulls with flower wreaths on their necks paraded around Gibeon before being led to be slaughtered, and Baal was often represented by a statue of a bull.

"I don't know," Zeb said. "Yahveh told Mosheh what was happening and declared he was going to wipe out our people. Mosheh begged for the Israelites' lives, rushed down the mountain, and smashed the golden calf."

"But Mosheh's intervention wasn't enough," Simeon said. "Adonai sent a plague as judgment and many died."

Someone called Uncle's name from outside the gate.

"I must go," Uncle said. He hugged Danel and Donatiya, then picked up his bundle and headed off, leaving Danel and Donatiya to start training Zeb and Simeon in the art of making bread.

* * *

"Let's go out to the fields," Danel said. "I want to show you the wheat and barley before it becomes the grain I showed you."

Zeb and Simeon had asked lots of questions as Danel and Donatiya had led them through the process step by step. Their first loaves were now cooling, ready for them to take next door for their host.

Outside the walls, Danel noted all the people working in the fields. He presumed many were Israelites beginning the task of learning how to farm crops.

Simeon saw some friends and darted off to join them. Danel now had his chance but he didn't want to ask his most pressing question first. "Zeb, is your name short for something?"

"My full name is Zebulun. It's the name of one of the twelve tribes of Israel, as is Simeon's name. All the tribes are named after sons of our ancestor Yaakov or his son, Yosef."

They strolled toward the grain fields and Danel pointed out the differences between the barley and wheat. "It'll be easier when they have the heads of grain as they look quite different then."

Zeb peered at the plants. "I'll take your word for it."

Danel glanced around to make sure they wouldn't be overheard. "I knew someone with a pale streak of hair like yours."

"It is quite common in our family," Zeb said. "Where have you seen it?"

"Her name was Rivkah," Danel said.

Zeb drew in a sharp breath and looked at Danel. "Where did you meet this Rivkah?"

"Next to a stream near Gilgal," Danel said, his blood pounding in his ears.

"She did not mention meeting anyone with your name," Zeb said.

Danel looked at the ground. "I called myself Keret."

"That was the name she mentioned. She did wonder if it was your real name."

"I didn't dare to use my real name," Danel said. "A friend and I went to the Jordan to see what we could learn of your people."

"To spy, you mean?" Zeb asked.

Danel's cheeks heated. "I guess you can use that term. I'd recently discovered my grandfather and uncle spied on the Israelites forty years ago when you sent twelve spies of your own into Canaan."

"My grandparents are ashamed of those days, because most of our people refused to obey Adonai and enter Canaan. They forgot victory had nothing to do with the size of our army. If Adonai wants us to do something, he will enable it to happen."

As Danel had already seen at Jericho and Ai.

"Like your uncle and grandfather, my grandparents, Kheti and Nophret, are an inspiration to our family," Zeb said. "They have been faithful to Adonai when so many haven't."

"Why do you think they've remained faithful?" Danel asked.

"Perhaps it is because they grew up worshiping the Egyptian gods. When they chose to follow Yahveh, they were choosing to leave all they were familiar with and start again. They often tell us Yahveh is the only God worth following. The only God who loves and rescues and cares for all, even the foreigner."

Rivkah and Zeb talked about their god as if following such a god was a privilege and a delight. None of these words had any place in Canaanite religion. Remembering Talliya, Danel shivered. The words he associated with her were fear and darkness and death. Had she foreseen what was to come with the arrival of the Israelites? Was that why she was afraid?

"I sent a message back with the other Israelites asking the whole family to come here," Zeb said.

"Do you think they will?" The thought made Danel simultaneously want to throw up with anxiety or do a cartwheel right here in the farmlands.

"Grandfather Kheti often talks about growing wheat and barley, and fruit and vegetables. He says he longs to dig in fertile soil again. I think they'll come."

"There's a deserted house near ours, but it will take hard work to make it habitable. The owners have been gone a long time."

Danel touched the amulet at his waist. He wouldn't tell Zeb that sorry tale. The youngest daughter had been sacrificed in the hope of saving her pregnant mother's life. All that had happened was that the husband had lost his entire family. He hadn't been able to handle the grief and had ended his own life. The house remained empty because Gibeonites feared the house. Zeb's grandparents didn't sound like the sort to be afraid.

CHAPTER THIRTY-FIVE

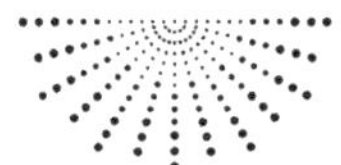

Zeb and Simeon had mastered the basics of baking quickly, leaving Danel more time to help Donatiya sell to customers. He wouldn't risk Zeb or Simeon on the stall, for the people of Gibeon were still getting used to the presence of Israelites. Still adjusting to the fact that Hivites, who'd been free for generations, were now the slaves of the Israelites, even if things still seemed much the same as they'd ever been.

Danel washed his hands and then went and took the next order—four loaves of barley and one of wheat. "Something special today?"

The woman nodded. "My son's intended is bringing her parents to complete the marriage settlement details."

Special indeed. The family would have been preparing for days to make a good impression.

There was a sudden blast of a trumpet. Danel dropped the loaf he was holding onto the stall and looked up. He sniffed. There was no smell or sign of smoke but there must be some emergency. A second blast sent the blood pounding in his ears. If there was one more blast, Danel would have to leave immediately.

Before he could say anything to Donatiya there was a third, more urgent blast. Already only the customers' backs were visible as they scurried for the gate.

"Donatiya, go inside and keep Grandfather calm."

Zeb and Simeon came into the courtyard at a run. "What's happening?"

"Three blasts is an immediate summons for all able-bodied men to assemble at the chief's hall, I must go."

"We're able-bodied," Zeb said.

"You are, but I don't know if it includes you. Simeon, please go and get your landlady and bring her here. I'll take Zeb. He'll let you know what's happening as soon as he can." Danel grabbed a waterskin and his bow and arrows and set off at a run, Zeb at his side.

Already the laneways were deserted, although Danel could see worried faces peering out at them as they ran toward the center of town. The closer they got, the more they had to slow down until eventually they were jostled on every side as they squeezed their way forward.

They couldn't see or hear much this far back. Danel tugged Zeb's arm. "There's some trees over that direction. Let's see if we can reach them." They pushed sideways, working their way around with some apologies as they stepped on people's feet, eased clear of the crowd, and found trees that hadn't yet been filled.

Danel hung his bow and quiver over a broken branch and put the waterskin on the ground.

"Give me a boost," Danel said.

Zeb made a cradle with his hands. In moments, Danel was in the tree and once secure he lowered his hands to haul Zeb up. Soon they were seated with a clear view of the steps leading up to the chief's hall.

The chief came out the main doors of the hall, accompanied by the best of his soldiers and all his sons in full fighting gear. Danel's heart rate increased. What was the emergency?

The trumpeter blew a short blast and the crowd fell silent.

"We have received news," the chief said. "The kings of Jerusalem, Hebron, Jarmuth, Lachish, and Eglon have gathered to wage war against us because of our treaty with the Israelites."

"I knew that treaty was a mistake," someone muttered at the bottom of the tree.

"Shut up and listen," snapped another.

"Adoni-Zedek of Jerusalem has called the other Amorite kings together to attack us. They'll be here in just over a day. We will send messengers to Yehoshua to ask for aid, but we do not know if the Israelites will come." The chief looked out over the crowd. "Each man must report to his leader for instructions."

"Can I fight with you?" Zeb whispered.

"I don't know," Danel said.

The chief peered out at the crowd. "Danel, grandson of Keret, report to me immediately."

Tension gripped Danel's neck, but he waved to let Yassib know where he was.

"You heard him," Danel said to Zeb. "Come with me."

They scrambled down from the tree and walked against the flow of the rapidly thinning crowd. Gibeon had been at peace with Jerusalem for years. It had always been a risk that in saving themselves, they would make enemies among the other Canaanites. Canaanites who now regarded Danel's people as traitors.

By the time Danel and Zeb arrived at the stone forecourt, there was a group of young men around the chief. His bodyguard kept an ever-watchful lookout.

"We are going to send messengers to call for Yehoshua's help," the chief said.

"But will he come?" asked one of the other men.

That was what they all wanted to know. This situation allowed Yehoshua a way to wriggle out of the peace treaty. The Israelites could delay their support or simply refuse to come. Once the four

Hivite cities were wiped out, Yehoshua could then appease those who'd been angry about the treaty.

"We must make the effort to enlist their help whether they come or not," the chief said, voice tight.

A ripple of fear ran down Danel's spine. So the chief thought the Canaanites would outnumber them.

"You will need to be ready to leave before the shadow crosses the courtyard." The chief looked around the group. "I know many of you will be eager to serve, but we need men who know the way to Gilgal and can talk with Yehoshua."

The crowd shifted as those at the back stood straight.

"Does anyone know if any of the Israelites can ride a horse?" the chief asked.

Danel sighed. If riding was essential for this task, it counted him out. Presumably Yassib would again get his chance to shine, for he knew the way to Gilgal and had been riding since he could walk.

A name was shouted out. The chief snapped out a message for the chosen Israelite, and the messenger departed at a run to collect him.

"I'm sending two groups of four, in case one group is waylaid," the chief said. He chose four men to ride and instructed them on the route to take—not the most direct route.

Yassib scowled. He'd obviously hoped to be in the group.

"Don't worry, Yassib. I still have something for you to do," the chief said. "I want you, Danel, and two Israelites to run the shortest route to the Israelite camp. You need to find two Israelites who can run like deer and keep running until you reach Yehoshua."

Yassib punched the air, grinning, and pushed his way over to Danel.

"I can run," Zeb said from his position next to Danel. "And Simeon is also a runner."

The chief nodded, strain deepening the lines on his face. "We have our two groups," the chief said. "The rest of you join your leaders to prepare the city for battle."

Once the others had left, the chief turned to Yassib and placed a hand on his shoulder. "Run well! Run safe!"

* * *

*D*anel's eyes were on the rough ground in front of him. He looked for the smoothest path and kept to it, knowing how easily he could twist an ankle, meaning he'd have to be left behind to fend for himself.

Simeon and Zeb had turned out to be a wise choice as runners. They had good memory for the terrain from their recent trip and had already saved them effort by leading them on easier routes through the hills.

"Water break at the top of the hill," Danel panted.

Yassib nodded but said nothing, probably saving his breath for the climb. Yassib pushed past a branch, and Danel was too slow to catch it before it swiped his cheek. They were running under the cover of trees as much as possible. They must make it through to Yehoshua.

They came out of the grove of trees and there was a clear run toward the top. Yassib hesitated and looked each way, then headed for a line of rocks so they'd be less visible. Danel was soon wiping his sweaty forehead, as running next to the rocks was far hotter than under the trees. Reaching the top, he and Yassib pulled to a stop and bent over, hands on knees, to catch their breath.

Zeb and Simeon weren't far behind. A breeze lifted Danel's hair. They'd recently filled their waterskins at a stream, so Danel poured some over his head. He sighed as the cool water soaked his hair, then perched against a rock and looked back from where they'd come.

"Look!" Danel said, with a catch in his voice.

A vast army could be seen, already close—much too close—to Gibeon, for the familiar pools of water glinted in the sun. *Keep Grandfather and Donatiya safe.* Danel hoped Elohim would accept prayers from a Hivite.

"Time is running out." Yassib stood and replaced the stopper in his waterskin.

"I wonder how the riders are doing," Zeb said as they followed Yassib's example.

"They'll be faster, but the horses are going a longer route and horses can get injured too," Yassib said. "We will try and beat them."

"We must cover as much ground as we can before dark," Danel says.

"There should be a moon," Zeb said.

"Pray there won't be too many clouds," Danel said.

"Oh, I'm praying," Zeb said.

Danel had been watching Zeb closely since he'd arrived in Gibeon. Every morning, Zeb would pray on the widow's rooftop. Simeon hadn't seemed so devout at first, but Zeb's influence meant Simeon soon joined in.

They were now running downhill, and there was no danger of being seen by the army, so Yassib simply chose the easiest route and Danel, Zeb, and Simeon ran to keep up.

They heard the rush of water before they saw the stream across their path. Yassib picked up a hefty branch and used it to find the most stable rocks. Danel watched and followed Yassib's lead. They continued on their way without much difficulty.

As he watched the path, Danel thought about the stories Zeb had told as they worked together. Zeb had shared as many as he could remember. Of how Adonai created the world and the first people. How A'dam and Havvah had rebelled and evil had come into the world. Danel had traveled with Noach and his boat, and with Avraham from Ur. He'd asked Zeb many questions and was beginning to see why Zeb and Rivkah loved following Yahveh.

A family of quail dashed across the path in front of their pounding feet and fled into the thick bushes.

Danel had begun to think he too might be able to follow Yahveh until Zeb had talked about some of the laws that had been given on Mount Sinai. Mixed in with many laws that thrilled Danel with their justice and care for the poor and vulnerable, Zeb had mentioned that Yahveh hated divination. Danel could understand that but it was Zeb's words about divination that had sent despair coursing through him. "Yahveh forbids us to go to a diviner. In fact, he commands that if we do, we must be stoned along with the diviner."

As Danel ran he could hear the words repeating in his mind, "Stoning for any who consults a diviner." Having been close when Achan was stoned, he could imagine no worse fate. Was it fair that his visit to Talliya meant he couldn't join Yahveh's people? Maybe that was what Talliya's words had meant. A death by stoning would explain her strong reaction.

The shadows were lengthening on the ground, and Danel had to watch more closely. If he was injured out here, the others would have to leave him behind.

They stopped at the next stream to pour water over their heads and drink. A tiny waterfall splashed water onto bright green moss and ferns. It would be a great place to linger on a hot afternoon, but they must press on, Gibeon would soon be surrounded. The city had reasonable water supplies, but if the Amorites had found a way to send fire over the walls, then the city would not last long. The strain in the chief's voice suggested he must wait for the Israelites' support. But would the Israelites come? That was still unknown.

The path ahead wound between large rocks and Danel followed Yassib as he twisted and turned. A stone shifted under Danel's foot, and he lurched to the side wrenching his ankle.

"Careful," Simeon said behind him.

Danel stopped, pointed his toe, and swiveled his ankle. "My foot is fine." He took a few tentative steps and jogged carefully for a few steps before increasing his speed again. Yassib had disappeared into the next stand of trees.

The sun was low in the sky when Yassib stopped on the bank of another stream. "Eat something," he said. "But only a few mouthfuls. Too much and we won't want to run. Zeb, how close do you think we are?"

Zeb frowned. "I'm not sure. I'm hoping one of the patrols might find us and lead us in."

As they'd done last time.

"How many patrols are there?" Yassib asked.

"Lots. Yehoshua knows we're vulnerable with all our women and children and herds," Zeb said. "The patrols keep our men fit and alert."

"Yehoshua is wise." Yassib took some dried figs out of a pouch around his waist.

They were soon running again. Danel's thoughts drifted back to Zeb's stories. Zeb always freely admitted if he didn't know the answers to Danel's many questions. Zeb had also told him about the many festivals that were part of the cycle of the seasons. Each festival reminded the Israelites of their history. One of the reasons Zeb said his family hadn't rebelled against Yahveh—as many of the Israelites had—was that Zeb's family had weekly gatherings where they retold the stories of Adonai's dealings with his people and discussed how the stories applied to their situation. Danel envied Zeb's family. Danel had loved his father, but Papa had been too busy making sure they survived to have time to spend telling stories.

Zeb held his hand up, put his finger to his lips to tell them not to make any noise, and then pointed.

Through the trees, Danel could see a fire.

Using gestures, Yassib indicated that he and Simeon would approach the fire, hoping it was one of the Israelite patrols. Danel and Zeb must go to the far side, in case it wasn't Israelites. That way at least two of them might reach Yehoshua.

Danel and Zeb made a wide circle around the fire and waited in the darkness. At last, Danel heard the hoot of an owl followed by another. It was the way he and Yassib had communicated since they were children.

Within moments Yassib had introduced them to the men of the patrol, and they were following the Israelites toward the main camp.

The patrol led them to Yehoshua's tent and Yehoshua came out almost immediately, obviously realizing anyone calling at night must have an urgent message.

Yassib stepped forward and introduced himself as a son of the Gibeonite chief. "We have run from Gibeon to deliver my father's message, 'Do not abandon your servants. Come up to us quickly and save us! Help us, because all the Amorite kings from the hill country have joined forces against us.' By now the army will already be camped outside our walls."

"Who is that with you?" Yehoshua asked.

Danel, and the two Israelites came forward into the light.

"Zeb, you have run with these others?" Yehoshua asked.

"Yes, sir. We saw the armies with our own eyes," Zeb said. "And we've been running all day."

"Have the trumpeter call the leaders immediately," Yehoshua said. "And ready my weapons."

Danel's shoulders relaxed. Yehoshua would honor the treaty.

CHAPTER THIRTY-SIX

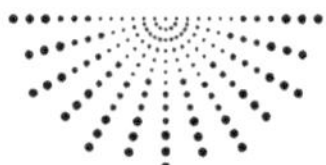

Moonlight bathed the landscape in silver and gray and danced between the dark shadows. Somewhere nearby, a nightingale poured out its heart in song. Danel walked amid the Israelite army. An army who'd mobilized and set off in the time he'd taken to have a meal and a short nap. Danel hadn't expected to fall asleep amongst the chaos of an assembling army but he'd been too exhausted to stay awake. Yassib said it was probably best to get moving again. If they slept all night, they'd have been too stiff to move in the morning.

With such an army, there was no need to move stealthily for their passage through the Canaanite hills couldn't be kept quiet.

Zeb reported that some of the leaders had objected to going to help Gibeon, but Yehoshua had been firm. He'd admitted he was at fault over the original treaty because he hadn't taken the time to ask Adonai for his guidance, but since the treaty had been signed, the Israelites must honor it. Danel couldn't imagine Yassib's father ever saying he'd been wrong about anything. He'd consider it a sign of weakness. Weakness that would give any others who aspired to leadership a chance to attain the position.

Next to Danel, Zeb was stumbling with exhaustion. He had remained with Yehoshua apart from a brief visit to his family. Zeb had given one piece of news that Danel mulled over as they marched. This time, Yehoshua had made sure to consult Adonai. Adonai had said, "Do not be afraid of the Amorite armies; I have given them into your hand. Not one of them will be able to withstand you."

Why would Adonai protect the Gibeonites? Were they, as Rahab had been, somehow now under Adonai's protection? Rahab had believed Adonai would conquer Jericho, and she'd cast herself on his mercy. Was that what it took? Choosing to trust and place themselves under Adonai's care, to seek his direction and follow it?

Danel glanced to his other side, where Yassib was marching with no apparent tiredness. He said soldiers must be able to sleep anywhere and anytime. He'd slept well and not woken until the last of the army were leaving the Israelite camp. Then he'd bounded to his feet and trotted forward. Danel envied Yassib's energy but was glad none of the seven messengers who'd reached Gilgal without incident had been left behind. One man, whose horse was lame, would leave it behind to recover in the camp but he marched close by.

"Father is here somewhere," Zeb said. "I'll make sure to introduce you if we can find him."

Danel didn't think it would be possible. They were marching to war, not going on a summer stroll. In the morning, there would be the confusion of battle and many might lose their lives. Yehoshua believed this battle would be won, but there was no guarantee Danel would be protected. Danel touched the amulet he still wore around his waist. He hadn't dared to take it off, just in case it offered some protection. Talliya had predicted Danel would lose everything. Maybe tomorrow would be that day. He shivered in the damp darkness. If tomorrow was to be the end for him, he hoped he would die with courage, defending his city and family. He would hate to leave Donatiya, but Uncle would make sure she was looked after, and Grandfather might not even notice he was missing. Danel sighed and kept going.

Ahead there was the neighing of one horse after another. "The scouts are returning," said a soldier a short way ahead of Danel.

Yehoshua had sent scouts to see if they could find a more hidden way, and to discover whether the Amorites were camped for the night or attacking Gibeon under cover of darkness.

Everyone kept moving but all chatter ceased as they waited for the news to be passed back. The news came back to them slowly and in snatches.

"The walls of Gibeon still stand."

The tightness in Danel's belly relaxed. His family was still alive, and the Amorites hadn't worked out a way to get fire into the city.

"The Amorites are camped outside the city."

Maybe they were planning a siege. This was good news, as it gave the Israelite army more time.

"The scouts have found a way that allows us to get close without being seen."

Did all this positive news mean that Elohim was indeed with this venture? Danel prayed it was so.

Even if I die, save Donatiya.

If Donatiya survived, Danel would have kept at least part of his last promise to his father.

* * *

*A*s Danel stood above the enemy camp in the darkness, his heart beat loud in his ears. He couldn't see the army below in the gloom, but there were many fires and glimpses of tents.

A pale banner waved far in front of him, and the men around him moved forward at a fast trot like a river overflowing its banks. All around him was the jangle of weapons held at the ready.

Somehow, unbelievably, they weren't noticed until they were close to the Amorite camp. There was one scream and then another. A trumpet gave a half-hearted blast choked off halfway.

Danel ran down the slope toward a pale purple-streaked dawn. He'd been directed to stand off to one side with the other bowmen. There were more screams and crashes and curses. Bile rose in his throat at the thought of shooting at people who had so recently been almost neighbors.

The shouts and screams were intensifying. A man ran right through the fire near his tent, and the air was full of shrieks and the smell of burning flesh. Someone tried to clamber on the back of a donkey, but the animal took off, dragging the man behind him.

Danel reached his post, planted his forward leg firmly and drew his bow, but it wasn't necessary. The Amorites were running around in confusion as if they were blind. Some of them ran right at the Israelites and were killed before they seemed to realize what was happening.

Most of the Amorite army abandoned their camp and ran away up the road toward Beth Horon. The Israelite army pursued them and cut them down with almost no opposition.

A yell went up from the walls of Gibeon, and Danel stood with his mouth open as the chief and Yassib's brothers led their soldiers out to join the pursuit. Fear clutched at Danel. Ai had behaved as Gibeon was now doing. Perhaps Ai's soldiers had wanted to prove themselves, rushing in without thinking of the city behind them with its gates swinging open.

"Zeb, we must get them to close the gates. Just in case," Danel said, voice strained.

"In case this is like Ai?" Zeb asked.

Danel didn't bother answering. His weariness forgotten, he ran toward Gibeon. If only the gatemen would believe him. Donatiya and Grandfather must not die as the people of Ai had. Zeb's footsteps pounded after him.

Danel dashed through the gate and looked around wildly for the head gateman. The man was standing with his hands on his hips and a self-satisfied smirk on his face as though this chaos was his doing.

"You must close the gates," Danel said, skidding to a halt.

"Must?" said the gateman. "Who are you to tell me what I must do?"

"I am nobody," Danel said. "But I'm here to warn you that Ai was defeated in such a way. When their army were drawn out by a fleeing enemy, they left their gates open. A hidden enemy entered and burned down the city."

"What? Say that again more slowly," the gateman said.

Why could the man not grasp things more quickly? Danel took a shaky breath and repeated what he'd said.

"Well, I don't know," the gateman said. "I can't just open and close these gates for anyone."

"He's right you know," one of the other gatemen said. "That's what happened at Ai. Yassib told me so himself."

"Yassib and I watched the battle of Ai," Danel said. "We saw the trick. We Gibeonites aren't the only ones who can trick others."

"Weren't you one of the messengers sent to bring the Israelites?" A man limped toward Danel. "And this man was one too."

Would these men not get a move on? The Amorites, if they were coming, could be here at any moment.

"Yes, Zeb and I were two of the messengers, along with Yassib," Danel said. "If the chief gets angry about closing the gates, you can blame me."

"You can be sure I will." The gateman rubbed his head. He probably hadn't had much sleep last night either.

"Close the gate," the other gatemen said. "It isn't that hard to open it again if the chief needs us to."

"The responsibility is yours," the head gateman said. "But this better not be a scheme so you can avoid doing your duty." He peered suspiciously at them.

"Shut us outside then," Danel said. "We'll return to battle."

"Deal." The head gateman gestured to the younger men and they sprang into action.

Danel and Zeb allowed themselves to be swept out of the gates. The gates closed with a crash, and Danel released a shaky breath. He was likely going to look a fool, but better a fool than the alternative.

He and Zeb walked away from the gates but Danel turned to scan the top of the wall. He'd love to let Donatiya know he was alive. Someone hollered his name, and Danel squinted toward the sound. A man waved, one of Danel's neighbors. He'd injured his leg and could no longer fight.

Danel went closer. "Let my sister know where I am."

"She's selling bread faster than she can bake," the man shouted back. "Says people still have to eat, and the soldiers will be hungry when they return."

Danel shook his head in admiration of his sister's business sense and then set off with Zeb at a steady lope to chase their army.

* * *

"All of these men are Amorites," Danel said, trying not to smell the carnage or look at the faces of the dead and dying. He'd been fighting nausea since Zeb had insisted on checking among the dead for his father or people he knew. So far, they'd only seen Amorites.

"Can we get off the track? We'll catch up faster if we run there." Danel traced the route with his finger.

Zeb let Danel lead the way. He must have seen Danel's pale face but he made no comment. They set off at a fast trot across the clear ground. Danel's bow, quiver, and waterskin bounced across his shoulders.

It didn't take them long to catch up with their own army. The Amorites must still be out in front, running for their lives.

"We can't let the Amorites get away," Zeb said. "Or we'll have to fight them again another day."

Behind them there was the rumble of thunder.

"That's going to make things hard," Danel said. A wet bow wasn't much use. A sourness rose in his throat. He'd have to pick a weapon off one of the bodies.

"It looks like it's going to blow over," Zeb said.

The wind whipped Danel's head and tunic, and the sky darkened as clouds obscured the sun. Green-tinged clouds scudded above their heads then raced ahead of the Israelite-Hivite army. There was another rumble and a flash of lightning, and the way ahead was covered in darkness.

"That's it then," Danel said. "They'll get away now."

"Keep running," Zeb panted. "Until we know for sure."

They passed the rear soldiers of their own army. Around them, men worked to finish off the injured scattered all over the ground.

Ahead of them Danel heard a cheer and then another. Why would their soldiers be cheering? Danel and Zeb pushed forward.

A shout rang out and then another. "Hay—"

"What are they saying?" Danel asked as he stopped. The way in front was blocked by their own army. He took a few deep breaths and cupped a hand around his ear.

"Hail!" Zeb's voice vibrated with excitement. "Adonai has sent hail on the Amorites."

Danel followed Zeb as he continued to weave his way to the front.

More cheers went up and now Danel could see. The front line of their own army was ahead, then there was a gap. Ahead of them, the Amorite army was almost hidden by the hail. Danel had never seen a storm that was so localized. The air was still where he stood, but lightning cracked over the Amorite army. A tree whipped to and fro in the gale, and giant head-sized lumps of hail bounced out of the storm toward Danel and Zeb.

The hairs at the back of Danel's neck stood on end. Who was this god? A god who could control the lightning, wind, and hail. Who could direct the hail to not fall on his own people but move it forward and deploy it like an army. Danel shook his head as though not believing what he was seeing. This was Yahveh. The same god who could open the way through the waters and make the walls of a city crumble to dust.

This god wanted this land to give his people, but did his plans include Danel and the cities of Gibeon, Beeroth, Kephirah, and Kiriath Jearim? There was no doubt in Danel's mind that Yahveh had known about the trick they'd played on the Israelites, but he'd not revealed it to Yehoshua. What was Yahveh's plan for the Hivites? Was it a plan for their good, or did he yet have some twisted trick of his own to play?

CHAPTER THIRTY-SEVEN

The hailstorm cleared up almost as quickly as it had come. The wind stopped howling, the lightning disappeared, and the clouds gathered their trailing skirts and dispersed as though they'd never been.

There was a collective gasp from the watchers, then a horrified, terrified moan. Danel pushed his way through the crowd. Ahead was a tangled mass of bodies. Many had their arms raised to protect their heads, but it had been as much use as holding up a piece of cloth. Danel fell to his knees and vomited, acid burning his throat.

Rivkah had said that her god was loving and kind, but that was only part of the story. This god was also judge, and it was terrifying to fall into his hands. Terrifying to displease him in any way. Yahveh had judged the Egyptians forty years ago, and now he was judging the land of Canaan. Yet Danel's people were not too different from the Amorites. They had their peace treaty and now knew the Israelites would honor it, at least while Yehoshua was alive but did Yehoshua speak for his god? What if this god had already planned for the destruction of Danel's people? The breath of his nostrils could smite them and they'd be gone in a moment. Was that what Talliya had meant? The loss not just of Danel's bakery, and home, and life, but the loss of his people as well?

Footsteps crunched on the pebbles behind Danel.

"Are you alright?" Zeb asked.

Danel poured out some water from his waterskin into his hand, swilled out his mouth, and spat. "I'm not sure." He grasped the tree in front of him and hauled himself to his feet. "This god of yours terrifies me."

Zeb nodded, his face as gray as the sky had been.

"He's supposed to. My people, we have short memories. We forget all God gives. Too often we walk our own way, without God. Like at that first battle at Ai, or forty years ago in the desert, when we didn't trust God's directions. But God …" Zeb glanced down. "It's hard to put it in words. Like our life, our breath, God gives us what we need to live. He gives us food, land, law. Without God, there is …" He shifted his gaze to the horror which the hail had made of the Amorites and sighed. "I often find myself wanting to focus on God's kindness and compassion, forgetting his judgment, because in my heart I am determined to go my own way."

"Isn't that natural?" Danel asked. "To want to go your own way?"

"That's the excuse we give, but Adonai is holy. He calls us to be like him," Zeb said.

"Holy. I don't know this word," Danel said.

"Pure, perfect, flawless. I don't know how else to explain it," Zeb said.

"But that's impossible!" Despair filled Danel's chest.

Zeb looked ahead to where the Israelites and Gibeonites were setting out to follow the remainder of the Amorite army. "I'd love to talk more about Adonai, but we've got Amorites to pursue."

The much-reduced Amorite army were cresting the top of the next hill. Danel took another drink, and checked his bow and arrows were still in place. "I need another weapon." A bow was only useful from a distance. If he was faced with an Amorite, he'd need a dagger or sword. The best place to obtain a weapon was from a dead Amorite soldier.

Zeb pursed his lips. "I'll go and get both of us something."

Danel breathed out a gusty sigh. He hadn't been sure his stomach could stand close contact with the dead men.

They weren't the only ones with the idea but Zeb was soon back with a long dagger. "No need to clean it," Zeb said. "None of their weapons have been used, and I still haven't seen a single Israelite casualty."

The hairs on Danel's arms rose. There were no Israelite casualties because Adonai was fighting for his people. Adonai had whittled down the Amorite army. Would Hivite and Israelite armies now have to complete the job? If so, they'd have to hurry. Night would soon fall, and the Amorites could more easily escape in the dark.

* * *

*D*anel still had not come into contact with the Amorites. Maybe he didn't want to. This wasn't turning out to be a bowman's war, for the Amorites never turned to stand and fight. Instead, they fled. More often than not, they died because they tripped and fell, or because the faster ones left the slower ones behind in their haste. Any isolated groups were quickly surrounded and killed.

But some Amorites would escape. The pace of battle was too slow for the hours of daylight left. Far ahead, Danel could see men climbing the hills toward the high pass. Once they were through the pass, they could escape along the far side of the hills. Though the mountain way was longer, if they reached their cities, they'd be behind strong walls. Not invincible walls, for the defeat of Jericho had proved that even walls could turn to dust, but the war could drag on and on, and the Hivites would remain vulnerable to repeat attacks.

"Zeb, I've got an idea." And Danel quickly explained. If some fast runners with bows could get to the pass ahead of the Amorites, they could shoot and turn them back toward the pursuing swordsmen.

"The commander of the bowmen is just there," Zeb said. "Let's see what he thinks."

Danel started to run. If the idea was to work, they'd need every moment they had.

The Hivite commander heard them out. "Yes, I think it might work."

He barked out orders. Before Danel had quenched his thirst again, a group of bowman were gathered. The commander pointed at the top of the ridge. "Aim for that reddish rock. If the Amorites are there before you, go further up—to that rock there. Everyone clear?"

To Danel's relief, an experienced bowman was appointed their leader. He'd know how to refine the plan once they were in position.

As they turned to go, someone yelled. "Sun!"

Danel turned toward the voice to where Yehoshua stood on a high rock. "Sun! Stand still over Gibeon, and you, moon, over the Valley of Aijalon."

Danel gasped at the audacity of Yehoshua's prayer.

There was no time to watch if Adonai answered the prayer. No time for anything but running. Zeb matched Danel's pace. Danel watched the path in front of him but also checked the position of the Amorites. The Amorites had been too busy running to fight, but they'd love to get their hands on some Hivites.

An arrow whistled to the south, and an Amorite toward the back of their army stumbled and fell. Zeb gave a weak cheer. The commander of the bowmen must be giving them backup. The more the Amorites were slowed down, the more chance Danel and the other runners had of getting to the narrow pass before the Amorites.

The sound of the runners' pounding feet and panting breaths surrounded Danel. Beside him, Zeb tripped over a small log, but righted himself and kept running.

Their leader stopped and checked where the Amorites were. They would soon be ahead of the Amorites, whose pace had slowed as they no longer dared run in the open.

Danel checked where the leader was and veered further to the north to follow.

If he survived, Danel would be ready for a long rest. A fly buzzed in his ear and he flapped his hand to shoo it away, but it was soon following Danel again. Annoying as it was, there was no time to deal with it. Danel concentrated on running. Every now and then he checked that the other bowmen were close.

Ahead of them, the lead bowman held up his hand, then notched an arrow. Danel and the others did the same, spreading out to check none of the Amorites had reached this height. Danel exhaled when they found the area deserted.

The leader counted the runners. "Danel, climb the rock and check where the Amorites are."

Danel ran to the back of the rock and clambered up. He dropped to his stomach and crawled the last part of the way. Below him the Amorites were moving slowly up the hill with the Israelites close behind.

Danel scrambled back to the leader.

"That's the better vantage point. Up there." The leader pointed. "If Astarte smiles on us, we'll find water."

Zeb grimaced at the mention of the goddess.

It didn't take long to reach the protected position. They found a trickle of water near a rock and were able to both quench their thirst and cool their heads. The more experienced bowmen in the group indicated where Danel and Zeb should stand, and the leader gave final instructions.

"Don't shoot until we see the first group clearly. Shoot low. We don't want to shoot any of our own soldiers."

That would be a waste.

"They'll be coming up over a crest," the leader continued. "Hopefully the first ones will turn back before the ones behind them know what is happening. Chaos is what we want to create."

They stood braced and ready for action. Sweat trickled between Danel's shoulder blades. He glanced up at the sky. "Zeb, does the sun look like it is going down?"

"You heard Yehoshua's prayer," Zeb said. "He prayed Adonai would stop the sun. Why should you be surprised that Adonai would listen?"

Why indeed? There seemed no limit to the kinds of miracles this god could do.

"Adonai has excellent ears," Zeb said with a chuckle.

"Silence!" hissed their leader.

It felt like there were locusts hopping in Danel's belly. The Israelite and Gibeonite armies had avoided deaths up to now, but Talliya had predicted total loss for him. Was not war the most likely place for sudden death?

The first of the Amorite soldiers appeared, paying little attention to what was in front of them. Danel's heart pounded in his chest and his hand shook on the bowstring. Their leader drew back his bowstring and with a twang released his first arrow.

A line of arrows whistled across the clearing. The Amorites looked around wildly and grabbed each other, but they were too late. Five fell and lay on the ground, unmoving. The others fled, heading back the way they'd come.

"Get ready to shoot again," their leader said.

Danel and Zeb already had their second arrows ready. When the braver—or more foolhardy—of the Amorites cautiously poked their heads above the crest, they were met with more arrows.

"Don't waste arrows," the leader said. "Our job is just to stop them escaping."

Down the hill, out of sight, they could hear the screams and gurgles of the dying. Two Amorites moved in a crouching run toward them. The leader shot the first, and the other fled back the way he'd come.

All through the next hours they only shot an occasional arrow. Theirs was an easy task, and they could even take turns to rest and refresh themselves. Only once, in the unnatural brightness some-time during what should have been night, did they have to regroup and fire a steady volley to repel a desperate mob of Amorites. Most died, and a few escaped toward the north. They might, if they were lucky, reach the shelter of their cities.

At last, when Danel was dropping with fatigue, the leader sent him with another Gibeonite out to check whether it was safe. They were able to report that the Israelites had completed their victory and were headed back toward where they'd left Yehoshua.

* * *

The sun was finally descending as Danel, Zeb, and the other bowmen rejoined the main army. Danel and the other soldiers foraged among the bushes and found edible plants or berries while they asked for news. Yehoshua had apparently been to Makkedah and back.

"The five Amorite kings were found cowering in a cave," a soldier mumbled around his mouthful of berries. "Yehoshua had ordered those who found the kings to block up the entrance of the cave with large rocks and stand guard,"

"And?" Zeb took a swig of water from an abandoned waterskin.

"When Yehoshua reached the cave, he had the entrance unblocked and the kings brought out," the man said.

"Yehoshua made the commanders of the army stand with their feet on the kings' necks." Another man demonstrated what had happened. "Then Yehoshua said, 'Do not be afraid; do not be discouraged. Be strong and courageous. This is what the Lord will do to all the enemies you are going to fight.'" The soldier made an exaggerated slash with an imaginary sword. "And the kings were killed and their bodies hung up on poles."

Danel was glad he hadn't been there. That would have been the fate of the Hivites if there'd been no treaty.

There was a trumpet blast, and Danel looked around to see what it meant.

"Yehoshua is calling us," said the talkative soldier.

Danel and Zeb went towards the high rock they'd seen Yehoshua standing on earlier.

"There's my father." Zeb called and waved.

They pushed through the crowd, and Zeb threw his arms around his father and was hugged in return. Once he broke out of the hug, Zeb introduced Danel. "Abba, this is the baker I'm working with."

Zeb's father looked Danel up and down. "You're younger than I expected."

"My parents died young," Danel said.

"I'm sorry to hear that," Zeb's father said. "We'll talk more once we've heard what Yehoshua has to say."

Yehoshua waited until the army was crowded round the rock. Those at the front relayed his words to those at the back. "Today Yahveh has given us a great victory." Yehoshua pointed to the setting sun.

By Danel's calculations, it had stayed in the sky all night.

"Never has a god listened to a man's prayers as ours has. He sent confusion and the hail and halted the sun so we could defeat the

Amorites. We must never forget it is not who we are or the strength of our legs and arms that matters. It is that we always go into battle at Yahveh's bidding."

Yehoshua looked around the exhausted army and then bowed toward Yassib's father, who was standing with Yassib and his other sons. "You may now go home in peace." Yehoshua switched his attention toward his army commanders. "We will send men to get food from Gibeon. Then we will pursue the Amorites back to each of their towns. There is still work to do."

Work which Danel no longer wanted to do. His senses were glutted with the sounds and smells of death. Would he ever be rid of the stink? This day was going to give him new nightmares. He was alive, but he would see the blood, the bodies, the butchered torsos when he closed his eyes.

He remembered himself as a child, stick in hand, sparring with Yassib, his head full of dreams of the warrior he wanted to be. He'd only seen shiny swords and the townsfolk gathered to hear the elders tell tales of glory. But he'd never imagined this day. Not at all. Now he wanted nothing more than to smell baking bread and to hear his sister humming as she did her morning chores.

CHAPTER THIRTY-EIGHT

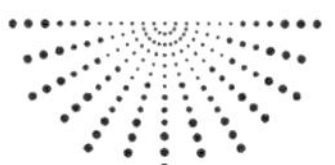

**One moon later,
Gibeon**

anel heard the slam of the front gate and running footsteps and his heart leaped. He'd been waiting for what felt like weeks.

"They made it. They're here." Zeb burst into the bakery where Danel had been keeping himself busy with mundane tasks. "Come and meet my family."

Danel wiped sweaty palms on his tunic and followed Zeb and Donatiya out into the glare of the sunlight. "Don't leave them standing in the street. Bring them in."

"They've left Abba and Grandfather outside the walls with the flocks and herds. I think it would be easier to take them straight to the house you told them about," Zeb said. "Then we don't have to move their things twice."

The chief had given permission for Zeb's family to move into the house once it was habitable. Until then, some of the family planned to camp in the garden, while Zeb's grandparents would stay with the widow next door. Simeon had decided baking wasn't for him and had moved elsewhere to learn farming. The family filled the laneway with donkeys and a heavily laden pair of oxen. Danel was introduced to Zeb's mother, two younger sisters, and a younger brother, all in rapid succession. "And Rivkah you know of course."

Like all the female members of the family, Rivkah was veiled. "Keret, I presume?" she murmured.

Danel's mood plummeted. So she hadn't forgiven him? Danel couldn't blame her, but it hurt all the same. He'd been dreaming of this meeting for days but instead of warmth, an icy blast was coming his way.

Danel refused to let Rivkah see his hurt. He held his head up and reached for the donkey's bridle. It jerked its head and backed away from him. Rivkah stepped forward. "Looks like you'll need some help."

His face warmed. "This way," he said to cover his embarrassment. He led the party up the laneway.

Danel walked through the gate he'd recently mended. "It's been abandoned for a long time and will need a lot of work."

"This will be fine after living in a tent for forty years," Zeb's grandmother said with a laugh. "There's nothing hard work can't fix."

Zeb and the boys unloaded the baskets from the livestock, then took them back to the widow's home. She had empty stalls prepared.

Zeb's mother said, "Why don't you show us around."

Danel had checked the house over thoroughly before going to the chief. The structure was sound, but it leaked in places and needed more mud between the stones.

"This is better than I expected." Zeb's mother walked around the main part of the house and looked out each of the windows. "The area around the house is spacious. Is there a well nearby?"

"You can use ours for the moment," Danel said. "Zeb and I already built you a bread oven out back, and the stalls for the livestock can soon be mended. There is plenty of grass for livestock outside the walls."

"How do you keep them from being stolen or attacked by wolves?" Rivkah asked.

"The town livestock is usually managed in big groups with many shepherds," Danel said. "Families with only a few animals keep them inside the city."

"Are the outside stairs safe?" Rivkah pointed up to the roof. Like most Canaanite homes, the roof was flat with a low parapet around its edges.

"I checked them yesterday." Danel led the way up the stairs.

"This is a fine view." Rivkah's mother took off her veil.

Danel could see where Rivkah got her looks from. Her mother was still beautiful, with a warm smile and eyes that were full of life. She gazed around with interest. Danel pointed out the chief's hall and the different city gates. "We'll show you around later. For now, where would you like to put your things?"

"Do people sleep up on the roof?" Rivkah's mother asked.

Danel nodded. "Most of us. We could probably rig up your tent as a covering for rainy nights."

"That would suit us well." She sighed. "It will be a big adjustment to settle here, but other Israelites came with us and that will make things easier."

Five other families had come and the chief, feeling generous toward the Israelites after recent events, had given them enough land to farm.

*D*anel coughed as straw dust went up his nose. Rivkah and Zeb had been helping in the bakery every morning. In the afternoons Rivkah's family worked hard at filling the gaps between the stones so the wind no longer whistled through their new house.

Having lost his parents and with only one sister, Danel loved being part of this big family. If only Rivkah would return to being that fun-loving girl he'd met near Gilgal. She still showed that part of herself to her family but she became stiffly polite when he was around. A big family in a small space made it impossible for him to catch her alone for a moment to apologize for everything including not using his real name when they'd met at Gilgal.

Rivkah and Danel were working on the final corner of the house. Should he try to start a conversation, or would she just rebuff him again?

He bit his lip. "Have you been using your slingshot lately?" It was a stupid question but it sort of slipped out.

She snorted. "That's the only question you could think of?"

Danel's face warmed. "I often think back to our talks. You told me so many stories and taught me much about your people."

There was a long pause. *Come on, Danel, Say something!* He wanted to keep this conversation going, but his mind seemed stuck.

"I noticed the altar in your home seems unused," Rivkah said.

Danel shoulders relaxed. Rivkah wasn't stuck for words. "I stopped making offerings after Yassib and I came back from Jericho and Ai." He shrugged. "They seemed pointless. It was obvious our gods can't compete with yours."

"But you haven't taken the altar down completely?" she asked.

Danel shook his head. "I didn't want to upset Grandfather." And he didn't have anything to replace his gods. He sighed. "So much has changed lately ..."

"Even more has changed for us," Rivkah said. "We've been

constantly on the move since leaving Egypt. Our family jumped at the chance to settle down here. Perhaps more of our people can settle soon."

For her people to settle, it would mean many would have to die. It wasn't easy to accept. Danel understood it in his head, for there was much evil in the land and there were many times he'd wished for divine judgment in the form of a lightning strike on evil peoples' heads. People like the men who kidnapped girls, sent their children to the flames, or grew rich through corruption. Yet what about ordinary folk? Folk like Grandfather and Uncle Hammurapi. He didn't want to see them wiped out. He could rejoice that the people of their four towns were safe but his relief was always tempered by news of others who weren't so lucky.

Danel swallowed. They still hadn't talked about how he'd used his grandfather's name rather than reveal his own. He took a deep breath. "I'm sorry I lied about my name."

There was a pause while Rivkah slapped the mud and straw mixture into a particularly big gap.

"I was angry when I found out," Rivkah said.

His breath caught in his throat. Did she mean she wasn't any longer?

"I felt you'd used me to get what you wanted." She sniffed and kept her head turned away from him.

"I'm sorry I did that. Once I met you, the fun went out of spying because I didn't want to deceive you. I tried to not say anything I shouldn't, but not being able to talk freely tore me up inside."

"Good to hear you don't lie easily." She smoothed the mud between the stones.

"I tried a few times as a child. My father walloped me so hard I decided lying was too painful."

Rivkah laughed, the sound Danel had been missing for too long.

"I too got disciplined for lying," she said.

Danel wiped a drip of sweat off his eyebrow with the back of his arm. "What did you do?"

She flushed. "Stole Zeb's honey, then said I hadn't." She stood back, looking for any gaps in her work. This was the final section of wall to complete. Then the outbuildings for the livestock could be rebuilt.

Had Rivkah accepted his apology?

"I don't know why I lied about my name," Danel said. "I got nervous thinking about what I had already revealed and whether I might have compromised our whole purpose."

"That makes two of us," Rivkah said.

Danel looked at her and raised an eyebrow.

"Part of why I was angry with you was because I was afraid," Rivkah said.

"Afraid of what?" Danel asked.

"Afraid I may have been partially responsible for you being able to trick Yehoshua," she said.

Danel waited, hoping Rivkah would say more.

"I worried I'd revealed something that allowed you to trick us."

"You didn't," Danel said. "You were too careful. It was seeing the miracles of the crossing of the River Jordan and the crumbling of Jericho's walls that convinced Yassib and myself that military tactics wouldn't work."

"My main worry was that I'd wrecked Adonai's plans."

"Do you think it's that easy to wreck his plans?" Danel asked.

"I know the answer now, but it wasn't until I took my worries and fears to Grandpa Kheti that I understood this truth."

Danel wiped the mud off his hands, and fetched some water to offer Rivkah. "Could you tell me what he said?"

She had a good drink and sat down. They'd been working steadily since soon after the midday rain.

"Grandpa asked me if I believed I was big enough to wreck

Adonai's plans?" She laughed. "When he asked like that, I knew I'd been arrogant. It is like an ant thinking it can divert a river."

Danel smiled at the imagery.

"Of course, being my grandfather, he immediately told me stories to remind me of people who went their own way but Adonai's plan still went ahead."

"Such as?" Danel asked.

"I'll tell you the story as we work. You'll need to mix some more mud and straw to finish this final wall."

Danel got to his feet, scooped up clay, and added the right amount of straw. Then he stood on the pile and marched in place to mix the two ingredients together. "Are you going to help me or tell me the story?"

"I'll leave you to the stomping." She perched on a log. "Grandpa reminded me of the story of Avraham. Do you remember me telling you about him?"

Danel's face warmed. He remembered everything she'd told him.

"I remember he and his wife couldn't have children, yet Adonai promised them they'd become a great nation." Uncle Hammurapi and Zeb had also told him some of the story.

"Grandpa reminded me that there was a famine in Canaan after Avraham and Sara had been there for a while. They headed to Egypt to get food. Avraham told Sara to say she was his sister because she was so beautiful he was afraid he might be killed so someone could steal his wife."

Danel stopped marching. "That's a terrible way to treat your wife."

"I totally agree. It was a bad, bad decision by Avraham but even his bad decision couldn't stop Adonai's plan. Pharaoh did take Sara into his household, but Adonai protected her."

Danel wrinkled his brow. "How?"

Rivkah chuckled. "He struck the household with a plague. The next morning, Pharaoh asked Avraham why he had tricked him with the lie about Sara being his sister. Then Pharaoh sent them on their way."

Danel stared at his feet. The mud was thoroughly mixed now. He'd always thought Avraham was some sort of Israelite hero, but he sounded like an ordinary man.

"So although Avraham lied and failed to protect his own wife, Adonai protected her and ensured any child she had would be Avraham's. Grandpa was right. Nothing can stop Adonai's plans. Certainly not someone as insignificant as me."

Danel smiled at Rivkah. "No one who knows you would think you are insignificant."

She threw the rag she was holding at him. "Come on. We still have one section to go."

"And you're reminding me we still have unfinished business," Danel said.

She raised one elegant eyebrow. "We do?"

"We were going to see who was better with a slingshot."

"Anytime," she said with a grin.

"What about now?" he asked.

"I'm ready whenever you finish that wall," she said, going over to the bucket to scoop out water and wash her hands.

* * *

anel went home to invite Donatiya to come with Rivkah and her two younger sisters. Together they headed toward the river where he and Yassib liked to fish.

Danel wasn't sure if he was pleased when Yassib greeted them as they approached. He'd prefer that Yassib didn't meet Rivkah. How could Danel compete with Yassib's charm?

As she used to at Gilgal, Rivkah had brought the family laundry. She handed it to the younger girls, and they happily moved a little further on and set to work.

"Best of five?" Rivkah asked Danel. "What about if we aim at that mark on the tree across the stream?" She pointed it out to him, and he agreed.

If she could hit that target, then she was good. Very good.

"And if you can get a stone in the hole, it's worth triple," she said.

He squinted at the tree trunk. He'd mistaken the hole for a shadow.

She handed him the sling. "Take a few practice shots first, as you're not familiar with my sling."

She wanted to see how much competition he offered.

Danel stepped forward and whirled the sling a few times, feeling its weight and the way it hung. Then he added a stone, one of the less smooth ones, to the leather pocket, whirled, and threw. The stone hit the tree with a thud. He grinned. It might not have hit the target, but it wasn't a total embarrassment, and he was deliberately not showing her what he could do. It was better to lull her into a false sense of security.

He threw two more practice shots then offered her the sling. "You first."

"Hmm" she murmured but took the sling.

Without hesitation she fixed her eyes on the target, whirled the stone, and released. The stone connected just below the target with a thud.

It was as he feared. She was an expert.

His first shot also missed the hole, by a slightly wider margin.

Her second shot hit the target as well. His was in the target area too but not as accurate as hers.

"Looks like we're evenly matched," she said. She was being generous. Her third shot hit the edge of the hole but didn't go in. She flashed a smile of triumph.

"Did you make the sling yourself?" he asked before his third shot.

"I did."

It was beautifully balanced. Would she make him one if he asked?

He placed his foot forward for the shot and whirled the sling. Just before he released the stone, a hare dashed out of the bushes and sprang across his line of sight. His stone went wide and missed the target all together.

"That was unfortunate," she said with a barely disguised grin.

"You probably arranged for the hare to appear," he said.

"So you'd like to think," she said. "Now no jogging my arm." She positioned herself, and her fourth shot was as consistent as her others.

The only way he could save face was if he could get his stone in the hole. He squinted at it and rolled his shoulders to relax them. Then he swung the sling and released it. The stone whizzed toward the tree and disappeared into the shadow.

"Did it go in?" he asked.

"No, it's teetering on the edge."

Just his luck. Then he grinned. "But it's blocked you getting one of yours in the hole."

She didn't hesitate but swung and released. There was a click as her stone hit his and sent it into the hole. "Well look at that," she said. "They're both in."

If this shot was representative of her skill, she'd been playing with him the whole time, and skillfully enough that he hadn't suspected.

"Come on, Donatiya," Danel said. "Do you want to have a go?"

Donatiya got to her feet. She and the others spent time learning the technique. Rivkah was endlessly patient with the younger girls.

As they walked back home, Danel asked Rivkah, "Do you think your grandfather would tell me more stories if I asked him?"

Her smile made her eyes dance. "I think he'd be delighted."

CHAPTER THIRTY-NINE

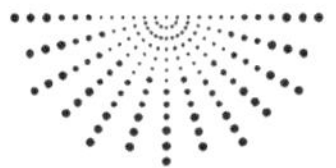

Three moons later

Danel and Yassib were sitting, backs against the trunk of a tree, with their fishing lines in the river.

"Have you heard the news about Talliya?" Yassib asked.

Danel's chest tightened. That was a name he'd hoped never to hear again. Since the battle, his nightmares had slowed to an occasional bad night. He'd begun to believe if he didn't think about Talliya's prophecies, then maybe they wouldn't be fulfilled.

"When she heard that the Israelite god hated divination and would stone anyone involved in it, she left our area in a hurry and fled to Lachish."

"Isn't Lachish one of the cities Yehoshua has just captured?" Danel asked.

"It's one of a string of Yehoshua's victories. He put everyone to the sword with no survivors."

Danel gripped his fishing pole. "Has it been confirmed that Talliya was among the dead?"

"No, but I don't see how she could have escaped." Yassib turned to Danel. "Maybe the reason she was so fearful when she saw you was that she'd seen her own death."

"Maybe," Danel said, not yet convinced.

The nightmares returned that night. A few nights later, Danel sat up panting in the dark before dawn. Why, oh why, did Yassib have to mention Talliya? Reaching under his tunic, Danel rubbed the smooth stone of the amulet. It gave him a sense of security.

Yassib, with his constant optimism, might believe the fear Talliya had shown was fear about her own death, but she had predicted great losses for Danel as well. He'd woken up the morning after the battle outside Gibeon, astounded to still be alive. He'd been grateful for every day since. He'd managed to temporarily dampen down the fear but it still struck him at unexpected moments.

Now the full terror had returned, gnawing at him like a lion with its prey. If Danel didn't die in war, would it be by some other, more mundane means? His death would be a terrible new grief for Donatiya and Grandpa.

Danel wrapped his arms around his knees and peered up at the stars overhead. The stars Rivkah's Grandpa Kheti said Adonai had made. *Adonai, your creation is magnificent. You are indeed great and mighty. I don't want to die. How can a dead man worship you?*

A breeze rustled the leaves of the fig tree, and he shivered.

Donatiya turned over on her mat. "Are you okay?" she whispered, keeping her voice low so as not to disturb Grandfather.

"Fine." Danel didn't want to burden her with his fears. "I'll get up and get started."

He went downstairs. After Danel's apology to Rivkah, things had been good between them. They'd bantered their way through their work in the bakery. She now helped Donatiya with the selling because she was so good with the customers. Finishing the final repairs on her family's house had also given them plenty of opportunity to talk together. Yassib teased Danel mercilessly about

Rivkah, but Rivkah was as far out of reach as the stars above Danel's head. He could not link her with his future—or, rather, his lack of one.

* * *

"Danel and Donatiya, are you ready?" Grandfather Kheti asked.

"Come in," Danel called from inside the bakery. He was just about to start kneading the dough for tomorrow's bread. "We're always ready for another story."

Some time ago, Kheti had come to ask Danel a question. Seeing they were still cleaning up and preparing the dough for the next day, he'd sat himself down. As they talked, Kheti had told them a story as he did with his own family. Donatiya had asked Danel if they could regularly hear stories, and he'd been more than happy to agree.

Kheti had started his stories at creation. Some of the stories Danel had heard from Zeb, Rivkah, or Uncle Hammurapi, but most were new. Each helped him gain a greater appreciation for this god of the Israelites. A god who was both mighty and good, a god who cared for his people like a mother hen looked after its chicks.

Kheti sat down on his usual stool. "I've decided not to tell you a new story today."

"Oh." Donatiya sounded disappointed. "I love our story time."

Kheti patted her shoulder. "Instead, I have some questions to ask." He took a moment to make himself comfortable. "Have you noticed what is common to all the stories?"

Donatiya wiped down the precious hot stone she'd baked the flatbreads on. "Well, the first thing is obvious. They all reveal more of Adonai."

"And what else?" Kheti asked.

"None of the people were perfect." Danel said. "Not one. Each story shows how humans go their own way and end up making a mess of things."

Kheti nodded. "What else?"

Danel paused in his kneading, thinking back to the stories of Noach, Avraham, Yoseph, and Mosheh and Aharon. "Yet Adonai rescues his people and fulfills his plans, no matter what."

"And what are Adonai's plans?" Kheti asked.

Danel had been thinking about this for days. He had no doubts about Adonai's existence. How could he, after watching multiple demonstrations of his power? Some of the men of Gibeon had called the hail during the battle a coincidence, but no one in their right mind could call the sun stopping anything but a miracle, and that had obviously happened in response to Yehoshua's prayer.

"He wants to save his people," Danel said.

Kheti shifted on his seat. "Yes, but from what?"

"What do you mean?" Donatiya asked.

Kheti rubbed his bushy white eyebrow. "If someone who can't swim falls in the river, then they need to be saved from drowning and be pulled to safety."

"So do we need to be saved from ourselves?" Danel asked, hesitation in his voice.

"Partly," Kheti said. "Do you remember what happened to A'dam and Havvah in the garden?"

"They were tricked by the snake." Donatiya paused from refilling the oil container. "He lied to them."

Kheti shifted his position. "And what was the snake's purpose?"

"Oh, that's easy," Donatiya said. "He wanted them to stop trusting Adonai. To convince them to rebel against Adonai and go their own way."

"So that the relationship between them and Adonai would be broken," Danel said. He'd initially been disappointed that Kheti wasn't going to tell them a story today, but this questioning was helpful.

"You've been listening well. Adonai is always working to restore the relationship between himself and his people," Kheti said.

"But we are not his people." Donatiya's voice was hushed and sad.

Kheti stroked his snowy-white beard. "During the plagues, I thought I had to be a descendent of Avraham to be included among Adonai's people."

Danel's throat tightened. Somewhere deep inside, a spark of hope flared. As he'd gotten to know the Israelites, he'd always been standing on the outside looking in, like a man standing outside in the dark and looking toward a lighted window. He opened his mouth to ask his question but Donatiya beat him to it.

"How do we become one of his people?"

Kheti smiled and looked at them both. "Do you remember what I said about my family? My brother and my mother repeatedly refused to listen to Adonai or follow his ways."

Kheti's experiences had been unforgettable. As Adonai rained down plague after plague upon Egypt, most Egyptians had either ignored Adonai's word or been stubborn and rebellious like Pharaoh. However, Kheti's father had listened to Adonai's warning and brought in the livestock, saving them from the hail. Then he'd painted lamb's blood on the doorposts to protect the family from further deaths during the final plague. Nophret had also done her best to convince her family to listen, but they'd refused. As a result, both her father and brother died on the same night.

"My father listened to Adonai's warnings and took action to save our family." Kheti shook his head. "If only more of my people had done the same."

Kheti had wept the day he told Danel and Donatiya about the final plague.

"Choosing to leave Egypt and follow the Israelites was the hardest choice I've ever made," Kheti said. "There were no guarantees that we'd ever be accepted."

Rivkah said Rahab was having a rough time of it. Many people remembered her past and spoke behind her back or turned away from her.

Kheti coughed, and Donatiya fetched some water. Kheti swallowed a mouthful. "But we wanted to follow Adonai more than we wanted to stay in Egypt and more than we cared about how others treated us."

Kheti took another mouthful of water. "Every person must decide how we'll respond to Adonai. With indifference, with rebellion, or with acceptance."

Donatiya had remained by Kheti's side. "How do we show we want to follow Adonai?"

Kheti laid a hand on Donatiya's shoulder "He'll know your heart, but you could also talk to him and tell him. Every father likes to hear his children's voices." It was easy for Donatiya to make the decision to follow Adonai, but Adonai hated divination and Danel had consulted Talliya. He might wish he hadn't, but knowing how Adonai viewed such practices, Danel could not speak up. Not if it meant his death. He shuddered. And it wouldn't be any death but death by stoning. Donatiya would be devastated and never live down the shame.

He must keep silent. For both their sakes.

CHAPTER FORTY

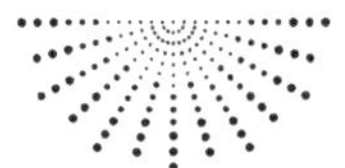

One moon later

"Danel, come and inspect the sesame with me." Kheti poked his head into the bakery.

Danel looked up in surprise. It had only been a few days since their last inspection. Perhaps Kheti was beginning to show his age at last. Age that had not been evident in all the moons of work on the house, nor as he supervised the preparation and planting of their new fields.

He and Nophret were the only ones in Rivkah's family who had farming experience. They'd planted wheat and barley as well as sesame and poppy seeds. Danel had promised to buy the crop if it was fine enough quality for the bakery. Next season, if Talliya's prophecy had still not been fulfilled, Danel would also be planting his own crops. The arrival of new settlers and the profits made from the increase in sales at the bakery had enabled Danel to buy some land which had become available.

Danel checked that everything was finished and issued a few last-minute instructions to Zeb and Donatiya, then followed Kheti out the door. A walk after baking most of the day was something he always welcomed.

They went through the side gate of Gibeon and headed toward the fields.

Their progress disturbed occasional grasshoppers, who scattered before them with a whirr of wings. Once they reached the fields, Danel ran his hand over the feathery heads of grain that already promised a good harvest.

"I never see a crop like this without praying." Kheti looked at the cloudless blue sky. "It was a day like this when the hail fell. Later, the locusts came to devour whatever was left."

They stopped to look around them.

"You might be wondering why I invited you to come and inspect the grain when we'd done it so recently," Kheti said.

"I was surprised," Danel said.

"It is hard to find a quiet place inside Gibeon," Kheti said.

Danel swallowed. Why would Rivkah's grandfather want to talk with him? The fear that had stalked him ever since he'd first had the nightmares swirled in his gut and he touched the smooth stone hidden at his waist. Would he ever be free of this darkness that grew and spread day by day?

"I am praying for you. Your uncle reported on his last visit that he has trusted in Adonai and now your sister also rejoices in her newfound faith, but you hold yourself aloof, although you seem to thirst for what they have."

Kheti paused for a long moment to stare toward the hills. His lips moved. Was he praying?

Kheti looked at Danel. "I sense some darkness around you. A bondage." Kheti shook his head. "Back in Egypt, I pitied the Israelite slaves my family owned. I believed I was free, but I was wrong. It seems contradictory, but the only way to freedom is to serve Yahveh. We must turn toward his light to cast out our darkness."

Danel's throat constricted. If only it was that easy. He longed to have the joy Donatiya had. Joy that burst forth in songs of praise.

"I cannot follow Adonai," Danel said, voice cracking.

"Cannot or will not?" Kheti asked gently. "What would keep you away from what you yearn for?"

Yearn. It was a good word for what Danel felt. Cut off from the people he most loved. Overwhelmed by fear. Danel stared at the ground. Afraid to look up in case he saw the compassion in Kheti's eyes. Afraid he'd break down. Afraid, afraid, afraid. What might life be like if he were free? Yet how could he speak of what might get him killed?

"What lie do you believe?" Kheti mused. "I once believed many, and each one made it hard for me to come to Adonai in trust. Made it hard to submit myself to him and his ways. I tried to rely on my own strength."

Danel sighed. The desire to tell Kheti what he had done was strong but so was the fear of what would happen if he did. Yet of all the Israelites, Kheti was one who might understand, for he'd once worshiped the gods of Egypt. *Adonai, give me courage.*

"Did you ever visit a diviner in Egypt?" Danel asked.

Kheti raised an eyebrow. "Is that what this is about? Dangerous people, fortune tellers and diviners."

Danel nodded miserably. "It was before I met Rivkah. Before I knew of Adonai and his ways."

Kheti sat himself down on a large rock on the edge of the field. "Tell me about it."

Danel explained his original dream, about Talliya and the powers she was believed to have, and what had happened on the day he visited her.

Kheti listened intently.

"Ever since I heard her words, I've believed I would die soon," Danel said.

Kheti cleared his throat. "I begin to see the reason for something else that was puzzling me. It was obvious you and Rivkah think highly of each other, yet you didn't talk to her or us. Was this the reason?"

Danel's face heated and he nodded. It had become increasingly difficult to be around Rivkah and not want more than mere friendship.

"I couldn't pursue anything deeper with Rivkah if I was going to die. It wouldn't be fair."

"What exactly did that woman say?" Kheti asked.

"She said I would lose everything," Danel said with a catch in his voice. Everything he held dear. His home, his bakery, his very life. With all those things, Rivkah would be lost to him as well.

Kheti stroked his beard. "Do you begin to see why Adonai forbids his people to go near diviners? Their prophecies are like millstones that crush the life out of people. You've lived in fear ever since you heard her words, have you not?"

Danel nodded miserably.

"And that is the intent. It's like the snake in the garden. The lies and half-truths are designed to create a barrier between you and Adonai, and between you and other people. The snake wants you to be full of doubt and fear. That is why diviners must be stoned and why those who visit them are also condemned."

Danel gulped. There was no escape.

"Don't look like that," Kheti said. "The rules about visiting diviners are for those who claim to know Adonai. You visited her before you knew anything of Adonai." He put a hand on Danel's shoulder. "Adonai understands our weaknesses and fears and he has made provision for unintentional sin."

The tension in Danel's shoulders eased. "He has?"

"Adonai has specified offerings that can be made for such sins."

Thank you, Adonai that you have made a way. "I can do that."

"At Mount Sinai, when Adonai appeared to Mosheh and gave him the Law and explained how we could live as his people, he gave us a sacrificial system that restores our relationship with him. I don't fully understand how Adonai forgives but I trust that he has." Kheti brushed an ant off his leg. "We must believe we are forgiven. I often find myself feeling guilty again, as though no offerings have been made. I have to remind myself over and over that whether I understand how the sacrifices work or not, Adonai has forgiven me."

A breeze rippled across the field of grain and Kheti stared ahead. "You were told you would lose everything. In one sense, you already have."

Danel turned toward Kheti. "What do you mean?"

"You have lost your position. Officially, you have become wood-cutters and water carriers, although Yehoshua has found another use for you. And you have lost your gods."

"My gods were no loss. I feel like I've gained in every way."

"Yes, but divination is designed to leave you fearful, to lead you astray."

That had certainly been the case. "How do I fight fear?"

"You remember who holds the future. Trusting in divination puts you under its power and overshadows you with fear. The more you trust the more your fears will multiply and the further you will walk away from your Creator." Kheti shook his head. "Eventually you will no longer know what Adonai wants you to do."

"Are you saying the ultimate cure for fear is to keep close to Adonai?" Danel asked.

Kheti's smile spread, creasing his face into a myriad of wrinkles. "None of us knows when our lives will end, but we live knowing that Adonai knows. That is enough. No follower of Adonai needs to let fear win, but we must choose to walk with Adonai day by day."

Kheti peered at Danel. "Yahveh is holy, and we must whole-heartedly follow him."

Danel wanted to hide from the old man's piercing gaze.

"What are you going to do about the altar in your house?" Kheti asked.

"We haven't used it for ages," Danel said.

"But what would one of your neighbors think if they saw it?"

Danel squirmed. "That we've neglected it?" He said with a light tone.

"They might, but having it there would not lead them to conclude that you were following Yahveh. And—" Grandpa Kheti said. "I know its presence bothers Donatiya."

"Will you help me remove it?" Danel asked.

"We'll do it together. We'll also remove anything else you have in your home. Yahveh is worthy of all your devotion. You must not rely on anything or anyone other than him."

Danel was acutely aware of the amulet beneath his tunic. He'd bought it as a just-in-case, but the longer he wore it, the more important it had become. It gave him a sense of security and the feeling that he'd done all he could to stay alive for Donatiya's and Grandfather's sake. It was so small a thing. Surely it didn't matter. Did it?

Kheti was praying again. Maybe he knew about the amulet that hung heavy around Danel's waist. Danel would feel naked without it but wasn't that the point? He must come to Yahveh stripped of everything, for it was Yahveh who was worthy of his love and devotion, not some lifeless object. Certainly not something that he'd bought from a temple where Baal and Astarte were worshiped. Danel gagged.

"Kheti," the words were hard to speak. "Help me. I must remove my amulet."

"It is not me that you need to ask for help. Pray to Yahveh, he is stronger than any power in this land." Kheti placed his hands on Danel's shoulders. "Call out to him."

Danel had watched battles and fought in one, but now there was a fiercer battle inside him. "Yahveh, help! Free me from my past."

The first two words had been almost impossible to utter but it was becoming easier. "Free me from my allegiance to the gods and practices of this land. Thank you for saving Donatiya and Uncle. Please rescue me. Help me rely on you for everything."

It felt as if the amulet was dragging him down. Danel reached under his tunic and ripped at the cord binding the amulet round his body. For a moment it resisted his efforts. *Yahveh, help me.* With a snap the cord broke and the amulet fell to the ground with a dull thud. Danel stepped away from it. Joy coursed through him. "It is done. Would you destroy it?"

"I'd be delighted." Kheti gave Danel a little push. "Don't wait for me. There are people at home who will be excited to hear about your decision."

Danel smiled as he hadn't in far too long, and ran back toward Gibeon's gate. "Today I choose to trust Adonai," he said as his footsteps pounded along the ground. "Today I trust Adonai."

Even as Danel had made his pledge, the last of the fear that had wrapped around his heart loosened its hold. This wouldn't be one-choice-fixed-fear-for-good. No. It would be a decision he needed to make every day. A decision to keep his eyes fixed on Yahveh and his ways.

He had a lot to learn and a circumcision to undergo. He suspected it would take a lifetime to learn Yahveh's ways but that didn't matter. He'd chosen a new life. A new life that promised meaning and purpose and freedom.

A life worth living, and a life worth passing on to others.

ENJOYED TRUST AND TRICKERY?

A book can never have too many reviews. My first novel has now passed 1000 ratings and each one is valuable.

This book is independently published which means the only way it will be discovered is if readers tell others. Online reviews are a concrete way of doing this.

How to write a review – easy as 1-2-3

1. A few sentences about why you liked the book or what kind of readers might enjoy this book. Even one word turns a mere star rating into a review.
2. Upload your review - the same review can be copied and pasted to each site. https://www.storytellerchristine. com/blog/reviews-the-how-and-where/ tells you where and how for the priority sites.
3. If you loved the book please also share your review on social media or by word of mouth. Anywhere you can spread the word is appreciated.

HISTORICAL NOTES

Names of the characters

Canaanite names have been hard. The only names we know are gods or goddesses and a few other, very rare, examples. I have a very small number of male and female names to choose from but I have done my best to make them authentic for the time period.

One of the difficulties about writing a story where many of the incidents are well known is figuring out how to make the story fresh. I decided to call the biblical characters by less familiar names to make us enter their world with new eyes. I consulted several places for how to better anglicize the Old Testament names.

Names of God

You might have noticed that I used both capitals and non-capitals when referring to God. If it is written as god (lower case) then the character is not a believer (yet).

I have tried to use the names that followers of God used in the days of the story. Hence names like Elohim, Yahveh, the Creator, and Adonai.

Many of you will know that Jewish folk today don't use the

name Yahveh as a mark of respect. However, this custom probably developed much later than the events in this novel.

Canaanite gods

The three main goddesses were Anat (goddess of war), Astarte, and Asherah. I have chosen to use the Greek form, Astarte rather than the more Canaanite form of Ashtart, because Astarte is already less familiar to us. Astarte was the goddess of fertility and love. Baal is the male equivalent.

The Old Testament often uses the words Astarte and Asherah interchangeably but Asherah was the consort of the supreme god, El.

Who were the Gibeonites?

We tend to call these people by the name of one of their cities - Gibeon. However, four cities are mentioned as being included in the treaty - Gibeon, Kephirah, Beeroth, and Kiriath Jearim.

Joshua 9:7 and 11:19 calls them Hivites. The Hivites were one of the nations clearly listed in the peoples within Canaan to be wiped out (see Exodus 23:23; Deuteronomy 20:17).

However, several other early Bible translations have these people called Horites or Hittites. After reading the evidence for each of the positions, I have called them Hivites. The Hivites seem to have been a widely scattered people and it is likely that the northern branches were wiped out but that the peoples of these four towns did survive.

The Hivites are counted in David's census (2 Samuel 24) and form part of Solomon's labor force on the temple (1 Kings 9:20-21).

A balancing act

Genesis 15:16b states the reason that Avraham had to wait to receive his promised land and inheritance was because, "... the sins of the Amorites had not yet reached their full measure." That is,

God did not randomly wipe out the people of Canaan. He waited until they were so evil that judgment must result (like in Noah's time).

My difficulty was that I didn't want to wallow in the evil in this novel, both for my own sake but also because this series has some quite young readers. How could I show the evil and thus that God's judgment is just and yet not write an R-rated book? What I've done is hint at the issues - widespread corruption, kidnappings, child sacrifice ... Ancient Canaan would have been like Sodom and Gomorrah. Not a place any parent would want to raise their children.

Battles

I found the details in Joshua 8 and the battle of Ai quite confusing but have done my best to be as accurate as possible. Here too I have attempted to keep the story suitable for younger readers.

STORYTELLER FRIENDS

Becoming a **storyteller friend** (https://subscribe.storytellerchristine.com/) will ensure you don't miss out on new books, deals, and behind the scenes book news. Once you're signed up, check your junk mail or the promotions folder (for gmail addresses) for the confirmation email. This two-stage process ensures only true friends can join.

Facebook: As well as a public author page, I also have a VIP group (https://www.facebook.com/groups/242910632748639) which you need to ask permission to join.

BookBub (https://www.bookbub.com/authors/christine-dillon) - allows you to see my top book recommendations and be alerted to any new releases and special deals. It is free to join.

DISCUSSION QUESTIONS

- Who were your favorite characters? Why?
- What were significant steps in their spiritual journeys?
- What were significant barriers?
- Did you learn any new things about the ancient cultures?
- Did you learn any new things about the biblical stories?
- What were the original beliefs of Danel and his family?
- Without written scriptures, it would have been easy to forget the Lord. How did believers remain in the Lord?
- What attracted Danel towards knowing the God of the Israelites?
- Choose a character and trace their faith journey.
- Which faith journey do you most relate to? Why?
- How did this story encourage or inspire you?
- Have you struggled with why God instructed that the Canaanites be totally wiped out? How does Genesis 15:16b and Chapter 20 of this story help you?
- Take the time to explain why it was the death penalty for anyone involved in divination. What are the implications for us today?

- What did you learn from this story that you can apply to your life today?

Please feel free to write your own discussion questions. I would love to see them and am happy to include them for others if you give permission.

FICTION BY CHRISTINE DILLON

Prior to writing Biblical-era fiction, I wrote a 6-book contemporary Australian set of novels.

I prefer you to buy the ebooks/audio directly from my online PayHip store (https://payhip.com/ChristineDillon#). It uses PayPal or Stripe (Visa/Mastercard).

Book 1 is also available in Dutch under the title: *Verborgen Genade.*

Of course the books are available from a wide range of other stores.

The *Light of Nations* series will likely be at least twelve books. The best way to hear about upcoming books is to subscribe and become a storyteller friend.

ACKNOWLEDGMENTS

Although, my first series of novels were contemporary Christian fiction, I am feeling very at home in the new genre. I've always loved history and research (one of my hobbies is genealogy) and I've been telling oral Bible stories since 2004.

Many years ago, I spent a year looking at the Old Testament and the many opportunities that non-Israelites had to get to know the God of the Bible. That study was probably the genesis of the idea for the *Light of Nations* series. Throughout the Old Testament, other nations interacted with the Israelites and many showed superior faith to the Israelites. Think of Rahab, Naaman, Abimelech, and Ruth.

In Isaiah 55:11 it says,

> my word that goes out from my mouth: It will not return to me empty, but will accomplish what I desire and achieve the purpose for which I sent it.

I do not think this means that God's word will always lead to trust in him but it will achieve its purposes whether salvation or judgment. Who were some of the people impacted by the witness and words of God's people? I didn't want to write about the familiar stories like Rahab and Ruth because many books have been written about them. I wanted to write about some of the nameless others who represent people that we will meet in God's kingdom where people will come from the east and west to form that multitude of nations around the throne of the Lamb. As Revelation 7 says,

> There before me was a great multitude that no one could count, from every nation, tribe, people and language, standing before the throne and before the Lamb…they cried out in a loud voice: "Salvation belongs to our God, who sits on the throne, and to the Lamb."

My favorite part of the process of these novels is the research because I can spend lots of time delving deeply into the scriptures and thinking about what daily life might have been like back in Old Testament times.

I am thankful for my beta readers, Lizzie, and Laura.

My proofreaders continue to be highly efficient - Stephanie, Suzanne, Elizabeth, Lizzie, Kim, and Anne. Though excellent at their job, it is amazing that errors can still remain. Please contact me if you see any as one advantage of self-publishing is that I can easily sort these out.

As ever I am grateful for Iola Goulton who has edited all my novels. This time was tougher as first she got Covid and then I too was diagnosed the day she returned the manuscript to me.

Designing historical covers for obscure people groups is not easy. Thank you Joy Lankshear for all the expertise you bring and for your endless patience as people in my VIP group comment on them.

And thank you to my readers who have followed me into this

new genre and read my stories with such enthusiasm. I appreciate those who take the time to review and especially those who learn to wrestle with unfamiliar technology to do so.

Onwards and upwards to the next book and following our great saviour and king.

NON-FICTION BY CHRISTINE DILLON

1-2-1 Discipleship: Helping One Another Grow Spiritually
(Christian Focus, Ross-shire, Scotland, 2009).

Telling the Gospel Through Story: Evangelism That Keeps Hearers
Wanting More (IVP, Downer's Grove, Illinois, 2012).

Stories Aren't Just For Kids: Busting 10 Myths About Bible Storytelling (2017).

This book is free for subscribers. It's a taster book and includes many testimonies to get you excited about the potential of Bible storying. All these first three books have also been translated into Chinese.

Sword Fighting: Applying God's word to win the battle for our mind (July, 2020).

This book is also available in German under the title: *Siegreich Sein: mit Gottes Wort.*

ABOUT THE AUTHOR

Christine writes both fiction and non-fiction. Her non-fiction concentrates in the areas of evangelism, discipleship, and spiritual growth/warfare.

Christine worked in Taiwan, with OMF International, from 1999 to 2021 and still works with OMF, but now based out of Australia.

It's best not to ask Christine, "Where are you from?" She's a missionary kid who isn't sure if she should say her passport country (Australia) or her Dad's country (New Zealand) or where she's spent most of her life (Asia - Taiwan, Malaysia and the Philippines).

Christine used to be a physiotherapist, but now writes storyteller on airport forms. She spends most of her time either telling Bible stories or training others to do so.

In her spare time, Christine loves all things active – hiking, cycling, swimming, snorkelling. But she also likes reading and genealogical research.

Connect with Christine
www.storytellerchristine.com/

bookbub.com/authors/christine-dillon